ROYAL

How to prepare for command performances of
The Sleeping Beauty and *La Bohème* and the
circumstances thereof

Jonathan Diack

WINNER OF OEP 2021 PRIZE FOR BEST BOOK ON THE ARTS

Delightful odyssey in a fabled country in the early twentieth century. Behind the scenes, while an orchestra is being rebuilt, villainous and romantic figures pursue conflicting interests in the forthcoming season of ballet and operatic productions. General readers will enjoy the intriguing story as much as lovers of classical music

> \- Dr J Keay, *Tasman Times*

Fascinating, and wickedly funny. \- James Stratford, *OEP Chronicle*

Rachmaninov will be pleased at the inclusion of his magnificent cantata Spring (*Vesna*), surprisingly ignored these days by the great orchestras and their choral societies.

> \- Trumpeter, *KK Gazette*

ABOUT THE AUTHOR

Jonathan Diack is an experienced British writer, editor and journalist. He is also an accomplished pianist, and has written extensively about the importance of classical music, opera and ballet in society. Recently appointed editor of Old English Press, he lives in Yorkshire.

ABOUT THIS BOOK

First published in 2021

ISBN 9781838423438

Published by Old English Press

CHAPTER 1

There is a place reserved in heaven for conductors who fail to remember that the national anthem should be played on arrival of the monarch not the monarch's mistress. When the time comes my predecessor, serenaded by harps and sampling the profusion of grapes in the celestial gardens, will have time to reflect upon the circumstances of his dismissal. If only, for example, he had turned from the podium to check the royal box or paid more attention to the whispers from the audience.

The incident was not the only reason for his discharge apparently.

'Too highbrow,' said the man in the frock coat seated at the desk in the oak-panelled office overlooking the Thames.

'How so?'

'Palestrina, Monteverdi, Scarlatti, to excess.'

'Oh.'

'Aggravated by persistent disregard of authority.'

'Ah.'

'Not much of a mixer either.'

'Oh dear, but,' I said searching for something to say in Leigh-Winter's defence, 'a talented artist nonetheless.'

'Manners are so important,' said the man in the frock coat. 'The master of music is a member of the court, residing and dining in the palace. You wouldn't have any trouble on that score, however. No trouble at all, that's perfectly clear.'

He thumbed through the papers on his desk, pausing to read the letter from Adrian Boult which thanked me for taking over a midweek concert during a mix-up of engagements. The letter kindly avoided reference to the London critics who had described the occasion as average.

'Please remind me of your attitude to contemporary music,' said the man in the frock coat.

He ran through a list of prominent living composers including Elgar, Ravel, Richard Strauss, Sibelius and questioned me on each, searching for evidence that I was sufficiently cosmopolitan in taste to limit the amount of Palestrina, Monteverdi and Scarlatti in my programmes. I assured him of my view that concerts should be balanced to reflect the complete range of classical music and that the complexity of the music should match the sophistication of the audience.

'Well then, that's settled,' said the man in the frock coat sitting back in his chair, placing his fingertips together and regarding me benevolently. 'There'll be an interview over there, of course. A mere formality in your case. You can probably name your price. The country's very wealthy, you know. May I submit your name, with our recommendation?'

I nodded.

'Excellent,' he said rising and accompanying me to the door. 'The master of music's responsibilities include the administration of the opera house, which adds to the enjoyment. You have obviously surmised that the musical taste of the court is not very advanced. I should be inclined to avoid anything too challenging. Advice which, suffice to say, was ignored,' sniffed the man in the frock coat shaking my hand, 'by your predecessor.'

Ten days later I was in Ardaniia, a small and picturesque country with terraced fields, olive groves and vineyards backed by hills which for centuries had protected the citizens from invasion and spared the nation's valuable natural resources, predominantly silver and copper, from plunder. The language was as Romanesque as the architecture and accessible with a reasonable command of French or Italian. English was taught in schools and spoken at court.

The capital city of St Frett looked down over a blue deep-water bay. Busy with ships of all sizes, the harbour served to foster the trade that had enriched the country since Phoenician times. Clippers and steamships laden with precious metals from the hills departed for passage through the Mediterranean to the Americas and northern Europe and returned with cinematograph projectors, gramophones, porcelain water closets and the other essentials of modern life. On behalf of the palace the royal yacht, magnificent in blue and gold regalia, paid regular goodwill voyages to Marseilles, Athens and Naples and returned with consignments of spices, cheeses, balsamic vinegar, truffles, wine and smoked hams.

The road curved gently as it climbed from the harbour. Through the pine trees lining the route there were splendid views of the countryside bathed in warm sunshine and suffused with the aroma of wild herbs. The spontaneous gaiety of the peasants waving from the fields at the liveried coach transporting me upwards impressed me.

Disembarking within the walls of the medieval castle which towered above the city I was greeted by a smartly-dressed equerry who escorted me into the palace, along a wide corridor hung with tapestries to the lord chamberlain's office, chatting suavely as we went.

'You'll probably miss the cricket here, but the hunting's good in winter,' he told me.

'Really.'

'You ride, of course?'

The lord chamberlain was equally urbane. Stately and erect he shook my hand, enquired about my voyage, expressed interest in my first impressions of the country and responding to my observation that the peasants seemed contented explained that the country was in the process of transition to democratic government. The palace had retained control of the principal offices of state but the erection of a parliamentary building with bell tower and clock and the corresponding award of voting rights had enervated the peasantry, never very restless.

Beckoning me to accompany him the lord chamberlain crossed the room to the door in the panelled wall opposite the main entrance, placed his ear against the wooden surface and stood for a few moments listening.

'The king should have finished his dispatches by now. He is anxious to meet you. Are you ready, shall we go in?'

He knocked on the door and slowly opened it.

'Mr Robin Landour, your majesty,' said the lord chamberlain. 'He arrived this morning from England.'

I followed the lord chamberlain through the door and bowed, inclining my head.

The room was elegantly furnished with a view over a courtyard's ornamental trees and a fountain. At the head of the table in the centre of the room sat a rotund figure with bright mischievous eyes and plump pink cheeks, the pinkness accentuated by the white silk scarf around his neck. Behind him stood a pair of pageboys in blue velvet suits, apparently risen from the vacant chairs beside the king. There was no sign of documents on the gleaming surface of the table, just a pack of playing cards.

The king gazed amiably in my direction examining me with an expression of polite curiosity while the pageboys at his side endeavoured to mask their discontent at the disruption to their game. My name meant nothing to the king, that was evident. Out of the corner of my eye I saw the lord chamberlain move his arms up and down simulating the actions of a conductor.

The king suddenly slapped his thigh. 'Tchaikovsky!' he beamed.

'A favourite composer, sir,' I murmured.

'We rather enjoy *The Sleeping Beauty*,' said the king.

'Yes, sir.'

'And *Swan Lake*.'

'Yes, sir.'

The beaming smile gave way to a wistful look which I interpreted as homage to the beauty of Tchaikovsky's music but which might equally have reflected the pleasurable shape of ballerinas in motion. The wistfulness was succeeded by a brief glance up and down my person after which the king nodded and reached for the pack of cards. Accompanied by the lord chamberlain I reversed out of the room.

'I shall arrange for a contract to be drawn up. Meanwhile, do you drive?' said the lord chamberlain.

'Yes.'

'Motor vehicles are stabled along the west wall of the castle. Please help yourself.'

In this manner the selection process for master of music and conductor of the Ardaniian symphony orchestra was brought to a conclusion, and my appointment approved.

CHAPTER 2

In terms of terrifying experiences facing a new orchestra for the first time is not unlike arriving at your preparatory school clutching a teddy bear and suitcase tearfully aware that you will be called stinker by the other boys and lifted by your hair from the floor by lugubrious masters for failing to conjugate Latin verbs in the correct sequence. Clauses in your contract of employment to the effect that as conductor you possess the authority to dismiss instrumentalists without recourse, intended to protect you from open scorn, are of limited value when the entire orchestra walks off the stage in disgust at the inadequacy of your technique.

I prepared myself for the fateful meeting by reconnoitering the opera house the day before. The building stood at the head of the city's central square, handsome and solidly imposing with Corinthian columns and a copper-clad dome which had become oxidised and gleamed green in sunlight. Wide steps ascended to a marbled foyer from where the rich and influential proceeded upwards to the royal circle and the rest dispersed sideways to the stalls or further upwards to the dress circle and gallery. There were no private enclosures except for the royal box in the centre of the auditorium which possessed its own entrance, separated from the royal circle by ornate partitions.

The booking office was to the left of the entrance and the cloakrooms to the right. Plush corridors led from the foyer to the orchestra's common room on one side of the building and to the master of music's chambers on the other. Escorted along the west corridor by the general manager, Signor Soprianti, a well-fed Italian in grey spats and a black frock coat, I found the chambers to be a set of attractive rooms overlooking the city with its own rehearsal studio and a Steinway grand piano. A cheerful young steward with dark hair was ostentatiously dusting the desk.

'Welcome to your new quarters, sir. Valentino's the name, at your service, sir,' said the steward bursting into a rendition of *Rule Britannia*.

'Maltese,' explained the general manager. 'Trained in the British navy. Your predecessors found him satisfactory, but if you would prefer someone else . . ?'

'I'll let you know,' I said nodding at the young man to acknowledge his greeting.

From the master of music's chambers Soprianti led me further along the corridor to the twin doors used by the conductor to descend to the orchestra pit for operas, or step up onto the stage for concerts.

'You will be attended here, of course, at the time of entry,' said Soprianti opening the second of the two doors and ushering me onto the stage.

The arena was a comfortable size. Twenty five yards wide, I judged. Smaller than the behemoths at the Albert Hall and Covent Garden but agreeably proportioned and with a pleasant sense of intimacy. The orchestra's chairs and stands were in place, forming a semicircle around the podium. None of the players would be more than twelve yards from me, I noted approvingly. Equally satisfying were the elevated tiers at the back for the brass, timpani and percussion protecting the wind instruments and strings from direct blasts. With my finger I began counting the number of stands.

'Eighty-four,' said Soprianti. 'The complete orchestra will be here for tomorrow's rehearsal.'

Inspecting the sturdiness of the tiers I found a gap in the safety curtain which acted as the backdrop to the orchestra during concerts. Soprianti followed me through and switched on the lights illuminating the cavernous gloom. A thin layer of dust indicated the infrequency of activity in the rear half of the stage.

'How many operas are performed each year, on average?' I asked.

'Not many,' said Soprianti, 'nowadays.'

'Two, ten, twenty?'

'I need to check my ledger for an exact figure, but not many,' said Soprianti.

'Where are the stage hands?' I asked looking around.

'We hire them, as required, from the royal theatre,' said Soprianti.

I opened one of the prop cupboards and blinked at the sight of a backcloth hanging from the rails featuring a prison cell.

'*Fidelio*?' I said.

Soprianti nodded 'Maestro Leigh-Winter was preparing the production when he left.'

'Indeed,' I said grimly. Even sophisticated London audiences struggled with Beethoven's difficult and frankly rather dour opera. What on earth had my predecessor been thinking of?

'The date had not been fixed,' said Soprianti.

'Is that so,' I said.

Soprianti turned the palms of his hands upwards to emphasise, I assumed, the limits of his authority.

'What about ballet?' I said.

Soprianti shook his head. 'No dance performances, not here in the opera house.'

'Where then? I thought the king liked ballet?'

Soprianti turned the palms of his hands upwards again.

'You must ask Madame Prtenchska.'

I raised my eyebrows.

'The ballet school, across the park,' explained Soprianti.

I had arranged to meet LeBreq, the leader of the orchestra, and was pleased to encounter an affable middle-aged Ardaniian with a commanding presence amplified by a large grey moustache. The morale of an orchestra depends to a large extent on the success of the relationship between the conductor and leader, so I was relieved at his enthusiastic response to my plans for introducing contemporary music into the opera house programmes. Sensibly he requested, however, that the programme for the first rehearsal should focus on works from the orchestra's standard repertoire, to relax the players who were anxious to impress their new conductor. I agreed, refraining from letting slip that the new conductor was considerably more nervous about the forthcoming event than the players.

I slept restlessly. The rattling motion of the carriage on the cobble stones next morning as the horses trotted through the mist to the opera house did nothing to soothe the turbulent uneasiness in my stomach, nor did the creamy sweet brew of tea prepared for me in my chambers by the young steward Valentino which, he explained, was much favoured by officers of the British navy.

'May I take this opportunity of wishing you again a long and felicitous sojourn in Ardaniia, sir,' said Valentino as I swallowed the tea and made for the door, baton under my arm.

Accustomed to the chatter and bustle of English orchestras assembling for rehearsal I was taken aback to find the players already in their seats and even more surprised when they stood and applauded as I approached across the stage. The calm before the storm, I thought mounting the podium. Eighty-four pairs of eyes followed mine as I checked the relative positions of the wind instruments. 'Good morning, gentlemen. *The Marriage of Figaro,* from the beginning, please,' I said tapping the brass filigree on the podium.

For the next few minutes my mind went blank. I was vaguely aware that the players, taken aback by the absence of any introductory speech on my part and being launched straight into the music, stumbled through the opening bars of the overture before settling into the familiar work. In front of me I saw my hands and arms moving mechanically to the distant pulse of the music and then, gradually emerging from the darkness, my brain began registering the news that *the orchestra was following my beat!*

Of equal importance to the relationship between the conductor and leader of the orchestra is the effectiveness of the conductor's technique. Players will endure almost anything from the podium - insobriety, churlishness, narcissism, repetition of jokes, affectation - but the situation is hopeless if the orchestra is confused by the movements of the conductor's baton.

Growing in confidence I followed Beecham's general advice to conductors and played the piece through without stopping. After a few minor comments I let the orchestra play it through again, then moved straight to the Haydn symphony on the programme. I then repeated the sequence, leaving the orchestra to play to an empty podium during the third movement while I clambered to the dress circle to check the acoustics of the hall.

With the restoration of confidence on my part came confirmation of my suspicions that the Ardaniian symphony orchestra, which had obviously been very good in its time, was now past its prime. Weariness hung over the music like a cloud, punctuated by far too many mistakes. No matter, I told myself, mixing with the players after the rehearsal, nobody had walked out in protest at my style of conducting, nobody had failed to follow my beat, the core of the assembly contained a number of first class musicians and anyway, at this stage of my career, I could scarcely expect to have been awarded one of the world's great ensembles.

. . . .

The music library was on the second floor of the building. Soprianti escorted me up the marble staircase and introduced me to the librarian, Signora Furcello, a thin-lipped woman with steely grey hair pinned into a bun who stared contemptuously at the retreating figure of the well-fed general manager. Signora Furcello was the longest-serving member of staff. She had been hired by the late Dr Fruncke, conductor of the orchestra from 1902-1923, who during a post-war visit to La Scala in Milan, where she was employed as a junior librarian, had persuaded her to exchange the cold damp winters of northern Italy for the sunshine of Ardaniia.

'The library at La Scala was much larger, of course,' she said.

'But hardly less impressive, I'm sure,' I said, admiring the neat arrangement of scores on the shelves lining the walls as she led me through her domain. There were no signs of dust or cobwebs in this obviously efficient branch of the opera house. The room lay directly above the foyer. It looked down over the main square at the bustle of horse-drawn carriages, fluttering pigeons and cafés with colourful striped awnings

'Dr Fruncke assisted me with the layout. He died almost exactly five years ago today, a tragic loss,' said the librarian wistfully fingering the crucifix on her blouse.

'Of enviable reputation, and deeply committed to music of the baroque period,' I murmured. 'A commitment shared, I believe, by his successor and protégé Leigh-Winter.'

'Shall we say attempted rather than shared,' said the librarian sharply.

I enquired about the process for ordering new scores and was informed that complete sets could normally be obtained from Rome within three days, and within a week from London or Paris. Relieved I passed the librarian my list for the first concert.

'Ravel, Tchaikovsky?' she said examining the list, eyebrows raised, only just managing to disguise in her voice the opinion that Dr Fruncke would have turned in his grave.

'You already have a section on Tchaikovsky, I see,' I said.

'For the ballet school,' said the librarian. 'I order on the school's behalf.'

'Which reminds me. What exactly is the relationship between the school and opera house?' I said.

'Except for my role in ordering scores, none,' said the librarian. 'At least not yet. You know about the December booking, of course?

'No.'

'The gala performance at Christmas - Soprianti must have told you?' said the librarian

I shook my head.

Signora Furcello clucked her tongue and muttered something under her breath. Evidently the librarian did not think much of the general manager.

'The king,' she told me, 'has commanded a special performance of *The Sleeping Beauty* here in the opera house with orchestra, to celebrate Princess Sophie's seventeenth birthday. The princess will be dancing the role of Aurora. She's a student in the ballet school over there,' said the librarian pointing through the window at an elegant glass-panelled building set amidst the trees in the park beyond the square. 'Madame Prtenchska, the head of the school, is waiting to meet you and discuss the production. I expect she'll also want to talk about the problem.'

'Problem?'

'With the princess.'

I shifted uncomfortably.

'What kind of problem?'
'She keeps falling down.'
'Falling down,' I repeated.
'Loss of balance. Nobody dares tell the king.'
The muscles around my stomach tightened.
'Something of a challenge then,' I said.
'Isn't it?' said the librarian eyeing me sympathetically.

CHAPTER 3

The courtiers were accommodated in the group of arcaded single-floor residences near the castle walls in the northern quarter of the palace. The ground floor apartments were allocated to the lord chamberlain and keeper of the privy purse and other senior officials. Equerries, gentlemen-at-arms and assorted minor courtiers such as the deputy master of the household, the keeper of the king's pictures and myself were housed on the second floor. The third floor was reserved for the ladies-in-waiting and maids-of-honour whose virtue was protected by guards on the main staircase and unprotected as a result of the unsupervised servants' stairway to the rear.

The residences were built around a formal garden with espaliered trees and fountains. When the sun dispersed the morning dew the scent from the flowers drifted through the arcades. There were peacocks on the lawn and bowers of bougainvillea shading the garden seats which, I duly learned, should not be approached in moonlight without due warning lest the occupants be caught in disarray.

Each apartment was approached along an ornate passageway to a heavy wooden door bearing the occupant's name and title. The door opened onto a reception hall which led in one direction to the drawing room and in the other to the bedrooms. The drawing room looked out over the garden and depending on the orientation of the residence the bedrooms faced the hills to the rear of the castle or the rooftops of the city. An archway separated the drawing room from the dining room, and a swing door in the dining room led to the kitchen and domestic areas staffed by one or more servants depending on status. The servants entered the residence from the service door at the back.

The master of music was allocated a valet and housemaid, the latter shared with the keeper of the king's pictures. I preferred to dress myself so the duties of my valet, an ancient Greek whose face was largely obscured by a white beard and bushy eyebrows, were not onerous. He moved slowly with the invariable grace of his profession and informed me that years ago hot water was carried up the servants' stairway in brass containers, an exhausting and unpopular task since each bath required a minimum of ten fills. The practice had continued until a newly-appointed footman observed that the water supply which came from the streams on the heights above the castle could be stored and heated on the palace roof rather than in the basement cellars and thereafter distributed by gravity.

Hot water showers were subsequently installed throughout the palace including the courtier's residences and the royal quarters at the front of the castle. The king was so pleased that he knighted the official in the department of education responsible for incorporating physics into the school curriculum, and awarded the footman a purse of gold coins. Separately the young man received gratitude of a different kind from the several dozen nubile maid servants in the palace spared the arduous task of carrying innumerable heavy brass containers up endless flights of stairs.

Courtiers were expected to dine in the refectory when at home in the palace. Drinks were served in the anteroom beforehand. Gentlemen wore black ties during the week and white tie and tails on Saturdays. Places at dinner were allocated by the lord chamberlain who sat at the head of the long table. The keeper of the privy purse and master of horse, respectively the second and third senior officials, sat opposite each other in the middle of the table and Countess Grigorn, the chief lady-in-waiting, long-nosed and irritable, reigned at the other end with a cluster of other elderly high-born females. The rest of us were dispersed at random.

Attendance at breakfast was optional and the majority of courtiers ate in their residences. I spared my valet the task of transporting food from the palace kitchens and instead descended early to the refectory where I served myself bacon and devilled kidneys from the dishes on the side table. Conversation at breakfast was discouraged so I could prop my music scores onto a newspaper stand and prepare myself for rehearsals without fear of being disturbed by fellow courtiers anxious to discuss the weather or the latest rumours concerning sleeping arrangements in the palace.

The refectory was closed for lunch. Courtiers took themselves to the Grand Hotel or one of the smart restaurants overlooking the bay or lunched in their residences having despatched invitations to the residences of friends and favoured acquaintances, and sent their maids to the kitchens with detailed instructions regarding their requirements for poached sea bass, roast partridge, figs soaked in peach liqueur and similar delicacies to which residents of the palace were entitled without charge.

Flirtation was rife, the most active participants being the gentlemen-at-arms and maids-of-honour who sighed heavily on passing each other in the corridors and conveyed their passion more overtly during dinner with quotations from Shakespearean sonnets intended to confuse the countess, who played the role, being no longer an object of masculine desire, of saboteur. Wary of participating in the entertainment and focused intently on the challenges facing me in the opera house I fabricated a fiancée in England. By feigning disinterest in the opposite sex my intention was to convey the impression of chaste unavailability. I should of course have realised that youthful members of the opposite sex generally regard unavailability of the male as a challenge. Instead of protecting myself from the attention of the patrician temptresses in the palace by pretending to be engaged I became a target.

Last night, for example, I was waylaid in the hall outside the anteroom by a bevy of young ladies.

'We need your help,' they cried.

'With what?' I said cautiously.

'Music, silly,' they exclaimed.

'Ah, yes.'

'We're tired of gavottes and waltzes,' they cried.

'How come?'

'We want the Charleston,' they exclaimed.

The young ladies crowded round jostling me with soft shoulders while I explained that the military bandmaster was responsible for the provision of light music for dances, garden parties and other social events, that I had no jurisdiction over the bandmaster despite my title, and that they should speak to him not me.

'We have, and he won't.'

'Ah.'

'This is what we need,' they cried lifting their gowns and

demonstrating with a flurry of shapely legs the steps of the dance currently in fashion amidst high society in England and America.

A sharp intake of breath heralded the arrival of Countess Grigorn and her entourage for dinner. Nose in the air the countess swept past into the anteroom followed by her elderly companions whose eyes swivelled alternately and disapprovingly from the bare knees of the maids-of-honour to the embarrassed face of the newly appointed master of music.

CHAPTER 4

I commenced the process of getting to know the players by inviting the principals and senior members of the orchestra to lunch at the Hunting Lodge restaurant in the square opposite the opera house. Seated in the rear of the establishment under a lattice of heavy wooden beams, after several flagons of wine when the mumblings of polite conversation had progressed to relatively unguarded chatter, I invited each of my guests to announce their assessment of the shortcomings and virtues of the musical scene in Ardaniia.

The shortcomings included inadequate ventilation on the stage during concerts and rehearsals, corresponding humidity affecting instruments and tuning, uncomfortable chairs, excessive numbers of rehearsals, excessive durations of rehearsals, boredom from the under-use of orchestral resources particularly the wind and brass sections, absence of salary reviews, uncertainty of tenure and, although their comments were appropriately guarded in view of the fact their future was now in my hands, and I was paying for lunch, the quality of conductors.

From their accounts I pictured my predecessor Leigh-Winter on the podium, spindly and cadaverous, arms flaying, fingers stabbing. He demanded full attendance at rehearsals, started with the ubiquitous baroque element of his programmes, interrupted the music incessantly and invariably ran out of time leaving the major works under prepared and the majority of the players frustratingly idle. Professor Heinrich Schmidt, head of the music department at the university, who had taken the concerts after Leigh-Winter's departure, seemingly inspired a similar lack of regard.

'There was an unfortunate incident at last week's concert,' the principal oboe told me across the table.

'Involving the presence of an unexpected diminished ninth in the Monteverdi,' said the principal clarinet.

'Which you should be informed of,' said the principal oboe.

'Which caught most of us by surprise,' said the principal clarinet.

'Including Professor Schmidt,' said the principal oboe. 'If you didn't know him better, you would have said he looked puzzled, angry even.'

Aware that I was being watched and that the success of my relationship with the orchestra depended to some extent on my response to these confidences, and equally aware that the proper course of action should have been to deflect the direction of the conversation with a witty but nonetheless mildly stern rejoinder, I was hard-pressed to stop smiling at the image of the eminent professor, renowned for his work on baroque compilations, beating time to an unexpectedly discordant version of one of Monteverdi's masterpieces, with no way of stopping the performance or investigating the reasons for the amendments to the score.

'If that happens to me, I shall know who to blame,' I said to the principal oboe, an engaging moustached Frenchman.

The orchestra represented a cosmopolitan blend of nationalities, Ardaniian, Italian, German and French in almost equal proportions. Most of the players had been hired by Dr Fruncke who with the fervent support of his assistant Leigh-Winter, and Professor Schmidt in the university, was intent on creating the world's finest baroque ensemble. Outbursts to the orchestra during rehearsals conveyed the extent of his ambitions. "What will they say in London to such *Geräusch?*" "If you play like that when we reach New York, no *Schnitzel!*" To the disappointment of the players looking forward to the excitement of overseas travel Dr Fruncke dropped dead on the podium one winter morning while rehearsing *St Matthew Passion* with the university choir. The obituary in the local newspaper commented on the appropriateness of the setting in which he expired, which must have been of limited comfort to Dr Fruncke's widow.

Meanwhile the sixty year old king had fallen in love with a ballerina during a visit to Paris. The ballerina kindled his interest in the arts, particularly Tchaikovsky's ballet music. Leigh-Winter, the new conductor, was instructed on the king's return from France to modernise the orchestra's repertoire, an instruction he only partially implemented, dragging his feet and defiantly refusing to advance his programmes beyond Beethoven. Preoccupied with the country's transition to democratic government the king waited for an opportunity to rid himself of his master of music which came about when Leigh-Winter prematurely launched into the national anthem at a charity concert in the opera house, mistaking the king's mistress (the former ballerina, elevated to the rank of duchess) for the queen.

To the relief of the orchestra the palace ignored Professor Schmidt's credentials for the vacant position and consulted the Crown Agents in London resulting in my appointment, a comparatively unknown conductor, selected less for his international stature than evidence of reasonable table manners.

Calling for the bill I assured my guests that the concerns they had expressed during lunch would receive careful attention and we spilled out from the depths of the restaurant into bright sunshine. LeBreq, leader of the orchestra, was especially effusive in his thanks. 'A rare but most enjoyable event,' he said slipping on the cobble stones freshly watered by the city corporation carts employed to dampen the summer dust.

'One of many I hope,' I said catching his arm, hailing a cab and helping him into the carriage.

I crossed the square to the opera house, informed Valentino that I did not wish to be disturbed and stretched out on the comfortable chaise-longue in my chambers. The heady effect of the wine probably ensured I was snoring loudly when awakened by a hand on my shoulder to find a bulky bearded figure in starched collar and cravat peering down at me disapprovingly.

'Good afternoon,' said the bearded figure. 'Allow me to introduce myself, Professor Heinrich Schmidt.'

I arose from the chaise-longue and looked accusingly at Valentino who stood in the doorway, arms raised helplessly.

'Shall I sit down?' said to my visitor.

Without waiting for a response the professor seated himself in one of the armchairs.

'By all means,' I said.

'May I assume I am addressing Mr Robin Landour?'

'You may,' I said adjusting my coat, smoothing my trousers and sinking into the armchair opposite him.

'Recently from England, appointed to acquaint us with recent exciting developments in musical structure?' said the professor, the sarcasm scarcely muffled in his beard.

'I wouldn't put it quite like that,' I said. 'Incidentally, weren't we supposed to meet tomorrow?'

'Yes, but I was passing and decided to drop in unannounced, unaware you would be otherwise engaged.' The professor examined his fingernails. 'I hope everything is to your satisfaction here?'

'Thank you, yes.'

'The accommodation is comfortable?' he said looking round at the elegant quarters he had been denied.

'Yes indeed.'

'And the orchestra, how do you find it?'

'Excellent,' I said.

'Well drilled technically but undisciplined. You'll find that out soon enough. Leigh-Winter was never firm enough with them. In his position, I would have been much stricter. Spare the rod, and invite mischief, that's my motto. There was, for example, a disgraceful incident last Saturday.'

'Some confusion with the Monteverdi score, I gather,' I said.

'Confusion!' snapped Professor Schmidt. 'It was sabotage, plain and simple.'

'Is that so?'

'Pencilled changes to the third variation. I suspect the oboes, but one can never be sure. Watch out for them.'

'I certainly will.'

'Or the clarinets, troublemakers, the lot of them,' said the professor. 'Anyway, good riddance. It's your problem now. So, I expect you want to know what's happening at the choral society? We're making good progress with *Fidelio* . . .'

The hurt and resentment Schmidt must have felt at being denied the senior musical position in the country, and the unpleasant surprise of encountering a much younger man casually asleep in the master of music's chambers with wine on his breath, entitled the professor to display a certain amount of aggression. Despite my annoyance at being disturbed in slumber I took no pleasure at worsening his condition.

'I propose to defer *Fidelio*,' I said.

'Defer!' sputtered the professor.

'For a while.'

He stared at me angrily.

'What precisely does that mean - for a while!'

'Until the audience in this country is ready for the darker aspects of Beethoven's music.'

'Darker!' snorted the professor. 'Do you realise what you're saying, the implications . . ?'

He drew out a handkerchief and dabbed his brow.

'Have you any idea - the extent of our commitment to *Fidelio* - the costumes, sets and soloists - the hours of rehearsal time with the chorus and orchestra?'

'None of your work will be lost,' I said, 'merely preserved for future use.'

The professor continued dabbing his brow.

'You have the right, of course, but I must protest most strongly,' he said. 'If not *Fidelio*, which opera do you propose?'

'*La Bohème*.'

The professor jumped out of his armchair.

'Puccini!' he snorted, pulling furiously at his beard. 'Are you quite serious? When I said exciting developments I did not envisage lowering our standards to such a ridiculous level.'

'I'm sorry you feel like that' I said.

'Do you seriously expect me to invite the eminent Ardaniian choral society to associate itself with such overrated rubbish, such . . .' he spluttered searching for the word '. . . trivia.'

'I hope so, because otherwise I shall have to look for choral support elsewhere,' I said.

I met the professor's angry glare and held steady until he dropped his eyes.

'This is the palace's doing, isn't it?' he said, slumping back into the armchair. 'Puccini indeed!'

'*La Bohème* is my choice, not the palace's,' I said.

He left soon afterwards, only slightly mollified by my assurances that I valued the opportunity of working with a person of his eminent stature and that I looked forward to collaborating with him on performances of major choral works in the years ahead. I could hear doors being slammed as he marched along the corridor to the exit.

CHAPTER 5

From the opera house it was a short walk to the ballet school through the city park under the shade of cypress and mimosa trees into the private enclosure marked by an ornate wrought-iron fence and 'Royal Ballet School' signboard above the gate. Preparing myself as I mounted the steps of the Palladian-style building for yet another encounter with an elderly dragon on the lines of Countess Grigorn, chief lady-in-waiting at the palace, or Signora Furcello, the opera house librarian - the latest in a series of grey-haired females dedicated to the discomfort of my person commencing in childhood with a vindictive maiden aunt who repaid me for throwing porridge at her by leaving her considerable fortune to the local hunt - I was relieved to be greeted by a serenely graceful woman with compassionate eyes.

The walls of Madame Prtenchska's office were hung with paintings and photographs of ballerinas. Some of the images were of her as a young woman performing at the Imperial Ballet in St Petersburg. After the revolution she had moved to France to teach at the Paris Opera Ballet School. From there she was recruited by the palace to open a ballet school in Ardaniia.

Arriving with a small staff of ballet mistresses she selected the old orangery in the park for the school on account of the extensive wooden floors. The rest of the building needed attention but the condition of the woodwork was excellent. Within a short time of arrival she declared the school open. The king enrolled his youngest daughter Sophie, hurriedly followed by the country's nobility anxious that their daughters should not be left behind socially. It took longer to fill the places for boys. The sons of upper class families were expected to join the army not dance around the orangery in tights. Alert to the prospect of advancement the middle classes spotted an opportunity for mixing with the aristocracy and stepped in. By the time the builders had finished, enrolment was complete. Since then the waiting list for places had grown exponentially.

'You see, in addition to ballet, we instruct the students in academic subjects. We are a proper school.'

'School, as in mathematics?' I said.

'Certainly, together with art, music, science, geography and languages.'

'Languages?' I enquired.

'French for ballet,' said Madame Prtenchska, 'English for everything else.'

The students in the senior term, from the original intake, were now sixteen years old. They had reached the final phase of classical ballet training, with two years to go before qualifying as professional dancers. None of them had yet performed with an orchestra. Music for rehearsals was provided by piano. Music for the annual concerts held in the school's studio theatre for the benefit of the parents as provided by gramophone records. The Ardaniian symphony orchestra had always been too busy preparing for its own concerts, said Madame Prtenchska choosing her words carefully, politely declining to accuse my predecessor of finding reasons to avoid being associated with anything as frivolous as ballet music. This year however orchestral support was required because the king had decreed that the school should perform *The Sleeping Beauty* in the opera house at Christmas to celebrate the princess's seventeenth birthday.

'I shall be honoured to conduct the performance,' I said.

Madame Prtenchska sighed with relief.

'That's wonderful news,' she said. 'Maestro Leigh-Winter was always most sympathetic, but . . .'

'Evasive?' I suggested.

Madame Prtenchska smiled. 'He was hard to pin down, sometimes.'

'Evasiveness is a characteristic of early music specialists.'

'And you're not one of them?'

'Absolutely not. You may rely on the orchestra's full support.'

'What a relief. Thank you so much.'

Until now Madame Prtenchska's hands had been folded motionless in her lap. I noticed them stir.

'There's something you need to know,' she said.

The problem had manifested itself during the winter term. At first the ballet mistresses assumed it was just a matter of inexperience. The role demanded new steps and jumps. The princess needed time to adjust her technique to the mechanics of the choreography. But neither time nor extra practice resolved the problem. The ballet mistresses then considered the possibility that perhaps she had strained a muscle or ligament and, in the way of students, had been hiding the injury in order to avoid being rested. The school doctor ruled that out. Confusingly there was no pattern to the incidents. She might go for days without tripping.

The ballet mistresses would begin to think the crisis was over then, crash, she was on the floor again, picking herself up apologetically. To add to the mystery the princess herself could provide no explanation for the sporadic nature of the falls.

'The tragic thing is,' said Madame Prtenchska, 'she dances the part so beautifully. Would you like to see? The senior girls are rehearsing at the moment.'

She led me down the corridor past classroom doors with glass windows through which I observed children of different ages bent over their books. Ahead of us came the sound of piano music and the throb of dancers' feet.

'No titles,' said Madame Prtenchska swinging opening the doors to the main rehearsal studio. 'I shall introduce the princess as Sophie, and the other titled students by their first names.'

My visit had obviously been anticipated. The music stopped as soon as we entered the studio and the dancers lined up in front of us. I was introduced to the duty ballet mistress and the principal dancers, including Sophie, an attractive girl of medium height with wide blue eyes who giggled sweetly when I informed the class that the symphony orchestra would have to work just as hard as the dancers to learn the score of *The Sleeping Beauty,* with the singular advantage that musicians didn't have to wear ballet shoes and perch on their toes whilst performing.

Madame Prtenchska and I sat on a bench during the rehearsal. The class was practising scenes from Act 1 in which Aurora, after being presented to prospective suitors by her parents, accepts a spinning wheel spindle from an old woman in the crowd, pricks her finger and succumbs to the effect of the poisoned needle. The process of reacting to the poison is an extensive one involving a series of brilliant pirouettes. In real life the victim of a poison attack would seek assistance not start leaping exuberantly about the room but this was the theatre, the world of fantasy, in which the scene was designed to illustrate the unfortunate consequences of crossing a wicked witch. For the benefit of Madame Prtenchska and myself, Sophie, a real princess dancing the part of a make-believe princess, illustrated the consequences with great charm and performed the pirouettes without, as far as I could judge, a hint of instability

The pianist interested me. Curly-headed, much the same age as the students, the boy was alarmingly talented. Rehearsal pianists, referred to as *répétiteurs* in the context of opera and ballet classes, required mastery of sight reading and keyboard techniques. Opera and ballet scores reduced for the piano were complex documents, rightly so because the objective was to simulate in the rehearsal room the conditions on the stage. All three essential elements of the musical structure - melody, harmony and rhythm - had to be conveyed to the singers and dancers, often at breakneck speed, frequently in uneven spells fractured by shouts from the director or ballet mistress. On top of that, the pianist had to keep an eye on the performers to anticipate changes in tempo, particularly relevant in ballet. I observed that the curly-headed youth watched the dancers' feet carefully, scarcely glancing at the score. I would be hard pressed to match him, I reflected, ruefully aware that my own preparations for conducting *The Sleeping Beauty* should include a spell as *répétiteur* here in the rehearsal studio.

The importance of watching the dancers' movements was emphasised during the adagio in which Aurora is presented with roses by her four suitors. The length of the concluding passage of music is determined solely by the amount of time the ballerina, balanced on one foot, needs to exchange hands with each of the male dancers. Throughout the exchange Sophie was steady on her toes, and captivating to watch as she dropped her hand prettily into each of the extended palms.

'That was most impressive,' I said to Madame Prtenchska after the rehearsal.

'I'm so glad. What about Sophie?' she said. 'Did you notice anything?'

'Absolutely nothing. There was no sign, to my untrained eye, of any problem at all,' I said.

'It always happens so suddenly.'

'She looked very confident and composed,' I said. 'Perhaps the worst is over.'

'I do hope so. I dread the thought of informing the king. Still,' said Madame Prtenchska, brightening, 'at least you're here now. Men are so good at handling these sort of things.'

CHAPTER 6

Preparations in the opera house for the orchestra's first concert under my baton have slowed down. Relying on the proficiency of their sight-reading skills the players are finding the transition from classical to contemporary music more difficult than expected and are struggling with the intricacies of the Ravel's *La Valse* and Tchaikovsky's fantasy overture *Romeo and Juliet* which I have chosen to accompany Haydn's Symphony No. 98. The strings are mostly to blame and transparently guilty of failing to devote sufficient time to practice.

'Look here,' I said stopping the music for the third time during the electrifying ascent in the fantasy overture which heralds Juliet's death. 'The idea is that Juliet kills herself for love, not to seek refuge from the violin section of the Ardaniian symphony orchestra.'

The timpani and percussion sections on the other hand continue to please me with their near faultless readings of Ravel's score. The eruptions from the drums and cymbals contribute significantly to the climax of the work, and with luck will serve to mask a percentage of the errors from those players in other sections of the orchestra still grappling with the complex rhythmical structures loved by Ravel - structures more Spanish than French, as distant from the baroque period as the moon from the stars.

The three pieces I have chosen for the concert are each comparatively short. Allowing time for the intermission the concert will last no more than ninety minutes. The brevity is deliberate, intended to discourage members of the royal family, courtiers, aristocrats and other dignitaries from sneaking off early to the palace. The Saturday night ball is not scheduled to commence until the king returns from the opera house, but the champagne bar in the ballroom opens at sunset.

My objective is to stun the audience with the ravishing harmonies and rhythms of *La Valse* thereby containing them in their seats through the Haydn symphony, which some of the listeners will find more difficult to assimilate. Even if the king's attention wanders during the symphony I am confident he will stay the course because he will see in the programme the magical word TCHAIKOVSKY above the entry for the single work in the second part of the concert. After the intermission, as soon as *Romeo and Juliet* starts, he will become immobilised, spellbound, as the exquisite themes unfold. At least that is the plan.

'Two days to go,' I said dismissing the players on conclusion of the rehearsal. 'Those that need it, attend to your homework please. And don't be too proud to dust off your metronomes.'

The new chairs for the orchestra have still not arrived so after lunch I delved into the requisitioning process and ended up, not before time, undertaking a wholesale examination of the opera house's financial infrastructure. 'Don't worry about expense, you can spend what you want, within reason,' the lord chamberlain had assured me when I signed my contract of employment and although there was no reason to doubt the palace's intent I was experienced enough in orchestral management to know that there was no such thing as fiscal equilibrium in the world of music and the arts.

I called Soprianti to my chambers.

'Where are the new chairs?' I asked

'Coming soon,' said Soprianti, 'for sure.'

'In Ardaniia, as a matter of interest, what is the definition of soon?'

Soprianti spread his hands urbanely. I had not yet made up my mind about the opera house general manager. He was affable and apparently on good terms with everyone in the building except the librarian for which he could be forgiven on the grounds that Signora Furcello was unlikely to win any awards for congeniality any time in the distant future. Less apparent however was evidence of Soprianti's efficiency. I continued to nurse the uncomfortable feeling that the opera house general manager was not someone from whom I would wish to purchase a horse or second-hand motor vehicle.

'Soon means,' said Soprianti spreading his hands wider, 'soon.'

'You said the chairs would be delivered yesterday.'

'I expect there has been some difficulty with transport.'

'Tell me again,' I persisted, 'what happens to requisitions after they've been issued.'

It was very simple, explained Soprianti. After signature the forms were placed in the main office tray. Each morning the tray was cleared by the duty clerk and requisitions were forwarded to the purchasing department at the ministry of finance. The purchasing department acknowledged receipt by counter-signing each document, entering the estimated cost and delivery date and returning a carbon copy of the requisition to the opera house. This infallible arrangement, instituted hundreds of years ago in the mists of time, explained Soprianti, ensured that each transaction was completed to the satisfaction of all parties.

'What estimate was given for this delivery?' I said.

'They were supposed to be delivered yesterday.'

'In which case we have cause for complaint. Please let me see the copy of the requisition and I will pursue the matter myself.'

'Alas, the acknowledgement has not yet arrived.'

'Then where did the estimate come from?' I enquired.

'Experience,' said Soprianti.

I raised my eyebrows.

'In the event an acknowledgment is delayed,' said the general manager spreading his hands even wider, 'we make our own estimate, based on experience.'

'What is your experience of ordering chairs?' I said.

'You will recall,' said Soprianti, 'that the furnishing store representative who brought the samples for you to examine was able to confirm that the model you selected was available in stock.'

'So why haven't the chairs been delivered?'

The opera house general manager, having already extended his hands as wide as possible, shrugged his shoulders.

'Very well,' I said rising from my desk. 'Let us visit the ministry ourselves and find out. Follow me.'

I strode along the corridor to the coach yard door, skipped down the stone steps and leapt into the driving seat of the smart velvet-blue Citroën sedan allocated to me by the castle motor mechanics, complete with royal crest embossed in gold on the doors. I beckoned Soprianti into the passenger seat and set off through the afternoon traffic towards the cluster of government buildings on the opposite side of the park.

The Citroën was capable of 30 miles per hour without undue noise and vibration so I was able to overtake carriages without startling the horses although most of the animals tossed their heads as the car sped past, motor vehicles still being comparatively rare on the roads of Ardaniia. Beside me Soprianti clutched the dashboard, wincing on the few occasions I clashed the gears. To distract his attention from the ordeal of mechanised transport I enquired whether my predecessor had ever visited the ministry to register a complaint. Soprianti's response to the effect that Leigh-Winter was a frequent visitor alerted me to the possibility that we would be received by the purchasing department without much in the way of enthusiasm, if not downright hostility.

On arrival at the ministry we were escorted through a warren of corridors to an office marked 'Purchasing Supervisor' where the incumbent, an elderly Ardaniian with bushy grey moustache, half-rose from his chair, positioned as if ready to bolt from the room, an alarmed look on his face.

I extended my arm, shook his hand warmly and introduced myself as the new master of music.

'Forgive us for dropping in unannounced. You know Signor Soprianti, the opera house general manager?'

The purchasing supervisor remained half out of his chair eyeing us uncertainly until, realising that we were not shouting or banging his desk with our fists, slowly lowered himself down into the seat.

'What an extremely nice office,' I said, pretending to admire the grey walls of the room which was as austerely furnished and decorated as the others we had passed on our way through the drab corridors. I concluded that employees of the ministry of finance took great care to avoid ostentation lest doubt be cast on their integrity. To embellish their workplaces would be to invite enquiries into the source of the funds, a short step from demotion, dismissal or, in bygone years no doubt, execution. The sole adornment in the purchasing supervisor's room was a framed photograph of the king.

'My office is agreeably spacious,' admitted the purchasing supervisor cautiously.

'Yes indeed,' I said. 'Befitting for someone of your rank.'

I explained that in addition to the pleasure of making his acquaintance the purpose of the visit was to familiarise myself the requisitioning process worked within the ministry. For example, the opera house had recently raised a purchase order for some new chairs . . .

The purchasing supervisor reached into the filing cabinet beside his desk, extracted a bunch of papers and flipped through them, moistening his fingers intermittently.

'Yes, here it is, held in abeyance,' he said holding up a flimsy sheet of paper.

'Abeyance?' I said.

'Just so. It's customary in these cases.'

'Cases?' I said. 'What does that means?'

'Specifically, in this one, absence of funds.'

I looked at Soprianti.

Soprianti stared gloomily at the floor.

'We sent a memorandum to your predecessor several weeks ago advising him that the opera house purchasing budget had been expended, and that further funds were required,' said the purchasing supervisor.

'So we don't have any money?' I said.

'Only temporarily,' smiled the purchasing supervisor referring again to the papers. 'I see that additional funds were received from the palace last week, and are in the process of being transferred to the opera house account.'

'That's a relief,' I said. 'Presumably the funds can be used for the purchase of the chairs?'

'Certainly, on completion of the transfer.'

'You need to wait?'

'Until the account had been credited,' nodded the purchasing supervisor gathering the papers together and returning them to the filing cabinet.

'Even though you know that the funds have been received?'

'It's the rule, I'm afraid.'

Realising we had now reached the point at which Leigh-Winter would have become more than usually aggressive, I enquired, 'So how long before we get the chairs?'

'Soon,' said the purchasing supervisor.

CHAPTER 7

I have cancelled afternoon rehearsals. The players are half asleep, somnolent with wine after lunch in the local tavern. It is different in the mornings when refreshed by sleep and alert after black coffee they combine into the prospect of a fine orchestra.

In exchange I have lengthened the morning session by an hour and informed the players I expect them to devote appropriate periods of private practice to new works. Separately LeBreq, the leader of the orchestra, is establishing a committee of senior players to examine and report on the whole matter of rehearsal times and durations, including preparations for stage productions of operas and ballets.

This morning's rehearsal was certainly more productive. Defaulters from the last session have evidently concluded that despite my comparative inexperience I am capable of identifying attempts to free-wheel through complex passages of music. The quality of playing from the string sections showed a marked improvement. The percussion section continues to impress me.

To keep the players on their toes I have informed them that I intend to hold regular auditions for new recruits ostensibly to maintain an adequate reserve of extras but implicitly to warn defaulters that they face an uncertain future.

In due course I shall also address with the orchestra the matter of female instrumentalists. The fact that autocratic self-governing European institutions like the Vienna Philharmonic refuse women the right to participate in their music making is not, in my opinion, an argument for excluding them from the Ardaniian symphony orchestra. The orchestra I am now privileged to conduct exists under royal patronage. As executor of that patronage I have every intention of recruiting players by merit alone and in the process enlivening the orchestra with some feminine charm and beauty.

....

Princess Sophie has fallen again.

'Thank you for coming at such short notice. It was more severe this time. Nothing broken, mercifully, but the doctor insists that Sophie rests for a week,' said Madame Prtenchska when I visited the school after lunch.

The ballet mistresses were now outwardly worried at the prospect of Sophie falling during the gala performance of *The Sleeping Beauty*. I shared their concern. If Sophie collapsed in front of the country's noblest and most influential personages, the reputation of the school would be irreparably damaged. The king would be displeased at the embarrassment suffered by the royal family, disappointed that his daughter had failed to make the grade as a ballet dancer and angry that the school had attempted to conceal details of her disability. If the king then closed the school, a not unlikely outcome, Madame Prtenchska and the ballet mistresses faced the prospect of an unexpectedly early return to Paris or Moscow, their reputations tarnished, their chances of re-employment within the international world of ballet reduced by failure in Ardaniia. Impresarios like Diaghilev would show them the door.

'This doctor,' I said. 'Does he perform routine medical check-ups on the students?'

'Yes,' said Madame Prtenchska. 'Why do you ask?'

'Regular inspections?'

'Every year.'

'All the students?'

'Yes.'

'Including the princess?

'Yes.'

'After her last check-up, did the doctor report anything unusual?'

'No.'

Madame Prtenchska stared at me enquiringly.

'In which case, I suggest postponing the decision for a few days,' I said. 'There's still plenty of time. While Sophie is recovering, let me think about the problem. I have an idea.'

. . . .

The lord chamberlain beckoned me this evening to the fireplace, his customary position from which every night he surveys the assembly of courtiers gathered for sherry and cocktails, warming his posterior from the flames of giant logs in winter and, from habit, retaining the same place in summer. Tall and distinguished, immaculate in black evening dress, his presence dominates the room.

'I hear you've been to the ministry of finance?' he said.

My visit had come about while familiarising myself with the requisitioning process for the opera house, I explained. It had provided me with a valuable opportunity of meeting the personnel responsible for dealing with our purchase orders, and to understand the procedures and constraints at his end.

'Constraints?' said the lord chamberlain.

'I expect government officers are the same the world over,' I said.

'Pen-pushers, all of them,' said the lord chamberlain.

The unwritten rules of the palace discouraged conversation involving commerce or money in leisure hours so I endeavoured to change the subject with a whimsical response only to be reminded that the lord chamberlain was not bound by the same conventions as lowly courtiers. Hands behind his back, flapping the tails of his dress dinner coat as if to circulate the warmth from the non-existent flames, he continued to pursue the matter of opera house finances.

'I am despatching you a copy of the university music department's budget. Kindly examine it at your convenience,' he said.

'Of course. To what end?' I said.

'It might make sense to place the music department's finances under opera house control. Professor Schmidt would protest, of course, but the logic is hard to dispute. See what you think.'

'Very well,' I said, flattered but puzzled at the proposition.

'Incidentally, his majesty is looking forward to tomorrow's concert. I gather you've included something by Tchaikovsky, an admirable choice.'

Dismissed from the fireplace I retreated politely a few steps and backed into Lady Sarah Delchette, one of the maids-of-honour from the Charleston demonstration.

'My fault,' I apologised.

'No, mine,' she said. 'I was waiting for you. Have you spoken to the bandmaster yet?'

'Not yet.'

'Traitor.'

'I think I explained,' I said, 'that the military band is beyond my sphere of influence.'

'That doesn't stop you trying, does it?'

'It would be most unwise, in my opinion, and probably counter-productive.'

'Nonsense,' she said. 'Well then, you'd better make up for it at the ball. I shall keep a space open on my card.'

'Nothing would give me greater pleasure,' I said politely, reflecting that it was one thing to want to enhance a symphony orchestra with members of the fair sex, quite another to be lured into indiscretion by a fecund maid-of-honour. 'But unfortunately I shall be on duty in the opera house tomorrow night, returning late.'

'Not too late, I shall expect at least one dance,' she said departing in a swirl of silk and expensive scent to join her companions, glancing round as she crossed the room, conveying to me by the flash of her eyes the pleasures that awaited a successful suitor.

CHAPTER 8

I adjusted my tie and waited for the usher to open the door. In a few moments the baton in my right hand would initiate the martial pomp of the national anthem followed shortly afterwards, for the first time in the country, by Ravel's *La Valse*. Amidst the kaleidoscope of images in my head was the audience's turbulent reaction to Stravinsky's *Rite of Spring* a few years ago in Paris. *La Valse* was even more modern. Too late to change now, I reflected, the die was cast, if the audience booed and hurled tomatoes at the podium the blame was entirely mine. I would continue conducting until the barrage of missiles forced the orchestra to flee whereupon I would depart the stage at a dignified pace and compose my letter of resignation.

On the other hand, I reminded myself, *La Valse* was structured upon a familiar form of music and the variations to the form were ravishingly beautiful whereas Stravinsky had ripped open the heart of classical music and presented his audience with notes and rhythms so completely foreign to their experience that they had rebelled. Moreover the audience here was unlikely to throw vegetables at the orchestra without reference to the royal box and I could be reasonably certain the king would reserve judgement until after the performance of *Romeo and Juliet* in the second part of the concert, by which time Tchaikovsky should have cast a spell over the assembly.

The usher maintained his grip on the door handle. At my instruction the door was to remain closed until Soprianti signalled from the foyer that the king had arrived and was mounting the staircase with his retinue. Not until the king's feet were on the staircase was Soprianti to give the signal. Important personages such as monarchs were notorious for stopping in foyers to chat with reception committees hoping to encounter attractive females with whom to trifle or, worse, for ignoring reception committees altogether and heading off in the wrong direction or even disappearing into the nearest lavatory. Too many conductors had been left stranded on the podium waiting for important personages to empty their bladders.

'It's nearly a full house tonight, sir, much busier than usual,' observed the usher politely as we waited.

'Very pleasing,' I said.

'They've come to see king, sir. His royal highness hasn't been here for years.'

'Yes indeed.'

'And you too, of course, sir,' said the usher diplomatically

I glanced through the peephole beside the door. The stalls and royal circle were completely full. There were some gaps in the dress circle but even the gallery, slightly obscured by the haze of cigarette and cigar smoke, looked crowded. Most of the men were dressed in white ties or dinner jackets, and their wives in long gowns. Diamonds sparkled from the tiaras in the royal circle.

'That's the signal from the foyer, sir,' said the usher.

'Time to go then,' I said.

The usher opened the door, stood aside and in accordance with established practice clapped discreetly. The clapping sound and my appearance at the door generated a ripple of applause from the assembly which grew steadily as I strode across the stage. Nodding at the leader of the orchestra, I mounted the podium, bowed to the audience, straightened up and faced the royal box into which the royal family soon began to emerge, dowagers, elderly royal dukes, the queen in white gown and tiara and the king, splendidly attired with a purple and gold sash across his chest.

I waited until the king had reached the front of the royal box then swung round and raised my baton.

The Ardaniian national anthem was neither profoundly artistic nor factually correct. The text urged the people to rid the forests of tigers, bears and wolves which, even if they wanted to they could not, the animals in question having long since been hunted to extinction and the forests converted to vineyards. Nonetheless the anthem served admirably to introduce the music of Ravel to the audience because after the members of the well-dressed assembly had settled into their seats the leaden features of the anthem were replaced by the beauty of the dreamlike strands which open *La Valse*.

On the podium I could sense the change of atmosphere in the hall as the audience grappled with this extraordinary piece of music.

The dreamlike strands drifting mysteriously through the auditorium without discernible purpose were clearly quite different from the texture of music the listeners had experienced before, whispering mysteriously and punctuated strangely by low growls from the double basses and bassoons. It took several minutes before the listeners identified that the frequency of the growls was compatible with the title of the composition and that within the pattern of whispers and growls the rhythm of a waltz could be discerned.

The remarkable feature of the music is that the source appears to lie beyond the orchestra and that as the seductive loveliness of the waltz takes shape and the volume begins to increase the listeners are transported in their minds to the windows of a ballroom in which they can see figures of great elegance and beauty twirling under magnificent crystal chandeliers.

There is something disturbing about the picture, however. Intermittent variations in the pace and structure of the waltz indicate that the dancers in the ballroom are exposed to some kind of extraneous pressure, perhaps even duress, all the more bewildering for the sensuality of the music and the relentless increase in the pace and volume. Discomforted by the changing picture and accumulation of sound the listeners begin to realise the situation is moving in a sinister direction. Clutching the arms of their seats they brace themselves, instinctively guessing what is going to happen, and they are right, because as the waltz accelerates to its climax Ravel unleashes some of the most violent explosions in the classical repertoire.

I nodded appreciatively at the percussion section, lowered my baton and waited.

Behind me the hall was completely silent. I could detect no sign of movement. Stunned and confused the audience was trying to work out why such beautiful music had suddenly disintegrated, a reasonable question which only Ravel could answer. Then a voice from the rear stalls cried 'bravo!' Someone in the gallery began to clap, followed by several people in the dress circle. Slowly the rest of the audience joined in. I would not describe the reception as tumultuous but by the time I turned to face the audience a significant number of people in the stalls were on their feet applauding.

In the royal box the dowagers and elderly dukes looked unsurprisingly baffled. In front of them the queen was dipping her fingers into a box of chocolates. Beside her I could see the king leaning back in his chair stroking his chin, staring thoughtfully at the opera house roof.

I bowed to the audience and stepped from the podium reasonably confident that my passage across the stage, executed in accordance with the tradition that allowed conductors a few moments in the sanctuary of the wings puffing furiously at their cigarettes before returning to tackle the next item on their programmes, would not be marked by showers of rotten tomatoes.

Haydn's delightful 98th symphony was received appreciatively by the members of the audience accustomed to compositions of the baroque and classical periods, and with less fervour by the proportion of the listeners fed up with early music, drawn to the opera house by the pronouncements in the press that the newly-arrived conductor intended to introduce works by the great modern composers. Therein lay my challenge. To raise the level of attendance in the opera house while simultaneously sustaining the interest of both types of listeners. Hence my decision to employ classical romantic music as the bait, sandwiching into each programme examples of easily assimilated works by the great masters of the mainstream repertoire, gradually increasing the range and complexity of the concerts.

'His majesty seems to be enjoying himself, sir,' said Valentino producing a dry shirt and collar from the clothes cupboard in the interval.

'Good,' I said shedding my damp apparel, resolved to accelerate the opera house ventilation project having now experienced first-hand the uncomfortable levels of heat generated by a packed auditorium in summer.

'His majesty did not attend concerts during the last maestro's time, sir.'

'Why was that, do you suppose?' I asked

'From what I've heard he only likes ballet music. Personally I prefer operas. By the way, did I mention I am something of a singer myself? Just for future reference, if you get my drift, sir.'

Tchaikovsky's *Romeo and Juliet* overture, completed in 1880, shared with *La Valse* the distinction of being wholly ignored by Ardaniia. Indeed examination of the opera house register verified that this was the first ever public performance of a Tchaikovsky work in the country, a disgraceful omission by my predecessors. It was extraordinary to think that with the exception of those persons rich enough to have travelled abroad, or privileged enough to be attending the ballet school, or fortunate enough to possess a gramophone machine, none of the members of the audience sitting hushed and expectant as I stepped back onto the podium had ever heard a single note of the immortal Russian's music.

The king's undemonstrative response to *La Valse* failed to prepare me for his reaction to *Romeo and Juliet*. The work climbs through the vicious clashes between the Capulets and Montagues to the famous balcony scene and whereas the end of *La Valse* is to some extent predictable nothing prepares the listener for the tragic conclusion to Tchaikovsky's famous work in which the death of the young lovers is accompanied by music almost too wrenchingly beautiful to bear.

Once again the result was a stunned and silent audience only, this time, the first sign of movement came from the royal box. Rising to his feet the king stood for a while looking down at the orchestra, one hand on the brass rail, the other dabbing his eyes. For several minutes he remained in that position then, replacing his handkerchief in his cuff, he raised an arm in my direction, turned and departed from the box followed by the rest of the royal family amidst the sound of applause swelling throughout the auditorium.

'Most appreciative, the audience seemed, sir,' said Valentino relieving me of my baton and placing it in the leather case.

'Yes, fortunately,' I said sinking into an armchair.

'Begging your pardon, sir, but did Tchaikovsky write any operas?'

'Several. Why?'

'I like to keep up to date with vocal works. Being a singer myself, as I might have mentioned, sir.'

CHAPTER 9

Conductors who claim to be disinterested in the opinion of music critics are either untruthful or sufficiently renowned to get away with dismissing reviewers as minor irritants, akin to cowpats and horse flies. At my junior level, conductors take criticism very seriously and open their newspapers as gingerly as they opened their school reports years ago.

NEW BROOM SWEEPS IN   Sunday Gazette

A large audience gathered in the Opera House last night to hear Landour, the newly appointed master of music, conduct the symphony orchestra in a varied programme which included examples of the modern repertoire. The enthusiastic reception given to the later pieces, from Ravel and Tchaikovsky respectively, may be interpreted in a number of ways. Most probably the audience wished to convey by their applause a warm welcome to the young conductor, who stood well upon the podium and impressed the ladies with his square features. Alternatively the audience, confounded by the noise level, were perhaps expressing relief at the sudden restoration of normality, and the intactness of their ear drums. Or possibly the applause reflected the entertainment value of watching the percussionists in the orchestra flaying at their cymbals and gongs. Regrettably however, of all the options, it is exceedingly unlikely that the applause was founded upon appreciation of the musical technique on display, or lack of it.

Early in the performance of Ravel's *La Valse*, a work for ballet composed recently in Paris, it became apparent that the orchestra was struggling. The unorthodox rhythmical structure was clearly beyond the grasp of some of the players. Landour's reasons for wanting to introduce himself to the concert audience with an exhibition of dazzling cacophony are understandable, but it might have been wiser to have allowed more time for practice. The conductor was on much surer ground with Haydn's Symphony No. 98 and sensibly allowed the orchestra to lead the way with this familiar work. The troubles returned however with Tchaikovsky's attractive overture *Romeo and Juliet,* making its first appearance here in Ardaniia. The string sections transparently faltered over the harmonic intricacies of the score and the dramatic effect of the finale was lessened by some ragged play.

By the programme Landour selected for his opening concert he has made his long-term intentions clear With patience and practice the orchestra is certainly capable of rising to the challenges posed by the modern repertoire. The question is, how will the conservative establishment, deeply loyal to the classical period and steeped in the works of the great masters react to what prominent members of the artistic community outwardly fear represents change for change's sake ? Time will tell.

It could have been worse, I thought turning to the close-of-play cricket scores from England. The attitude was impartial, the assessment mostly accurate and I had been spared the kind of vituperative attack common amongst critics on the lines of "the noble heritage of the orchestra was demolished by the conductor" or "hopes of enlightenment as to the composer's intent died swiftly" or "the conductor mounted the rostrum confidently and dismounted a broken man". Politically the *Sunday Gazette* had carefully positioned itself between the baroque and non-baroque factions in the country and was in the enviable position of being able to wait and see which side ultimately emerged triumphant.

The newspaper was quite correct to find fault in the quality of musicianship. The orchestra had struggled at times. Much more practice was required. However, in the contest between the conservative establishment and the downtrodden populace starved of lighter music, last night's concert represented a triumph for the non-baroque faction. The ovations had had nothing to do with the conductor's so-called square features or any of the other critic's whimsical propositions, and everything to do with the beauty of the music. Starved for years of easily-discernible melody and dramatic texture the audience had voiced its approval for change. My task was now to bridge the gap between the opposing sides.

As for the king . . . Well, applause ringing in my ears, I had returned late to the palace from the opera house to be met at the main entrance by an equerry announcing that my presence was required in the ballroom.

'I rather want to turn in,' I protested.

'Royal command, I'm afraid,' said the equerry, seconded from the household cavalry and trained at Sandhurst.

'Couldn't you pretend you didn't find me?' I sighed.

'That wouldn't be right, old man,' said the equerry.

Straightening my tie I followed him up the wide staircase through the panelled doors into the crowded reception hall through a further set of doors into the ballroom magnificent with frescoed walls and an ornate minstrels gallery. The equerry forced a path through the throng of dignitaries and led me to the head of the hall where, under a canopy of purple and gold silk, stood the royal family and guests. The king turned in my direction as I approached, broke off his conversation and extended his arms.

'A thousand times, thank you!' he said grasping my hands, smiling broadly.

'I'm glad you enjoyed it, sir,' I said.

'Enjoyed it, we damned near expired of grief ! Play it again, will you, every Saturday.'

Still holding my hands he drew me into the royal circle and presented me to the queen. 'My dear, meet our new master of music, selected by me personally,' he said glancing impishly in the direction of the lord chamberlain.

Amidst the noise under the canopy the queen misheard the introduction. Plump and gushing, tiara askew upon her head, champagne spilling from her glass, she exclaimed how delighted she was to meet an expert in soil management, a subject close to her heart, the castle gardens occupying so much of her time. How long was I staying? I attempted to disassociate myself from the British agricultural delegation currently visiting the country but she was not to be persuaded and sought my advice on a number of horticultural issues including the spacing of plum trees. Only the arrival of more guests allowed me to escape.

Emerging from the clouds of cigar smoke and brandy fumes under the canopy, I encountered the corpulent figure of the royal physician.

'I've just been mistaken for a gardener,' I told him.

'Better than an undertaker, and more interesting than a hairdresser,' said the physician who several years ago had exchanged his Harley Street practice in London for a life of palatial splendour in Ardaniia.

'Actually, I've been looking out for you. I need advice on a problem of balance. Or loss of balance, rather,' I said.

'Instability? A common complaint here,' said the physician nodding at the adjacent cluster of inebriated elderly royal dukes. 'That and haemorrhoids.'

'Do your royal duties include the ballet school?'

The physician shook his head. 'That's Dr Fabricci. Why?'

I told him about Princess Sophie and my theory that there might be something wrong with her ears. A similar situation had occurred with my sister who had persistently toppled off her pony for no apparent reason when young and had been cured by a simple potion which cleared up her sinuses. Unfortunately I could not very well presume to ask the ballet school physician whether he had tested Sophie's ears without implying he was incompetent. I needed advice on how to proceed.

'I'll have word with the princess,' said the royal physician immediately.

'Excellent!' I exclaimed.

'Leave it to me.'

'Thank you so much. Could you avoid mentioning the matter to her parents? I don't want to involve the king, in particular, at this stage.'

'You may rely on my discretion,' said the royal physician tapping his nose.

I was retreating through the throng underneath the minstrels gallery where musicians of the military band led by the bandmaster resplendent in crimson coat were playing a waltz, when my progress was arrested by a voice crying 'Robin' and a slender arm slipped into mine.

'You're late. Never mind, come on, this way,' said Lady Sarah Delchette reversing my direction and drawing me towards the centre of the ballroom where couples were twirling to the music of the waltz.

Chivalry demanded that I did not wrest myself from her grasp. Briefly I thought of pretending to have broken my ankle but that would have involved dramatic skills beyond my ability. I was trapped. 'I dance very badly,' I said feebly.

'Nonsense,' she said turning when we reached the dance floor and presenting herself for me to place my arm around her waist, 'you're a musician.'

'Music and dancing are not necessarily compatible,' I said.

'What rubbish men talk. You didn't mind me calling you Robin just then, did you? I was being pursued by a hussar, you see, and needed help.'

'Not at all,' I said commencing the waltz stiffly to substantiate the claim that I danced badly.

'You can call me Sarah, if you want.'

'Thank you.'

'Go on then.'

'Thank you, Sarah.'

'We waved at you from the royal circle in the opera house tonight, but you didn't notice.'

'I was probably facing the orchestra. Conductors are inclined to do that, it simplifies our work.'

'Don't be so awkward, Robin. I meant we waved at you after that divine piece of Tchaikovsky, when everyone was weeping into their handkerchiefs. What nonsense about not dancing properly, you waltz very well,' she said.

Sarah's soft proximity was beginning to affect me so I decided the time had come to invoke my fictitious betrothal.

'My fiancée thinks otherwise,' I said.

'Ah, your fiancée. I expect she is very beautiful?'

'Indeed so.'

'Does she miss you very much, does she write frequently, expressing sentiments of great affection?'

'Within limits, yes, naturally.'

'Her letters are despatched in expensive scented envelopes, I expect. I must look out for them in the mail tray.'

'This hussar,' I said changing the subject quickly. 'In what manner were you being pursued?'

'His regiment is posted at the mountain barracks during the week, so he arrives at the ball hungry for affection,' she said. 'Rather too hungry.'

At that point the music stopped.

'Thank you for protecting me. You can escort me back to the residence after the last dance, if you like. The moon is beautiful tonight,' she said, her oval eyes fixed steadily on mine.

'Nothing would give me greater pleasure. Unfortunately I have another engagement.'

'Liar,' she said taking my arm as I returned her to the cluster of maids-of-honour assembled near the royal purple and gold canopy.

'A very important engagement.'

'With whom?'

'Countess Grigorn.'

'Never!'

'Indeed, yes.'

'I don't believe it!'

'The nature of our assignment must of course remain confidential. However if you promise not to tell anyone I shall read you the note I received from the countess shortly after the concert,' I said.

I drew an imaginary piece of paper from my pocket.

"My dearest, I cannot live without you. Come to my apartment at midnight and I shall show you my etchings. Your loving, Clarissa".

Sarah cuffed me like a kitten. 'Her name is Isobel not Clarissa!' she laughed.

Bowing, I took my leave and made for the exit. Above the babble of conversation in the ballroom I heard Sarah's voice exclaim to her friends 'What's so dangerous about walking back in moonlight?'

CHAPTER 10

The university consisted of an imposing array of buildings modelled on Oxford with quadrangles and spires set amidst striped lawns and trees overlooking the lake used for college boating and rowing activities. The music school was at the rear of the complex. No shortage of funds here, I thought, arriving at the entrance and admiring the fluted columns, alcoves and grand marble statues of important classical composers.

Prepared for a cool reception I made for the concert hall escorted by a passing student who on learning my name stammered a few words of welcome, which was more than I received from Professor Schmidt. The choral society was rehearsing Mozart's *Mass in C minor*. Schmidt nodded in my direction when I entered the hall but continued with the rehearsal.

I slipped into a seat and waited, admiring the arrangement of the hall structured in the form of an amphitheatre which allowed the audience closer than average proximity to the performers while maintaining the classical theme of the building. The acoustics were excellent. The stage was large enough for chamber music recitals and choral works with piano accompaniment, but not for a full orchestra.

Having put me in my place by continuing the rehearsal Schmidt eventually laid down his baton and introduced me to the choir in a guarded speech emphasising the responsibilities of persons in authority to protect the cultural heritage of the nation and expressing the hope that the relationship between the choral society and orchestra would continue to be one of mutual trust and respect. I was given no opportunity of replying because as soon as Schmidt stopped talking he raised his baton and embarked on the *Qui Tollis* section of Mozart's masterpiece. The chorus having now identified me as the person responsible for cancelling *Fidelio* looked down at me from the stage with the distaste commonly reserved for cut-throats and tax collectors.

Ignoring the atmosphere of hostility I settled into my seat and concentrated on the performance. By the time the chorus had completed the *Qui Tollis* section I had reached several conclusions. Firstly Professor Schmidt was, as I had anticipated, a lurcher, that is to say a conductor who exaggerates the composer's markings. So intently does the lurcher strive to achieve faithful reproductions of the score that the markings achieve greater significance than the time signature, and the music jerks along between extreme interpretations of volume and pace. The conductor in effect loses the wood for the trees. Ordinarily this would not concern me but Mozart had composed the mass for choir and orchestra, not choir and piano. At some stage the work would be handed over to the orchestra for production in the opera house and I would have to decide whether to accept the professor's interpretation or impose my own, a decision which, given the prevailing spirit of animosity, could conceivably result in the newly appointed master of music ending up in a dark alley with a stiletto in his back.

Secondly the choral society's soprano soloists, in all other respects fine singers with attractive voices and good upper ranges, were several years too old and several sizes too large to play Mimi in *La Bohème*. The role demanded a young woman, slim and pretty. The tenors were similarly unsuited for the role of Rodolfo, the starving young poet, though there were several possibilities for Marcello and Musetta amidst the basses and mezzo-sopranos.

Thirdly the elderly pianist accompanying the choir was as prim and dull as Schmidt himself and not the sort of person I wanted for concertos although out of courtesy, and bearing in mind the need for a continuance of mutual trust and respect, I would have to include him in the forthcoming auditions.

'What do think of the ensemble?' said Schmidt condescending to walk over during a break in the rehearsal.

'Very professional,' I said.

'We are preparing the mass for the Christmas season in the opera house, unless you intend to cancel Mozart performances too.'

'Not at all. The piece will fit in very well.'

'I have broken the news of *Fidelio* to the choristers and, under the circumstances, they have accepted the wasted months of rehearsal with good grace,' said Schmidt nodding at the assembly of mostly middle-aged singers glowering at me from the stage.

'So I see,' I said.

'Well then, at your convenience, I suggest we arrange a meeting to discuss the university's contribution to the . . . ' said the professor, searching for the correct words, '. . . spiritual aspect of your forthcoming programme.'

'Excellent, we can address resources and funding at the same time,' I said.

'Funding?' bristled the professor.

'We must ensure that your finances are not adversely affected by opera house performance costs.'

'We certainly must,' said the professor shortly.

'Meanwhile, I am looking for soloists, for piano concertos,' I said.

'Can you recommend anyone - a rising star in the college perhaps?'

'You need look no further than Dr Leisl, our accompanist today,' said the professor haughtily. 'The best pianist in the country by a considerable margin, in my opinion, greatly in demand here and internationally, and a regular soloist in the opera house during . . .' Schmidt just managed to stop himself from saying better times and substituted '. . . previous years.'

'Thank you. In which case, I shall invite him to the audition. Can you recommend anyone else?'

'What concertos do you have in mind?'

'Tchaikovsky, Rachmaninov.'

Schmidt's knees buckled theatrically.

'Dr Leisl's repertoire,' said the professor hoarsely, grasping a chair for support, 'is confined to serious music.'

. . . .

The name of the young *répétiteur* was Marcus Galle. He arrived as the sun was setting over the square. He shook hands with me shyly and looked round the room, his eyes settling on the Steinway which he stared at with mounting excitement. The shyness, I soon discovered, represented endearing bewilderment at being worthy of anyone's attention. He was fifteen years old, medium height, slimly built with curly hair. He told me he lived with his disabled father on the outskirts of the city, that his mother had taught him the piano, that she had died recently and he travelled to work each day on the roof of a coach-and-four.

In the absence of other alternatives, LeBreq having confirmed that Dr Leisl was the soloist normally selected by the opera house for concertos (Mozart, Bach, Haydn etc) and Soprianti having verified there were no other pianists currently on the list of the visiting virtuosi, I had turned to Madame Prtenchska and promised her that nothing arising from my interest in Marcus would prejudice his duties at the ballet school.

He played Chopin's *Première Ballade* for me from memory. The piece represents a graveyard for pianists insufficiently gifted to handle the melodic themes submerged within the complex infrastructure, and has probably been responsible for undoing more pianists at competitions and auditions than anything other work in the keyboard repertoire. Marcus played the *ballade* effortlessly. Not perfectly, that would have been impossible at his stage of development, but with such nonchalant ease that by the end I was convinced of his talent.

'Have a look at this,' I said handing him a score.

Marcus opened the heavily-bound volume.

'Tchaikovsky's first piano concerto,' I said.

Marcus turned the pages, scanning the notes, the locks of his brown hair tumbling over his eyes.

'Take the score with you,' I said, 'and work through it for a few days. Then we'll talk with Madame Prtenchska and discuss the possibility you auditioning with the orchestra. What do you think?'

Without lifting his eyes from the score, Marcus nodded enthusiastically.

I drove him home in the Citroën. The car climbed slowly through the network of narrow streets to the outskirts of the city in the looming hills. Through the side mirror I could see the harbour lights blinking thousands of feet below and it occurred to me that if the engine and brakes of the Citroën failed simultaneously we would descend like a projectile into the dark blue sea. Arriving at a small wooden house in an unpaved lane Marcus leapt out of the car and ascended the stairs ahead of me, waving the score at his father who was waiting anxiously on the landing, propped on a crutch.

'I might be auditioned for the orchestra!' he cried.

They lived on top of the small house in a few sparsely furnished rooms. There was a painting of a schooner above the fireplace, and some wooden carvings on the mantelpiece which Mr Galle explained represented his hobby since losing the use of his leg, and consequently his job as electrician, in an accident. The old upright piano by the window looked in need of attention. Sipping tea I invented a clause in the non-existing arrangement between the opera house and candidates for audition whereby the opera house paid for the tuning and repair of domestic pianos especially, though I did not mention this part, when the sole breadwinner in the candidate's family was a fifteen year old boy.

The Citroën stalled on the return journey down the hill. Resetting the handbrake I could hear the opening chords of Tchaikovsky's famous concerto drifting through the starlit night. Marcus was wasting no time.

CHAPTER 11

I am getting rid of the principal double bass, Andreas. I made the decision when reviewing the performance of individual members of the orchestra with LeBreq this morning. Andreas is Hungarian, an excellent musician but excessively self-important and insolent. His caustic comments from the rear of the orchestra have been troubling his contemporaries for years, according to LeBreq, and I have personally had enough of his asides of audible dissent at rehearsals. He is not the only troublemaker, but the worst. The others will be warned.

Sadly the time has also come to say goodbye to several elderly members of the orchestra struggling with the transition from baroque counterpoint to the harmonic and rhythmical challenges of contemporary music. And here's the problem. None of the players are protected by contracts of employment, nor eligible for pensions.

I care little for Andreas in that respect. He is young enough to rebuild his career elsewhere. But I am deeply troubled at the prospect of forcing loyal servants of the orchestra into poverty-stricken retirement.

Under the feudal process I inherited from Leigh-Winter, players are employed on a monthly basis. The appointments are renewed automatically unless otherwise decreed by the conductor who can dismiss players without warning or notice, and without remuneration except payment of outstanding wages. The players have no recourse or appeal.

It angered me that Leigh-Winter accepted and executed this one-sided arrangement. He must have been aware of the steps taken by orchestras elsewhere in Europe to improve working conditions for their musicians. At the very least players and their families were entitled to a reasonable measure of security. I felt strongly that in this modern age players should be protected by some kind of pension arrangement and be given fair notice of intention to terminate their employment.

It also crossed my mind that the newly formed government in Ardaniia might already be addressing the subject of worker's rights. One of the outcomes of the country's recent transition to democracy had been the introduction of an independent judiciary. Deciding to seek advice before sacking Andreas I visited the castle's office building after lunch.

The notice on the door said 'Advocate Royal - Visitors by Appointment Only'. Entering I was informed by the clerk at the reception desk that the advocate was out of the country. I enquired if another lawyer was available. The clerk admitted that the deputy advocate was in residence but, he said fluttering his hands in the direction of the notice on the door, an appointment was required. In which case I would like to make one, I said, announcing my name and title. The clerk's pen froze above the appointments diary at the words 'master of music'. He looked up from the desk, ink dripping from the pen, alarm registering in his eyes.

To my embarrassment Leigh-Winter's prime legacy appears to be a trail of terrified retainers. Within minutes I was shown by the hand-wringing clerk into a large office overlooking a cobbled courtyard. Books were stacked neatly to the ceiling in mahogany cabinets along the walls. The room smelled of vellum, sealing wax and expensive floral perfume. There was a wastepaper basket in the corner embroidered with a picture of the Eiffel Tower and a hat-stand with a straw bonnet and purple ribbon dangling from it. On the desk, facing outwards, was a bronze plaque engraved 'Yvette de Carbon-Ferriere, Deputy Advocate Royal'.

Disorientated at encountering a female at the desk I hovered uncertainly at the door.

The deputy advocate was dressed in an elegant cream-coloured suit. Her hair was gathered at the back in the modern style without a parting in the middle. About my age, she looked chic and disturbingly attractive. Informing me in a brisk voice that she had just returned from vacation in time to take over from the advocate royal who by now was in Switzerland on a walking tour of Alpine villages with his family, she invited me to sit down.

'Do I call you mademoiselle or madame?' I said in the sort of breezy voice men adopt in the presence of beautiful women.

Without comment she raised her hands to display slim ringless fingers.

That was the end of small talk. Her hazel eyes stared coolly into mine while she waited to learn the purpose of my visit, conveying no visible sign of annoyance at the disruption to her timetable but not much in the way of enthusiasm for my presence either.

The government was endeavouring to introduce legislation to protect the workforce from unscrupulous employers, she said after I had listed my enquiries. The employers, mostly the landowning aristocracy, were doing their best to impede the government's programme. A recent attempt to introduce trade union representation into the industrial environment had, for example, resulted in the overnight disappearance of several left-wing officials, reportedly in the cargo hold of a freighter bound for South America.

Contracts of employment were awarded to foreigners in high-ranking positions to avoid the expense and embarrassment of international wrangles. Contracts were not normally awarded to Ardaniian nationals. The palace's position on employment was that the kingdom rewarded its elite with remunerations at levels well above normal, levels at which its educated citizens were expected to make their own provision for retirement. The lord chamberlain would be unlikely to approve the concept of awarding employees notice of dismissal let alone the introduction of a pension scheme for the orchestra.

She smiled only once.

'If I ended up in court defending a case of unfair dismissal, would your office support me?' I asked.

'Probably,' she said.

'Just probably?'

'First, we'd check the king's view on the matter,' she said with a chopping motion of her hand, her eyes lightening briefly to accompany the smile.

On the way back to the Citroen I called in at the clinic.

Dr Dalrymple-Smith, the royal physician, was sitting with his feet resting on a container marked 'Clinical Waste' talking the duty nurse. Nurses spent most of their time patching up cuts on the arms, hands and fingers of the kitchen staff responsible for slicing fowl and filleting fish, distracted from their work by the pranks of the younger staff and the gossip of the older, said the physician ushering me into his surgery. His own work consisted mainly of listening to elderly dukes complaining of headaches. The surprising thing was, said the physician, that the old rogues were alive at all, in view of the astonishing volumes of liquor they consumed. They kept themselves comparatively fit, of course, said the physician, still playing polo, hunting deer and riding to foxhounds, exercising their livers beneficially by the motion of their horses.

Concerning the princess he had followed up my request at the ball by asking Sophie to attend the surgery on the pretext of a routine palace check-up. He had examined her ears and found nothing wrong with them, or her hearing. She had admitted to intermittent problems with her balance, but put it down to the stress of dancing a major role.

'I have prescribed some tablets,' said the royal physician. 'Placebos. Sometimes they work, sometimes not, let's see. I've dropped a note to Dr Fabricci, the school doctor.'

CHAPTER 12

Marcus performed the Tchaikovsky concerto for me this morning.

He is immensely shy in conversation but seated at the piano he becomes transformed and radiates the confidence of his prodigious talent. In profile he looks the part of a concert pianist. His posture is good, he sits upright, moving only his arms and fingers, eyes focused on the score or straight ahead when playing from memory, intermittently glancing down at the keys, expressionless except for the occasional hint of a smile to acknowledge the beauty or complexity of the music and unconsciously, on conclusion of the performance, sweeping his hair back with both hands in the manner attributed to Chopin and Liszt.

By contrast, my own comportment at the piano is slovenly. I crouch over the keyboard and contort my face. The severity of the contortions are directly proportional to the intricacy of the score and I have never managed to rid myself of the unfortunate habit. Worse, I still occasionally throw anxious glances sideways, ready at a moment's notice to remove my hands from the keyboard in order to escape the swishing descent of rulers aimed at my fingers by the assorted collection of savage tutors engaged for piano lessons by my parents in my childhood.

Marcus's progress is extraordinary. In just a few days he has memorized the first two movements and overcome almost all the technical challenges. I have lent him Rubinstein's version of the concerto on gramophone records and told him to listen to the way the great master unfolds the themes.

'Don't model yourself on Rubinstein's style,' I warned. 'Treat him as a guide, and watch how he handles the entries of the orchestra.'

Afterwards we proceeded to the ballet school, Marcus to resume his duties as *répétiteur*, I to pronounce my recommendations on Princess Sophie.

Madame Prtenchska's two senior ballet mistresses were present at the meeting. Madame Slymnova, the older of the pair, was the niece of Capitoline Samovskaya, dancer at Russian Imperial Theatre who married the famous choreographer Jules-Joseph Perrot, the creator of *Ondine* and *Giselle*. She followed her aunt to the Imperial Theater before moving to Paris to teach students at the Theatre du Chatelet.

Madame Tuillée, a person after my own heart, was renowned for refusing to dance or instruct the ballet *Coppélia* in protest at the Paris Opéra's refusal to pay salaries to its dancers when the hall closed temporarily during the Franco-Prussian war in 1870. The victims included Madame Tuillée's mother, and the young ballerina Giuseppina Bozzacchi who had been dancing the role of Swanhilda in *Coppélia*. Giuseppina died of starvation on the morning of her seventeenth birthday. Madame Tuillée's mother survived but wept every time she heard Delibes' music.

The ballet mistresses were as graceful and elegant as Madame Prtenchska and shared the director's compassionate eyes. I attribute the gentleness to the lifetime of endurance by ballerinas *en pointe*, balanced unnaturally in positions which stretch their muscles in directions they were never intended to be stretched, causing great discomfort and pain.

'At my request, the royal physician has examined the princess,' I told the ladies, explaining the circumstances under which the examination had been conducted and assuring them that the school doctor had been notified and Dr Fabricci's credentials were not in doubt. The results of the examination were negative in that they failed to identify any physical reason for the princess's falls. During the examination the royal physician had conducted an ear test but the results were similarly inconclusive. As a precaution against the possibility that her ears or sinuses might be responsible for the imbalance, the royal physician had prescribed some pills.

'Which unfortunately does not advance the situation,' I said.

'But it does!' protested Madame Prtenchska. 'We were worried that Dr Fabricci might have overlooked something. It removes the doubt, you see. Thank you so much.'

'Yes, indeed,' nodded the ballet mistresses.

'The pills are placebos,' I pointed out. 'If the princess recovers her balance, it will be difficult to tell whether the recovery is genuine, or motivated by psychological factors.'

'Does it matter?' said Madame Prtenchska. 'Surely the fact of her recovery would be enough?'

'I think it does matter. Without knowing exactly what's wrong, there's no defence against a relapse.'

My audience sat thoughtfully for a while.

'Moreover, I think we're agreed that the worst possible time for a relapse would be on the opera house stage at Christmas?' I said.

'Certainly,' shuddered Madame Prtenchska.

'Yes, indeed,' nodded the ballet mistresses.

'So allow me to pose a question. How many of the girls can dance the role of Aurora?'

There was another long silence.

'Several,' said Madame Prtenchska cautiously.

'Three or four,' said the ballet mistresses.

'Why do you ask?' said Madame Prtenchska.

'How many students can dance the Lilac Fairy?' I said.

The ladies exchanged glances.

'A dozen,' said Madame Prtenchska.

'At least,' said the ballet mistresses.

'The part of the Lilac Fairy is almost equally important, but easier to perform, am I right? ' I said.

The ladies nodded.

'Technically less demanding?' I said.

'Yes,' said Madame Prtenchska, 'but why do you ask?'

'Because I think Princess Sophie should switch roles.'

The ladies' hands leapt to their mouths.

I sympathized with them. They had promised the king that the princess would take the part of Aurora. Their livelihood depended on his goodwill. If that was withdrawn, what then? In their minds they visualised flames rising from the site of the ballet school, blackened rubble where the princess had once danced, striving nobly at her task before the failings of the perfidious persons responsible for her instruction had been exposed as impostors, persons for whom no punishment could be sufficiently severe . . .

'It would reduce the risk of an incident, to a significant degree, while maintaining a prominent role for the princess,' I said.

The ladies looked at each other.

'If you agree, I shall inform the king,' I said.

In the silence the ladies twisted their hands anxiously in their laps.

'What will you say to him?' said Madame Prtenchska.

'Properly presented, I expect he will accept the situation with good grace,' I said, far from confident that the king would do anything of the sort.

. . . .

With the fingers of one hand, on a typewriter borrowed from the main office, I prepared a confidential document entitled 'Advantages of Financial Security for Orchestra and Opera House Staff.'

The theme of the report was the need to improve and sustain morale. I listed the measures commonly adopted by major European orchestras to nurture their musicians. Contracts of employment were the most effective method. Spared the ordeal of insecurity, musicians stopped worrying about their families and children and concentrated on making music. By contrast here, in Ardaniia, the system of verbal appointments had arguably contributed to a perceptible atmosphere of restlessness in the orchestra. Without remedial action there was a danger of losing important players. Worse, for the country as a whole, young musicians would be increasingly likely to look abroad for employment.

The other important advance I proposed was the introduction of pension schemes. With appropriate investment, pension policies could be self-financing, I wrote. The benefits in terms of employee morale were substantial and would allow the orchestra to initiate painless retirement processes for elderly players wilting under the pressure of learning new and increasingly difficult compositions.

The lights were still on in the lord chamberlain's office when I reached the palace. The clerks had left for the night so I placed the manila envelope on a desk and was turning to leave when the door from the inner office opened and the lord chamberlain himself appeared.

'What's that?' he said nodding at the envelope. 'Your resignation?'

'Not yet,' I smiled.

'Professor Schmidt's?'

'No,' I said. 'Though it wouldn't surprise me if he walked out of our forthcoming meeting on the music school budget.'

'You haven't discussed the subject yet?'

I shook my head.

'But you're going to?' said the lord chamberlain.

'Any day now.'

'Is he being helpful?'

'Yes,' I lied.

'Very well, do it your own way, but keep him on a tight rein. Professor Schmidt is a cantankerous bully,' said the lord chamberlain. 'Now then, what's this?'

He sliced the manila envelope open with a paper knife, read the report, returned it to the envelope, dropped the envelope on the desk, withdrew a gold watch from his waistcoat pocket and examined it.

'Time to change for dinner,' he said switching off the office lights. 'Walk with me.'

Flames from the braziers on the castle walls illuminated the path through the gardens. Still warm from the sun which had dropped behind the mountains the flower beds diffused perfumes of thyme and roses. The lord chamberlain walked with his hands clasped behind his back. I did not disturb his thoughts. Silently we proceeded towards the residences. Reaching the pillared entrance to the lavish ground floor accommodation the lord chamberlain stopped and turned in my direction.

'No contracts of employment, no pension schemes,' he said. 'We're not ready for them yet. However I approve your proposal in principle. Go ahead, but implement the recommendations by different means.'

CHAPTER 13

The committee convened to review the sensitive matter of rehearsals has issued its recommendations which include a request for a two day break each week, on Sundays and Mondays, and an embargo on evening rehearsals except in an emergency. I have agreed to the recommendations on the condition that during the last two weeks of preparations for a staged production of opera or ballet the orchestra will be on call throughout the day, and evening, without any weekend break, if required.

The programme for this week's concert includes Mendelssohn's Violin Concerto, with LeBreq himself as soloist. The major new work is a compilation from Tchaikovsky's *Nutcracker* ballet, including the sumptuous *Intrada Pas de Deux,* for the benefit of the king and in keeping with my intention that the second half of each concert should be devoted to music of the romantic school.

There was a strange atmosphere on the stage this morning. The players were restless. I wondered whether news had leaked out of my intention to cull the troublemakers and retire elderly members of the orchestra. If so, where had the leak come from? Surely not LeBreq. Had I carelessly left a carbon copy of my confidential report to the lord chamberlain on my desk? Determined to act without further delay I telephoned the advocate royal's office for a further appointment.

. . . .

Yvette de Carbon-Ferriere's desk was even more submerged in paper and her greeting even less enthusiastic than on the previous occasion.

'I need your advice on the definition of a contract,' I said.

The most likely explanation for her coolness, I thought, was the irascible temperament of my predecessor Leigh-Winter. Noisily aggressive when displeased, he would almost certainly have come into contact with the advocate's office and prejudiced this chic and determined young lady's view a of conductors. Alternatively, I pondered as she reached for a law book from the shelf behind her desk, her coolness towards me perhaps represented genuine indifference to males ineligible for appointment to Ardaniia's elite household cavalry regiment, whose rich and titled officers gathered around her every evening in the anteroom like moths drawn to a flame.

From the law book she quoted aloud the definition of a contract, which more or less matched the definition in my own dictionary.

'Thank you but, more specifically, at what point does a verbal agreement become a contract and, on the same lines, when do *ex gratia* payments linked to years of service become a pension?' I said.

Perhaps her attitude was simply a manifestation of overwork. After all, the advocate royal was on holiday leaving her solely responsible for the legal affairs of the court and, because the ministry of defence had not yet been handed over to the government, for all matters associated with military regulations. She was too busy for the frivolousness of flirtation.

In support of the overwork theory, a clerk hurried into the office and presented her with a note.

'Forgive me,' she said returning the leather-bound volume to the shelf. 'The lord chamberlain requires my presence.' I stood politely while she checked her hair in the mirror behind the hat-stand and adjusted her chiffon scarf wafting a hint of floral perfume in my direction.

'*Merci*,' she said as I opened the door for her.

A second later her head reappeared.

'Don't offer anything in writing,' she said.

'Right,' I said.

Her head reappeared again.

'Good luck.'

Driving back to the opera house I decided that her advice, though brief, matched my own assessment of the situation, namely that to comply with the lord chamberlain's directive I must confine myself to verbal commitments, such commitments being made face to face, in the absence of witnesses and carefully structured to avoid the words contract and pension.

．．．．

Over lunch with LeBreq I learned that the king's mistress, the French ballerina, had once been employed at the ballet school by Madame Prtenchska. The airs and graces assumed by the ballerina on promotion to duchess had made her so intolerably difficult to work with, so condescending in manner and so unpopular with the students that Madame Prtenchska had been forced to discharge her.

As to the infamous event resulting in Leigh-Winter's dismissal, on the evening in question the ballerina-duchess had arrived in the opera house accompanied by the king's uncle, Archduke George. Both were heavily inebriated. They weaved mistakenly into the royal box ahead of the royal family ascending the stairs behind them, catching Leigh-Winter by surprise who ill-advisedly launched into the national anthem without verifying the identity of the couple swaying unsteadily in the royal box in the space normally occupied by the king. The following morning the ballerina, demoted from duchess, and Leigh-Winter, demoted from master of music, were escorted to the steamer for Marseilles. The archduke left shortly afterwards, exiled to the royal family's estates in Austria, loudly protesting his innocence, shouting through the window of his carriage to onlookers in the street that the whole damned thing had been a case of mistaken identity, that he had been in bed with a dragoon major's wife at the time of the incident.

. . . .

I read out the list of complaints, added my own charges, and informed Andreas, the head of the double bass section, that his position was being awarded to another player

'What!' he said jumping out of the chair in front of my desk into which he had dropped uninvited when summoned to my chambers.

'Which unfortunately means an absence of vacancies for you in the orchestra.'

'What the devil . . !' snapped Andreas.

'Which means your services are no longer required, and your employment is terminated herewith.'

'You can't do that!' shouted Andreas.

'I require you now to collect your belongings and leave the building.'

The burly Hungarian slammed his fist onto my desk.

'This is outrageous!'

'You are a competent musician,' I said calmly. 'With due adjustment to your attitude you should have no difficulty in rebuilding your career elsewhere. At the end of this month your salary will be forwarded to your registered address. On evidence that you propose leaving the country, by virtue of possession of a steamer ticket, the messenger delivering your salary will disburse a further amount representing two month's severance pay.'

'I was hired by Dr Fruncke. You don't have the right to terminate my employment!' shouted Andreas.

'If you elect to remain in this country the severance pay will be held in abeyance for twelve months pending verification that you have not acted to the detriment of the orchestra during the year.'

'I shall inform Professor Schmidt!'

'You have ten minutes to collect your possessions. After that, if I see you in the opera house again the severance package will be cancelled.'

'I shall inform the police!'

'Close the door on the way out,' I said.

I dealt with the lesser troublemakers the same way, reading out the complaints and charges - negative contribution to orchestra's morale, arrogant attitude to junior musicians, sniggering dissent during rehearsals - and asked them for reasons why their employment should be continued. Knees wobbling in the manner of bullies everywhere they stumbled through their defences.

To each of them I said 'Your musical ability is not in doubt, but you are herewith on notice of dismissal, until such time that your contribution to the orchestra is seen to be positive.'

Then the compulsory retirements. Rarely have I felt so angry at Leigh-Winter as I did when forced to witness elderly servants of the orchestra shuffle into my chambers, heads down, resigned to a bleak future, convinced they were about to be condemned to the dark misery of destitution. The expressions of astonishment and relief on their faces when they learned of my intention to award them handsome bonus payments on their retirement in three months' time will long remain etched in my memory.

Finally the orchestra itself. Section by section I invited the principals to convey to their players the good news that salaries were being raised forthwith and that a discretionary award system was being introduced whereby players on retirement or resignation from the orchestra would receive *ex gratia* payments broadly based on the number of years' service. Pending appointment of Andreas's successor, LeBreq broke the news to the double bass section.

CHAPTER 14

The first thing I hear on arrival at the opera house each morning is Valentino's voice. I suspect he waits until I have switched off the engine of the Citroen before embarking on extracts from *Pinafore* or *Mikado* the sound of which accompany me up the steps and along the corridor to my chambers and stops immediately I open the door.

Greeting me with a theatrical bow he says, 'Begging you pardon, sir, I didn't hear you arrive. You quite caught me by surprise.'

He sings reasonably well but his voice requires training so I am inclined to ignore his attempts to attract my attention to his concert hall potential, at least for the moment. Right now I am in greater need of a steward than an amateur tenor.

My first task this morning was to inform the administrative staff of the new arrangements affecting their employment. I started with Peter Enkhle, the young and efficient Ardaniian orchestra support manager, who looks after the administrative arrangements for rehearsals, distribution of scores, seating arrangements, attendance records, storage of instruments etc. He works without supervision, gets on well with the players and does not trouble me unnecessarily. He beamed at the news of the pay rise and associated financial package and left the room grinning broadly.

Signora Furcello, the librarian, was next on the list and surprised me with her response to the award. Our meetings to date have been conducted in an atmosphere of frigid cordiality. She manages to convey without words, by merely adjusting the angle of her nose, that her venerated mentor, the late Dr Fruncke, would not have been seen dead with some of the composers whose works I presume to impose upon the orchestra. Moreover there is always an underlying hint of disdain, presumably instilled in her by Leigh-Winter, for English conductors.

So she caught me off balance by producing a handkerchief when I finished speaking. She twisted the piece of embroidered linen in her lap for a while then lifted it to her eyes which were suddenly full of tears. Indeed the flow of tears became so intense that I considered passing my own handkerchief across the desk.

'I prayed that something like this might happen,' she said when the flow had been stemmed. Her husband was an invalid, she explained. The pair of them had been living in mortal fear that she might become ill or that her skills as musical librarian might not be fully appreciated by a conductor of questionable discernment (viz. English) and that she might thereupon lose her job condemning them both to penury and starvation. I reassured her that in my opinion there was no retirement age for librarians, that her position was secure for as long as she felt capable of mounting the stairs and even then I would prefer to relocate the library to the ground floor than lose her expert services.

She stared at me long and hard from the door on departure. 'I am old-fashioned in my tastes, as you know, but I admit to having enjoyed last week's concert, especially your handling of the orchestra during *Romeo and Juliet*,' she said. The surprising confession was accompanied by what most people would have interpreted as a grimace but which I realised contained the elements of a smile.

Soprianti continues to irritate me. The opera house needs a suave personality in the foyer to greet the noble, rich and famous but not one quite so suavely idle and inefficient. To some extent the idleness can be excused on the grounds of the reduced workload during the summer season when the number of concerts and visits from touring companies is reduced. The inefficiency is less easy to condone. The only really clean parts of the building are the stage, library and my chambers, maintained respectively under the supervision of Peter Enkhle, Signora Furcello and Valentino. Elsewhere the condition of the opera house is most unsatisfactory. I have raised the matter several times with Soprianti but have yet to see much in the way of improvement.

The attitude of the general staff also leaves a lot to be desired. Ushers leap to attention as I approach only to slump back when I have passed. There are far too many of them anyway, another point of contention, and little in the way of evidence that they are gainfully deployed.

My displeasure at the situation is reflected in my decision to award the general staff, including Soprianti himself, a smaller pay increase than the rest and nothing in the way of *ex gratia* payments on departure. This is grossly unfair on the members of the general staff who work hard, including the booking office clerks and secretaries, but I have to draw the line somewhere.

Into my chambers, when I returned from morning rehearsals, marched Professor Schmidt, face dark as thunder, eyebrows lowered and chin thrust aggressively forward.

'What's this about the budget?' he demanded ignoring my invitation to take an armchair.

'Budget?' I parried cautiously.

Another leak. More awkward than the others, almost certainly direct from the lord chamberlain's office, and probably deliberate.

'Yes, budget. What the devil's going on?'

'Oh, you mean . . .'

'Don't pretend to misunderstand what I'm talking about!' said the professor. 'Whose idea was it to merge our finances? Yours I expect. I should have guessed it.'

'I can assure you . . .'

'You can assure me of nothing but deceit, sir!'

'You're probably referring to . . .'

'I'm referring to the hare-brained and insulting proposal to place the finances of a major university college under the control of a music hall conductor!'

'Come to think of it . . .'

'What experience do you possess of university administration, answer me that?'

'None really, although . . .'

'Do you have the faintest idea what the budget for an academic institution looks like?'

'Not exactly, except . . .'

'I thought so. This is an act of piracy, plain and simple. Pillage the students to finance a ludicrously extravagant programme of musical piffle which nobody wants! That's the objective, isn't it?'

'I wouldn't put it quite like that . . .'

'Then let me put it another way. Academic interests are significantly different from artistic interests.'

'I agree.'

'To merge the budgets of incompatible interests is to invite administrative paralysis.'

'I'm with you there.'

'What's more,' raged the professor, 'it most certainly will invite bitterness and warfare. For one, I will fight this preposterous notion to the bitter end!'

'I agree.'

'Not only will I fight . . .' the professor's voice trailed off. 'What did you say?'

'I agree.'

The professor stared at me.

'With what do you agree?'

'That the notion of integrating our budgets is impractical. I was not responsible for the suggestion, nor do I consider it feasible.'

'Impractical?' said the professor.

Wind removed from his sails, he sank into an armchair.

'So you don't support the proposal?' he muttered.

'No.'

'You're not going ahead with it?'

'No.'

The professor stared at his shoes for a while.

'When I said "piffle" and "music hall" just now I was rather exaggerating my position,' he said.

'I quite understand.'

'One can become carried away, in the heat of discussion, so to speak.'

'Think nothing of it,' I said dropping into the adjacent armchair. 'Now, shall we have some tea, and take a look at the schedule?'

In retrospect I think I prefer dealing with the professor in his normal aggressive state. At least I know what's on his mind. Subdued and repentant for his outbursts, he agreed too quickly to my suggestions. I fear there will be repercussions after due reflection on his part on the implications of his commitments. Nonetheless I think we have produced the basics of a workable programme, which includes the following choral works for performance in the opera house with the orchestra this year:

Handel *'Dixit Dominus'*

Haydn *'Missa in Angustiis'*

Mozart *'Requiem in D minor'*

Mozart *'Mass in C minor'*

Furthermore the professor has agreed that his senior year music school students should participate in the forthcoming auditions for vacancies in the orchestra and, grudgingly, that the university choral society would reconsider rehearsing for *La Bohème* next summer. He remains resolutely opposed to putting forward candidates for the Tchaikovsky piano concerto but he is too late anyway. The audition is scheduled for tomorrow.

It was a measure of the professor's subdued condition that he departed the opera house without slamming doors. I kept my ears open for crashing sounds in the corridor, but none came.

CHAPTER 15

The princess has not slipped, tripped or fallen since being examined by the royal physician. Accordingly I have postponed my audience with the king. My reasoning is that if Sophie's improvement is a result of the placebo tablets, indicating a psychological basis for the problem, it would be wiser to wait until she has finished the course of tablets. Recurrence of the falls would then provide a provide a positive diagnosis, strengthening the force of my recommendation. On the other hand it is possible to interpret my decision to postpone the audience as evidence of craven cowardice.

Buoyed by the pay awards the orchestra produced a fine performance at last Saturday's concert. Even the music critic of the *Sunday Gazette* was impressed. "The accomplished performance by the soloist, and the clarity of phrasing and mellow coordination of violin and cello strings, were admirable highlights of the Mendelssohn concerto." He was less complimentary about the *Nutcracker* compilation, calling the performance "loosely constructed". The audience disagreed with his verdict and greeted Tchaikovsky's delightful music with such rapturous applause that I was forced to replay the *Intrada Pas de Deux* as an encore. The royal family stayed until the end and the king raised his hand in approval before departing.

A less spectacular event this week but equally important was Marcus's audition. No other candidate had applied, nor did I expect one. Professor Schmidt had turned his back on the event from the start, effectively sealing off participation by the university and the country's influential musical circles. I was told of an excellent Hungarian pianist employed at the *Folies Belles*, an establishment of questionable reputation in the lower part of town. Further investigation revealed that the Hungarian was over-fond of liquor and inclined to slip off his chair onto the nightclub floor during the course of the evening, ruling him out on the basis that piano concertos are best played sober.

I had worked hard with Marcus before the audition, correcting wrong notes in the difficult first movement cadenza, rehearsing his entries, correcting his phrasing when he strayed from the markings on the score, all of which he bore with good grace and infinite patience although I would not have blamed him for arriving at our practice sessions with a note pinned to his chest saying "I would be extremely grateful if you will allow me to play through the work at least once without interruption".

During the actual performance of a concerto the conductor is at the mercy of the soloist who, by convention, dictates the tempo of the music. The conductor's job is to try and ensure that the orchestra completes the concerto on the same note as the soloist, preferably at the same time, and, if the soloist loses his way, to rescue the performance by reigning back the orchestra until the soloist catches up. Anyone who has ever tried reigning back a symphony orchestra in full flow with horns and trombones blaring and cymbals clashing will understand why conductors are selective in their choice of soloists.

I would never have taken the risk in England of transferring a *répétiteur*, however talented, direct from the rehearsal studio to the concert platform. The risk would have been too great. Here in Ardaniia, however, I was master of my own destiny free from the constraints of civic and corporate administrative oversight and the barbs of a vociferous press corps. The palace allowed me to run the orchestra without interference and the music critic of the local newspaper was too busy being impartial to pose a threat to my tenure, at least thus far. The only really serious risk was in damaging the boy's career by promoting him too early. I was confident of Marcus's technical ability, but could he handle the pressure of a public performance? More damning to myself, was I sacrificing Marcus on the altar of publicity, using his youthfulness to help promote my programme of classical romantic music?

I should not have worried. When the morning came for the audition he strode nonchalantly onto the stage, nodded at me from the piano stool and produced an exuberant and almost faultless performance of the Tchaikovsky concerto which earned the applause of the orchestra. The faults were all attributable to the same wrong notes in the first movement cadenza, errors which appear fixed in his mind and which nobody will notice anyway, except perhaps the Sunday Gazette's music critic. Even that was unlikely, unless the critic followed the music from the score.

I look forward to tomorrow night's performance with keen anticipation and am excited at the prospect of the audience's response to the young prodigy. The concert is sold out.

Next week the Neapolitan Touring Opera Company arrives to perform Donizetti's *Don Pasquale*. Curious as to the process of converting the hall from concert performances to stage productions, I summoned Soprianti to my chambers to talk through the arrangements. In preparation I drew up a list of the activities which I considered essential.

'Everything is taken care of already. Soprianti, he arranges everything,' said Soprianti, summarising for my benefit the procedure for the visit.

The touring company was bringing its own conductor freeing me of direct responsibility for the performances, which were scheduled for Thursday, Friday and Saturday nights. The conductor would arrive in the country earlier than the cast in order to rehearse my orchestra on Tuesday and Wednesday mornings. He would be accommodated in the Grand Hotel, the kingdom's most exclusive and expensive hotel, together with the company's soloists. The rest of the cast would stay in the Ocean View

Hotel, a three star establishment lower down the hill overlooking the port. The company would bring its own props. We would provide the stage hands, courtesy of the royal theatre. The stage hands would be responsible for setting up the orchestra pit in addition to handling the stage props and lighting during the performances.

When Soprianti had finished, I ran through the items on my list.

'Transport to and from the hotels?'

'Arranged.'

'Refreshments here in the opera house?'

'Yes.'

'Changing rooms cleaned and equipped for soloists and cast?'

'Done.'

'Booking office seating plans changed to reflect orchestra pit?'

'Arranged.'

'Bouquets for female soloists?'

'I tell you, Soprianti has arranged everything.'

'Insurance company notified?'

Pause.

'Press notified?' I said.

Pause.

'Arrangements made for reception at immigration?' I said.

Soprianti produced a notebook from his pocket and began writing.

'Medical support in event of emergency?' I said.

Another pause.

'It's done, but I will check, just in case,' said Soprianti scribbling in the notebook again.

In fairness to Soprianti, even if some of the items had merely slipped his mind, he would have recalled them in time to avoid, for example, groups of flustered Italian singers sitting on their suitcases at the steamer quay awaiting collection. This was not the first visit by a touring company. The Neapolitan Touring Opera Company alone had performed here at least a dozen times and presumably would not have returned to Ardaniia if their singers had been left sitting on the quay in the rain for indefinite periods. My respect for Soprianti's administrative abilities was such, however, that I felt more comfortable knowing the activities associated with touring company visits were recorded on a checklist, which I insisted be typed for general reference and circulation.

After lunch I took Soprianti with me to the royal theatre. The building was equidistant from the castle on the other side of the city looking directly down over the bay. Smaller than the opera house, the theatre was attractively proportioned with an elegant colonnade to the front. Posters in the noticeboards either side of the main door proclaimed nightly performances of *Le Tartuffe* by Molière, except on Sundays when the theatre was closed.

Soprianti presented me to the general manager, a pleasant Ardaniian who in turn introduced me to the director and producer. The former was a foppish young Frenchman in red chiffon scarf and black beret who smoked cigarettes from a long ivory holder, in caricature of *l'artiste de paris*. Despite the extravagance of his appearance he was lively and enthusiastic. I took to him at once. The producer, another Ardaniian, stout and middle-aged, was equally agreeable.

Proudly they showed me round the building pointing out features of importance. The booking office had recently been enlarged to cope with the demand for children's matinees, seats in the auditorium had been re-upholstered and a new hoist had been installed backstage to improve the speed of scene changes. The producer described how the labyrinth of ropes used for manoeuvring the props and curtains were operated and reassured me that he possessed sufficient manpower resources to meet all perceivable demands from the opera house for stage hands, even if the theatre itself was busy.

A trestle table was set up on the stage in our honour laden with earthenware wine jugs from which we were served by a group of giggling girls dressed up as rustic wenches. In this charming setting I outlined my plans for opera house stage productions, explaining that the extent of support required by the opera house for *The Sleeping Beauty* had yet to be determined pending resolution of a major casting problem with potential repercussions on the choreography, but that we would almost certainly lean heavily on the professional skills of the theatre for *La Bohème* next year.

'*La Bohème*,' cried the young French director excitedly, leaping up from the table. '*Mais c'est merveilleux!*'

'What happened to the Beethoven opera?' asked the theatre's general manager.

'I've postponed it,' I said.

The theatre's general manager and producer exchanged glances of what looked suspiciously like relief, confirming my view that *Fidelio* would have been an expensive disaster given the limited audience at the present time for such a challenging work.

'Alors!' cried the young French director hoisting a squealing girl onto his lap and raising his goblet with his free hand. 'Let us drink to the success of *La Bohème,* and the union of Mimi and Rodolfo!'

On the way back to the opera house I teased Soprianti with the suggestion that we install a trestle table on our stage. Soprianti, who clearly disapproved of the indecorous manner in which the royal theatre was administered, responded to my suggestion with stifled coughs and a cautious readjustment of his posterior in the passenger seat of the Citroen.

CHAPTER 16

I arrived early for Marcus's concert to find the coach yard full and the entrance blocked by a queue of people which stretched from the booking office to the gardens at the rear of the opera house despite the HOUSE FULL notices posted outside the building. The stable lads cleared a way through the queue and I manoeuvred the Citroen into the space marked RESERVED FOR CONDUCTOR hemmed in by lines of carriages with liveried coachmen watering and feeding their horses. Climbing the steps into the opera house I could hear the hubbub from the entrance hall, imperious voices raised in anger demanding to know why tickets were not available, complaining that sufficient seats should have been reserved for people of distinction, important people who had travelled considerable distances from their country estates to attend the concert.

Soprianti was at the door of my chambers wringing his hands. He had released the seats in the royal circle closest to the royal box despite the convention that space should be reserved in case of last minute additions to the royal contingent. Soprianti wanted me to release my allocation in the front row of the stalls. I refused, having already promised my spare seats to the ballet school to accommodate visitors from the Bolshoi school in Moscow. It was hard not to feel sorry for Soprianti as he hurried back to the booking house, hands grasping his hair. If the king arrived accompanied by more than the usual number of dukes, duchesses, equerries etc there would be trouble ahead in the royal circle.

Marcus was in the middle of the room standing with his arms

outstretched while the wardrobe mistress from the ballet school fussed around him. Her mouth was full of needles and her plump hands were adjusting the length of his sleeves. Unsure of the correct attire for a fifteen year old boy on a concert platform I had turned to Madame Prtenchska for advice. Hence the presence of the cheerful wardrobe mistress, clucking like a mother hen at Marcus who was trying to edge back to the piano to continue his warmup exercises. The wardrobe mistress had decreed that Marcus was too young for white tie and tails and should wear black tie and dinner jacket. The jacket was the source of the immediate problem. The sleeves were too long. They obscured his white shirt cuffs and interfered with his arm movements.

Observing the wardrobe mistress at work was Marcus's father. Seated at the window, wearing a brown suit with high collar that must have been fashionable half a century ago, he looked overwhelmed at the events which had overtaken his family. I spent a few minutes with him, enquiring about his health and making general conversation then instructed Valentino to make sure that he was kept supplied with drinks and that when the two minute bell sounded he, Valentino, was personally to escort the elderly parent to the seat in the front row of the stalls reserved from my allocation.

Valentino's other duties were to prepare champagne glasses for the guests invited to my chambers after the performance and to assist the ushers in denying entry to unwelcome visitors, a delicate task for which he was admirably suited being both snobbish by nature and acquainted with the social hierarchy in Ardaniia. My instructions to the ushers in the hall were that after the performance nobody was allowed entry into the corridor leading to my chambers until the king and royal family had descended the stairway, in case the king wanted to meet Marcus.

At the five minute bell LeBreq paid his usual visit to my chambers to inform me that the players had all arrived and the orchestra was assembling on the platform.

'Full house tonight,' he said. 'Newspapers have their uses, after all.'

He was referring to the front page article in a recent edition of the *Daily Gazette* which had described Marcus's early life at the piano, his tuition, his employment at the royal ballet school as an accompanist, his audition in the opera house and subsequent invitation to perform a concerto with the symphony orchestra, an invitation which would have thrilled his mother who tragically was no longer alive. The article had been composed largely by myself and supplied free of charge to the editor of the daily newspaper with a photograph of Marcus standing on the steps of the opera house holding a copy of Tchaikovsky's first piano concerto score.

At the two minute bell I told Marcus to stop practising, closed the lid of the Steinway and instructed him to wait until the lights had dimmed in the auditorium then slip into the empty seat alongside his father in the stalls.

A short thunderstorm battered the opera house during Schuman's *Rhenish Symphony*, the major work in the first half of the concert. The storm brought about a welcome drop in temperature in the hall but distracted me considerably seeing that I had forgotten to install the seat cover on the Citroen. Quite possibly I broke the record for the fastest performance of Schuman's famous symphony in the attempt to save my motor vehicle from filling with rainwater. Hurrying from the platform in the interval I found that Valentino had visited the coach yard at the onset of the storm, braving the rain and the restless hooves of the horses alarmed at the thunder, to fix the seat cover. He smiled modestly when I declared that his conduct in that respect had pleased me.

At the one minute bell announcing the end of the interval Marcus and I stood side-by-side in the wings adjusting our respective ties.

'I shake hands with Mr LeBreq first?' said Marcus.

'That's right,' I said.

'Then I bow to the audience?'

'That's right - and after that, you sit at the piano and enjoy yourself,' I smiled down at the boy.

We advanced in single file, Marcus first. The contrast between our heights must have emphasised the youthfulness of the soloist because the applause was mixed with aaahs and ooohs from the females in the audience.

Marcus shook hands with the leader of the orchestra, turned, bowed to the audience then matter-of-factly began adjusting the position of the piano stool. I waited until he had settled on the stool, positioned his hands over the keyboard and was looking up at me expectantly before I raised the baton.

Tchaikovsky's Piano Concerto No.1 in B ♭ minor opens with a series of loud chords from the orchestra. The soloist replies with a set of equally loud ones which, happily for him or her, are comparatively easy to play and serve to settle him or her down. Not that Marcus needed settling. He soared through the thunderous opening into the D ♭ major theme and from there on, with complete mastery of the notes, shoulders sometimes swaying to the music, curls of brown hair flopping over his forehead, flashes of an engaging smile on his lips, he held the audience enthralled.

The way he manipulated the second set of semiquavers in the D ♭ major theme (bar 1:4) took me by surprise. Tchaikovsky gives the semiquavers equal weight in the score although I wager he held them back too in a similar fashion in his own performances. The brilliance of Marcus's interpretation here and throughout the performance was well in advance of the interpretation he gave at the audition or at any of our practice sessions. His version of the magical trills at the close of the second movement (bars 46:9-10) raised the hairs on the back of my neck. Not for the first time in my professional life it occurred to me that extraordinarily gifted musicians possess some kind of spectral link with the composers whose music they play. Tchaikovsky was thirty five when he wrote the concerto, young in terms of his musical development. The great ballets lay ahead. The concerto is youthful in the sense it continues Tchaikovsky's experiments with methods of unfolding majestically beautiful themes. Half a century later Marcus was learning his art too, and the pair of them, the great composer and the gifted boy pianist, combined to produce one of the most lyrical and exciting performances I have participated in from the podium.

The roar from the audience nearly lifted the opera house roof.

Of the subsequent events that evening I cherish certain memories. Valentino turning pale at the door of my chambers whilst croaking 'They're coming'. The king bursting into the room shouting 'Where's the boy?' Marcus standing, wide eyed, being complimented on his performance by the king and receiving a purse of gold coins from the magnificently dressed rotund figure. The queen, in the perpetual state of intoxication with which I was to become familiar, whose sustenance was transported discreetly by her ladies-in-waiting within the voluminous folds of their costumes, bending over to stroke Marcus's cheeks with the backs of her long painted fingernails murmuring 'Such a talented child'. The lord chamberlain, to his great credit, taking the trouble to talk to Marcus's father and, when the royal contingent had departed and the room was filled with other guests voicing congratulations and downing champagne, the sight of Marcus, crushed against the piano by clusters of young ballerinas from the ballet school, squirming with embarrassment as the girls clamoured to embrace him.

CHAPTER 17

The refectory was normally empty on Sunday mornings. Revellers from the previous night's ball preferred to rise late and take breakfast in their apartments, tended by their valets who dispensed aspirins and sympathy in proportion to the severity of the courtly hangovers. The only person in the room when I arrived was the master of horse, hungrily consuming devilled kidneys. Collecting a newspaper from the rack I nodded at him and sat myself as far from the noble and invariably boring field-marshal as decorum allowed.

PROMISING DEBUT Sunday Gazette

An enthusiastic audience applauded a varied programme at the opera house last night. The house was packed and it has been many years since your correspondent witnessed a queue formed so late in the day, and for such a distance, stretching to the rear of the building, for tickets. The principal attraction was the soloist for the piano concerto in the second part of the concert, a young man of whom more later. The misery of the hundreds of disappointed music lovers turned away by the booking office and gathered outside the opera house windows in the hope of hearing at least some of the programme was compounded by a thunderstorm which left them drenched.

The programme commenced with *The Sorcerer's Apprentice* by Paul Dukas, currently professor of composition at Conservatoire de Paris. This is a jaunty and amusing piece of music which entertained the audience considerably and allowed the timpani and percussion sections of orchestra to display their undoubted skills. The string sections of the orchestra were less fortunate in meeting the challenges of the complicated score. Not for the first time your correspondent found himself wondering whether new works were being introduced without sufficient opportunity for rehearsal.

Schuman's *Rhenish Symphony* completed the first half of the programme. By now it has become clear that the orchestra's new conductor, Landour, intent on reclaiming the audience that has been dwindling recently from the opera house, proposes to maintain our enthusiasm with a mixture of light-hearted overtures and longer tragic-romantic pieces, into which are interspersed masterpieces from the classical era for the benefit of concert-goers of more profound discernment. Your correspondent does not complain of such tactics other than to express the hope that the masterpieces are treated in future with greater respect than the *Rhenish Symphony* which was played at such breakneck pace that the subtleties of work were sometimes lost.

The soloist in Tchaikovsky's first piano concerto was Marcus Galle, aged 15, an accompanist at the Royal Ballet School. Displaying commendable confidence and ably backed by the orchestra, the young man gave a moving rendition of the concerto which, in common with the Tchaikovsky works of previous weeks, was being performed for the first time in the opera house. There were some mistakes by the pianist in the difficult cadenza at the end of the first movement and his interpretation of music of such distressed beauty was in some places a little too youthful for the liking of your correspondent, who nonetheless shared with the audience a sense of excitement at the emergence of such significant talent. It is a long time since a soloist received a standing ovation in the opera house.

'What are you reading?' said the master of horse across the table.

'A newspaper, my lord,' I said.

'I can see that. Anything interesting?'

'Just a review of last night's concert at the opera house.'

'Oh, were you there? I gather it was rather good. Full too, apparently.'

'Fortunately I managed to find a place, my lord.'

The music critic was right about the tempo of the Schuman symphony for which I felt duly penitent. He was also right about the technical shortcomings of *The Sorcerer's Apprentice* but wrong in proposing dearth of rehearsal time as the reason. The problem lay principally with the string section where several elderly violinists were struggling with the rhythmical complexities of modern works. Perhaps I should go ahead and release the old retainers now, freeing them from the obligation to work through their periods of notice. Would they be upset at early departure? They deserved a dignified exit after so many years of loyal service. Whatever the solution it was evident I must get on with the business of recruiting new players for the orchestra.

Behind the critic's comments lay a mystery. What was the source of his technical expertise? From his comments it was apparent that his preparations for our concerts included close examination of the particular scores or detailed recall of the associated gramophone recordings. In the context of contemporary works such as *The Sorcerer's Apprentice* it was inconceivable that he had built up a library of scores or records in anticipation that the works in question might one day be performed in the opera house. A comprehensive library would have taken years to build. The cost would have been prohibitive knowing that the chances of my baroque-minded predecessors choosing to include *The Sorcerer's Apprentice* in their concerts were lower than the master of horse, replete with devilled kidneys, applying to audition for a vacancy in the orchestra. Yet the critic could not possibly have identified the wrong notes in the cadenza of the Tchaikovsky concerto without reference to a score. Who was assisting him? Was there a spy in our midst?

Stretching my legs later in the castle grounds I heard the sound of a girl singing. The sound came from the direction of the kitchens so I made a detour through the archway in the wall separating the kitchen block, laundry and servants quarters from the main palace buildings, and stood in the shade of a cypress tree listening. Her voice was sweet and pure. Her notes were perfectly pitched and held without a trace of vibration.

The kitchen windows stood high off the ground, presumably designed to ventilate and illuminate the building whilst inhibiting the staff from looking out and thereby distracting them from their work. Standing on my toes I could see only a thick layer of smoke from the ovens and grills, stirred by the blades of the ceiling fans.

The front of the building was busy with porters in heavy aprons unloading consignments of game, meat and fish from a line of ox carts. I followed the porters through the wide open doors into the kitchen which looked almost as large as the opera house auditorium. Under the layer of smoke the air was thick with the fragrance of roast fowl and rich sauces. Knives flashed along the aisles, wooden mallets hammered pieces of meat into shape, copper pans clashed on the stoneware surfaces and dimly through the hubbub and noise, from the direction of the sinks in the far corner of the building, came the sound of the girl singing.

'Can I help you?'

The stout woman curtsying with a minimum of deference and regarding me with hostile eyes wore a crown-shaped badge on her white apron. Her fists, I noted, were larger than mine and clenched. One blow and I would be catapulted across the kitchen through the windows amidst a shower of splintered glass. The combination of the badge and powerful fists left me no doubt that I was in the presence of the formidable royal cook, Mrs Drought, reputedly the only person in the palace of whom Countess Grigorn was afraid.

I announced my name and position and, nodding in the direction of the scullery, asked to meet the possessor of the voice whose song had attracted my attention.

The hostile eyes bored into me whilst the owner pondered the likelihood that my request represented yet another scheme by the gentlemen of the palace to lure her kitchen maids to their beds.

'I want to establish the extent of her musical background,' I explained.

Conveying by her expression that she found my explanation improbable Mrs Drought despatched a maid to the scullery, propped herself against a carving table and folded her brawny arms, indicating her intent to attend the interview. Years of experience had taught Mrs Drought that courtiers were not to be trusted.

The girl arrived drying her hands on her apron. Mrs Drought's concern was justified in as much as the girl was exceedingly pretty with soft pink cheeks and bright blue eyes which widened when I introduced myself. Her curtsey was noticeably more respectful than the version from the royal cook.

'What is your name?' I said as she straightened.

'Zoe, sir.'

'How old are you?'

'Eighteen, sir.'

'Where did you learn to sing, Zoe?'

'At home, that is to say, before my parents died, sir.'

'Have you had any formal training?'

'No, sir. Except for the music society.'

'You mean the university? Professor Schmidt?' I said astonished.

'The St Frett music society, sir.'

Seeing the puzzled look on my face, the girl said 'In the old town, sir.'

'I thought I knew all the musical establishments. I must pay the society a visit. How frequently do you attend?'

'Every Wednesday and Friday nights, sir.'

'Then I look forward to hearing you sing there. Assuming they let me in.'

'Of course they'll let you in, sir!'

The girl's laughter was gay and infectious, with just the right amount of worldliness. Departing the smoke-filled building I reflected contentedly upon the selection process whereby the role of Mimi in *La Bohème* might be played by a scullery maid from the royal kitchens.

CHAPTER 18

Enough, no more excuses. Princess Sophie has finished the placebo tablets and continues to maintain her balance which proves nothing other than she may, or may not, have recovered permanently. The summer months are running out and preparations for staging *The Sleeping Beauty* must begin. From my chambers this morning I telephoned the palace and arranged a preliminary meeting with the lord chamberlain.

'Three young gentlemen to see you, sir, from the music academy at the university,' said Valentino hovering at the door.

'Show them in,' I said.

I closed the files on my desk and sat back pleased at the interruption to the task of dealing with mundane administrative paperwork, a task reserved for Monday mornings in the absence of orchestral rehearsals.

Fresh-faced the three undergraduates filed into the room and stood in front of my desk. Their linen coats were pleated at the rear, with white cuffs at the sleeves and black shoes expensively buckled. Sons of affluent parents by the look of them, glossy and well-fed, suitably endowed for the grandeur of Professor Schmidt's prestigious academy.

I shook their hands and moved from my desk to the conference table.

'We can address the purpose of your visit more comfortably here,' I said nodding at Valentino who in accordance my long standing instructions for the handling of visitors stood at the pantry door awaiting confirmation whether or not to serve refreshments.

The undergraduates were enrolled in the university's piano and composition degree course. Banned by the university from participating in the audition for the Tchaikovsky piano concerto they had attended the concert on Saturday night and had been bowled over by the music. Tchaikovsky was not on the curriculum, nor were any of the composers of the modern and romantic schools they secretly admired. Their studies were restricted to the earlier classics. Nothing after Beethoven was considered worthy of serious attention in the music academy.

'When you say banned, by whom?' I said.

The undergraduates glanced at each other.

'Professor Schmidt?' I said.

The undergraduates nodded.

'Does he know you are here?' I said.

They shook their heads.

'Your visit is unofficial, then?'

The undergraduates nodded.

'So, how can I help?'

Not only had they been bowled over by the concerto but they were dismayed at being denied the opportunity of auditioning for the piece. The whole point of taking a music degree was to participate in the nation's artistic programmes yet they had been emphatically shut out of the most spectacular musical event in recent years. With no apparent prospect of remedying the situation, chained to a curriculum of ancient composers, they had decided to take the matter into their own hands and seek advice from the newly-appointed master of music.

'You want me to audition you now?' I said.

'Indeed, yes!' they cried, eyeing the Steinway which gleamed in the sunshine slanting through the mullioned windows.

'What do you imagine Professor Schmidt would say?' I said. 'Do you suppose he was pleased to learn from the newspapers that a young pianist untrained by the university, for whom the academy of music could claim no credit, received a standing ovation in the opera house on Saturday? Not only untrained but applauded for playing music the university does not think fit to teach? Moreover what now, do you imagine, would be Professor Schmidt's reaction if he learned that the newly-appointed master of music, responsible in his opinion for vandalising the integrity of opera house programmes, had been auditioning some of his star students behind his back?'

The undergraduates stared gloomily at the table.

'I admire the intensity of Professor Schmidt's position on romantic and modern music,' I said. 'He sees in Tchaikovsky and Ravel a loosening of the rules of counterpoint which have governed composition for the last two hundred years. It will take time to change his mind. Meanwhile I'm afraid you must be patient. You signed up for your courses knowing the terms of the curriculum, so you will have to wait until the opera house features Beethoven and Mozart piano concertos in its programmes again. Then, I promise you, you can apply to audition.'

'He always nominates Dr Leisl for auditions,' groaned the undergraduates.

I shook my head. 'I will insist on participation by university students.'

The undergraduates looked doubtful.

'If not, I shall threaten to award all concertos to our resident pianist, young Marcus Galle. Incidentally, are any of you as good as Marcus?'

They stared at each other.

'We shall find out, in due course,' I said shaking their hands and escorting the undergraduates from the room.

Valentino had scarcely finished clearing the cups and empty plates from the table when he was back at the door.

'A lady to see you, sir,' said Valentino

'Keep this up and I won't have to . . .' My voice trailed off as Yvette de Carbon-Ferriere entered the room, materialising like a rainbow, filling my chambers with colour. She was dressed in a lime-green dress with white buttons, and a pink scarf. Accompanying the rainbow came a mist of her exquisite floral perfume.

'You won't have to what?' said the deputy advocate pausing at the marble fireplace to admire the painting of St Frett castle attributed to an apprentice of Canaletto.

'Finish my paperwork.'

'*Oups!*' she said wagging her finger at me playfully, in marked contrast to her attitude during our previous encounters

'Is it so difficult?' she said removing the bag from her shoulder and placing it on the conference table.

Tongue-tied as usual in the presence of female loveliness I stammered something about the drudgery of official correspondence and was rescued by Valentino who, without waiting for my nod, delivered to the table two cups of coffee and a plate of expensive cakes purchased from the city's most fashionable patisserie, reflecting his view that my chambers deserved the finest available products in sufficient quantities to cater for emergencies and ensure a residue for anyone including himself who might fancy left-over delicacies for breakfast the following morning.

Yvette smiled sweetly at him, sliced a strawberry tartlet in half, passed one of the halves across the table to me, and sat down.

'I thought you would like to know that your double bass player, Andreas, has purchased a single ticket to Naples,' she said.

'Excellent!' I said.

'You won't have to go to court.'

'That's a relief!'

'And you won't lose your head,' she said simulating once more with her hand the chopping motion of an axe.

'Not for that particular offence anyway,' I said wryly. 'Do you happen to know the king personally? I mean do you meet him, in the course of your work?'

'Often.'

'Is he easy to talk to?'

'Yes, why?'

'Something has arisen, requiring my presence at an audience.'

'What kind of something?'

'It's better you don't know.'

Across the table her hazel eyes studied me.

'Don't lie to him,' she said.

'Right,' I said.

'Or flatter him. He hates that.'

'Very well.'

'And don't underestimate him.'

'What subjects should be avoided?'

'Criticism or manipulation of his children.'

'Ouch,' I said, stomach sinking.

'Are you sure you don't want to tell me?'

'Quite sure.'

She dabbed her mouth with her napkin and stood up. 'That was lovely, and I enjoyed the concert on Saturday, really wonderful. I wanted to congratulate you afterwards, but you weren't in the ballroom, as far as I could see.'

'The party rather dragged on here,' I said.

And then suddenly the room was empty. The rainbow colours had gone, the fragrance faded and I was left alone clenching my fists in annoyance. How slow and stupid of me! The transfer of strawberry tartlet across the table. The veiled hint about having looked out for me in the ballroom. I had just missed a golden opportunity of reserving a place on the beautiful young woman's dance card for next Saturday.

Soprianti was next to interrupt my paperwork, striding into the room hands spread.

'Everything for the opera, it is fine,' he said.

He ran through the list of everything that had not been fine when we last discussed the performance of *Don Pasquale* including accident insurance, first aid, liaison at immigration and so forth and then came up with a point I had overlooked, attendance in the royal box. The king did not like opera. The royal family did not like opera. Nobody in the palace liked opera, especially the *bel canto* ones from the few Italian touring companies approved of by my predecessors. A production of *The Tales of Hoffman* had once been authorised by Leigh-Winter who hurriedly cancelled the booking on discovering the promiscuous aspects of the libretto. Even then there was little interest from the palace.

'What happens to the royal box?' I said.

'Empty,' said Soprianti.

'Nobody inside?'

'Nobody. For Italian operas, the ambassador, he comes.'

'Where does he sit?'

'In the front row of the royal circle.'

'Well that's something, but not very welcoming, in a formal sense.'

'The singers, it is very upsetting for them when the royal box is empty. They love Ardaniia, they love the king!'

'Let me think about it,' I promised.

The sky darkens earlier every evening, reminding me as I motored through the emptying streets under the canopy of stars and deep blue sky that I must get to grips with the winter season programme. I parked the Citroen in the converted stables, informed the mechanic that the hand-brake needed tightening and made my way along palace paths to the lord chamberlain's office, where I had been summoned.

'Why do you wish an audience with the king?' demanded the lord chamberlain.

I cleared my throat.

'To advise him that Princess Sophie should surrender the leading role in *The Sleeping Beauty*.'

The lord chamberlain strode back and forwards across the office floor, exhaling heavily, hands clasped behind him, pausing at each turn to lower his head and frown at me through his long eyebrows. After several minutes of striding and frowning he moved to the window and looked out in the direction of the sea, where the moon was rising.

'Normally I would offer to act as an intermediary but,' he said turning from the window, 'given the nature of your petition, I think you should present it yourself.'

'I quite understand.'

The lord chamberlain fingered the chain of the gold watch in his waistcoat pocket.

'Very well, I shall request an audience with his majesty for Wednesday. Do you wish me to attend?'

'Probably not, all things considered.'

'I'm inclined to agree,' said the lord chamberlain.

CHAPTER 19

Flute trouble. For some time I have been aware of discordant undertones in the musical output from the flautists. I am fairly certain that the source of the trouble is the leader of the section but nobody else in the orchestra seems to notice the flat high-pitched emissions. LeBreq agrees with me that the flutes were off-key during the encore of Tchaikovsky's *Intrada Pas de Deux* a few weeks ago, but that is the limit of his complaint. It seems my ears are the only ones picking up the rogue emissions. Admittedly the emissions are intermittent and minor in the sense that the deviation from pitch is infinitesimally small but they are irritating and distracting nonetheless. I have spoken to the principal flautist who dismisses my concerns with a shrug of his shoulders claiming, with reasonable justification, that fluctuations in ambient temperature are a continuous problem for flute players but that his section is experienced enough to maintain pitch whatever the conditions in the hall.

I am reluctant to single out players during rehearsals. Some conductors are cruel enough to invite individual members of a section play alone in front of the orchestra in order to pinpoint technical errors. In my opinion the fact that the conductor has stopped the rehearsal, and explained why, is sufficient warning to the offender. In this particular case, were the offender not the leader of the section, I would make an exception to my policy. If the situation does not improve I will call the flautists to my chambers and rehearse them there alone.

Signor Bagnasco, conductor of the Neapolitan Touring Opera Company, has arrived. Trailing a black cape like his fellow countryman Toscanini he danced into my chambers this morning in small steps, arms outstretched, and embraced me fondly as if renewing an affectionate relationship. I hastened to deliver him to the stage where the orchestra was awaiting his arrival. I made a short speech of welcome, listened to the opening bars of the overture to *Don Pasquale* which Bagnasco conducted with flailing arms, like a seagull in a storm, then made myself scarce. In addition to his distinctive black cape Bagnasco adorns himself with a pervasive cologne which if nothing else should clear the auditorium of flies.

Deprived of my orchestra for a week I departed the opera house in search of the St Frett music society.

The old town lies at the feet of the castle conveniently placed in the familiar configuration that in more stressful times allowed the town folk to seek refuge within the castle walls at the first sight of marauding pirates. Many of the houses are still constructed from wood, with attractive eaves and overhanging timbers. Quaint, but a headache for the fire brigade, I mused, driving slowly through the narrow streets avoiding the squawking chickens, barking dogs and wide-eyed children who flattened themselves against the walls at the noise of the approaching internal combustion engine.

I found the St Frett music society amongst the old warehouses lining the upper reaches of the harbour. According to the faint letters on the signboard mounted high above the doors the building had once been a chandlery of sails and ropes. On the ornamental brick wall at the front a smaller signboard proclaimed "St Frett Music Society - Choral and Instrumental - Instruction Given". I pressed the bell next to the signboard. Receiving no response I opened the first of the doors and entered the building.

The dimly lit interior smelled of tar emphasising the nautical origins of the trade within the building. The smell was far from unpleasant and mingled with the aroma of lavender furniture polish. Wooden walls, empty of the sails and ropes once suspended from timber hooks, rose to rafters which supported a gabled roof with glass skylights, brown with age, through which the sun scarcely pierced. Rows of ornate wooden benches lined the wooden floor. Running my hand over the smooth mahogany surface I deduced the benches to be pews, presumably transferred from an abandoned church. The silky smoothness of the wood explained why the smell of tar was tinged with lavender.

The seats were arranged to face a sturdy wooden platform jutting from the distant wall. Unconventional in structure, extraordinary in its setting, the warehouse gradually manifested itself through the dim light into the shape of a small theatre or, more accurately on account of the grand piano and cello on the stage, a concert hall.

At the piano sat a sprightly old man in an oversized coat. Cradling the cello, with a red shawl around her shoulders, was an equally sprightly old lady. They were playing Brahms first cello sonata. Such was the level of their concentration and rapture and, incidentally, consummate skill that they did not hear the sound of the doorbell ringing or the floorboards creaking as I advanced through the warehouse towards the stage. Not until several minutes after I had slipped into the front pew to listen to the brilliant performance did the music come to an abrupt end.

'Bless my soul, a visitor,' they cried in unison.

I begged them to continue playing but the couple clambered down from the stage, apologising for not hearing the bell, smiling broadly, hands outstretched.

They were Jews from Leipzig. Hannah and David Lipsky. He had been the conductor of a regional orchestra, she a music teacher of violin and voice. Disturbed by anti-Jewish riots in the city before the war they had sold their house and possessions and travelled south to Ardaniia. The guards on the German side of the border looted their bags leaving them only just enough money to rent the warehouse in which we stood, then almost completely derelict. With the revenue from music lessons they eventually managed to purchase the building and convert the partitioned workshop area where sails had once been stitched and repaired into comfortable living quarters.

The continuing demand for music lessons (piano and wind instruments from Mr Lipsky, voice and string instruments from Mrs Lipsky) allowed them to respond to pleas from local schools and middle class families for a facility where amateur recitals and chamber music performances could take place at modest expense, the fees charged by the opera house and university being exorbitant to say nothing of the lip-curling response by the administrators of those establishments to the humble enquiries. The stage inside the warehouse had taken two years to construct using wood from an old hillside church whose foundations had collapsed The pews had come from the same site. Fire was a constant worry but the premises either side were built of concrete and brick, and by virtue of replacing the wooden roof with clay tiles they had managed to persuade a local insurance company to cover the contents of the building.

This information was conveyed to me with a gaiety that placed into perspective the sombre manner with which I regularly faced the challenges of life. The kindly couple insisted on showing me their living quarters and in a pleasantly furnished sitting room overlooking the harbour Mrs Lipsky served tea and cakes as delicious as those served by Valentino at, I could confidently predict, a fraction of the cost.

'This is such a pleasure, meeting you at last,' said Mrs Lipsky.

'We wondered when you would come to see us,' said her husband.

'And how you would react,' said Mrs Lipsky.

'React to what?' I enquired politely.

'Not everybody responds so positively, in such circumstances.'

'Or so gallantly.'

'Responds to what? ' I said puzzled.

'To my work,' said Mr Lipsky.

'I'm lost for words at your accomplishments, the expansion of your scope beyond music lessons - chamber music, school concerts, choral evenings, how could I not be impressed?' I said.

'My work with the *Sunday Gazette*, I mean,' said Mr Lipsky.

Choking on a biscuit I sat coughing while Mrs Lipsky fussed around making patting motions at my back.

'You are the music critic?' I managed between coughs.

'Why, yes. I thought you knew. I assumed that was the reason for your visit.'

'You must drink some water,' said Mrs Lipsky hurrying from the kitchen.

When I had recovered sufficiently I assured Mr Lipsky that my visit was disconnected with his writings, of which I had been unaware, and that in any event I had no quarrel with his assessments of the orchestra or myself as conductor, and confessed considerable awe at the range of his perception and expertise.

'The scores, where do you get them?' I said.

'Your library,' said Mr Lipsky. 'It has always been standard practice for the opera house to issue one copy of all incoming editions to the *Gazette*.'

'Why didn't I think of that!' I sighed.

'So, we are still friends?' said Mr Lipsky.

His wise eyes examined me earnestly.

'Of course,' I said.

'Frankness is the best policy, in all things, especially musical criticism.'

'You are completely right, though I would appreciate you not attributing musical faults to lack of rehearsal time.'

I told them of the problem with the elderly musicians in the orchestra struggling with the complexities of recent music, and how it would take time to find replacements for them, and how sometimes the faults were attributable to inexperience as in the case of the talented young pianist who had played the Tchaikovsky concerto or to external factors such as the weather, for example when I had raced through a symphony to avoid my motorcar filling up with rainwater. The Lipskys laughed and clapped their hands at my confession and declared how pleased they were that I was modernising the opera house programmes.

'Why then, if not to meet and rebuke the *Sunday Gazette* music critic, did you seek us out?' said Mr Lipsky.

'To enquire about Zoe, one of your singers.'

'The young soprano?'

'From the palace?'

'Yes.'

'A sweet girl.'

'Very gifted.'

'Gifted enough to sing Mimi in *La Bohème*?' I said.

The Lipskys looked at each other.

'When?'

'Next year,' I said.

'She will need lessons,' said Mrs Lipsky.

'The opera house will pay,' I said.

'She would not be ready for Paris or Milan, in a year,' said Mrs Lipsky.

'What about Ardaniia?' I said.

The Lipskys looked at each other again.

'It's not impossible.'

Before departing I discussed with the Lipskys the extent to which the St Frett choral group could contribute generally to the cast of *La Bohème*. In addition to the principal roles, singers were needed for the chorus in act 2 and the minor roles in the wintery scene of act 3. I was confident that the university choral society would eventually yield to the lure of opera house acclaim but less confident that Professor Schmidt's staid performers would be able to fill more than a proportion of the roles. The Lipskys appeared as excited as I at the prospect of collaboration.

'Your chief flute is playing flat,' said Mr Lipsky as we approached the doors to the street.

I stopped in my tracks.

'I knew it!' I said slapping my thigh. 'What a relief. Thank you for confirming my suspicions.'

'Definitely flat,' said Mr Lipsky.

'Another vacancy to be filled,' I said.

'What a pity we can't help. The best musicians in our small orchestra are all women,' said Mrs Lipsky.

I stared at her.

'Pity?' I said.

'Tradition,' said Mrs Lipsky. 'The national orchestra only employs male musicians.'

'To hell with tradition!' I said, apologising profusely for the unseemly outburst.

CHAPTER 20

Ten o'clock. I stood waiting in the public hall of the castle brushing specks of dust off my morning coat while admiring the shields and regalia on the walls. The doors to the throne room were flanked with guards in armoured breastplates carrying swords. An equerry was in attendance.

'Private audience?' said the equerry.

'Yes,' I said.

'His majesty won't be long.'

'Thank you.'

'When you enter, advance firmly to the throne and bow your head, like this.'

The equerry dropped his chin for two seconds, then straightened up.
'Don't speak until invited to by his majesty,' said the equerry.
'Right.'
'Reverse to the doors when the audience is over, bow again and exit.'
'I've got it.'
'His majesty will dismiss you by gesture or word.' The equerry flicked his fingers to demonstrate the gesture. 'Don't linger. If his majesty rings the bell beside the throne the guards will enter and remove you forcibly.'

The doors opened and a small neatly dressed man whom I recognised as the prime minister hurried out. We had talked briefly in my chambers after one of the concerts. He was knowledgeable about music and anxious that the national anthem should be improved or replaced. As he passed me now in the public hall he nodded and murmured 'Busy morning.'

The equerry coughed to attract my attention, indicating the open doors.

Obediently I advanced into the throne room which was altogether more imposing than the king's private study where I had been received on first arrival. It resembled one of the great Tudor halls in England. Strung between long narrow windows were the battle honours of centuries past, regimental banners, halberds, lances and the colourful regalia of knights in full armour. The throne was mounted on a circular dais. Suspended above it on golden cords hung the royal standard of Ardaniia, verdant green and purple with a white unicorn *passant*.

Dressed formally in ermine gown and crown the king looked larger and a great deal more powerful than on previous occasions. The mischievousness in his eyes had been replaced by something sterner.

Well?' said the king glancing at me briefly before bending down to adjust the position of his footstool.

I bowed my head.

'With your majesty's permission, I seek consent that Princess Sophie should dance the leading role in *Swan Lake* next year, in preference to *The Sleeping Beauty* this year,' I said.

'Why?' said the king.

'The role is better, sir.'

'Why should she not dance both roles?'

'I have dared to presume that Princess Sophie would not wish to take the leading position twice, sir.'

'Have you indeed?'

'The part of the Lilac Fairy in *The Sleeping Beauty* is of almost equal importance, and Tchaikovsky awards the role the most beautiful music in the ballet,' I said.

'You want my daughter to abandon the leading role and dance as the Lilac Fairy?'

'Yes, sir.'

'For any other reason?'

'She has been troubled with footwork recently. Perhaps worried by the responsibilities of the main part.'

'I see. Madame Prtenchska, does she share your recommendation?'

'Yes, sir.'

'Very well, permission granted,' said the king.

I cleared my throat.

'One further request, sir. Would you be kind enough to inform Princess Sophie of the decision yourself? Something on the lines that the royal family does not want to appear, in these democratic times, to be commanding the best positions. That way she will not think she is being transferred on account of her temporary footwork problems.'

The king stared at me.

'Have you considered a diplomatic career? I need a new foreign secretary.'

I responded with an appropriately whimsical disclaimer of aptitude at anything but music.

'Very well, I will speak to Sophie,' said the king. 'Anything else? Would you like me to insult the German ambassador, or invade France?'

Murmuring further demurrals I backed away from the throne.

As I reached the exit he called out.

'Come to dinner one night. The queen fancies you.'

Arrangements for the orchestra pit have been completed. Three rows of chairs have been removed from the auditorium and the panelling at the front of the stage disassembled to create a cavernous space for the percussion players. The trombones are on the far left of the pit, and the trumpets and horns on the far right. That way the blast from the brass section is directed straight at the audience not into the ears of the violinists. The wind section is sandwiched in the centre of the pit between the violas and the drums, cymbals etc at the back.

I am accustomed to facing the brass section in the pit, with the strings and woodwinds seated either side of the podium. Suitably elevated above the trombones and trumpets the blast from brass instruments hurtles past me at waist height having been channelled through the gap between the violins.

My first reaction on seeing the opera house arrangement was that the brass section would be more difficult to control and the output from the orchestra would be unbalanced. Bagnasco did not seem to be having any problems however when I slipped into the auditorium to listen to the orchestra during the dress rehearsal. On the contrary I found myself liking the split sound effect from the brass section. I also liked the way Bagnasco directed the singers. He had exchanged the ostentatious arm flapping style adopted earlier for the overture for short precise motions of the baton which were easier for singers to follow.

. . . .

The audience went well, I gather,' said the lord chamberlain beckoning me to the anteroom fireplace that evening.

'Fortunately the king accepted my recommendations,' I said.

"You have been commanded to dine with the royal family next Tuesday night. Grand Duke Rupert will be present. He monopolises the conversation so you won't have to say anything.'

'A great honour,' I said uneasily.

'On the other matter you raised, regarding empty seats in the royal box at the opera house, I am informed that Countess Grigorn keeps a gramophone and enjoys Italian music. She may be persuaded, what do you think?'

'Well . . .'

'Let's find out.' Motioning me to follow him the lord chamberlain walked across the anteroom to the group of magnificently-dressed elderly women gossiping near the tray of sherry wines.

'You know Landour, our master of music, don't you, Isobel?' said the lord chamberlain to the woman in the centre of the group, who turned and looked at me with an expression of disdain.

'The royal box is vacant for Saturday night's performance at the opera house. Landour wonders if you would be available to represent the court. What is it again?' said the lord chamberlain to me.

'The Neapolitan Touring Opera Company is performing Donizetti's

Don Pasquale,' I said.

'You would like that,' cried several of the ladies-in-waiting.

'Would I?' said the countess.

'Yes, you know, *bel canto*, like Rossini.'

'Perhaps I would,' said the countess.

'The point is, the king doesn't like opera and Landour feels, quite rightly, that the royal box needs a distinguished presence on such occasions.'

'Fanfare?' said the countess.

The lord chamberlain turned to me. Having studied the protocol for music on royal arrivals with great care, I was able to confirm that the countess was entitled to a single trumpet fanfare on entry to the royal box.

'And you would be accompanied by the Italian ambassador, naturally,' said the lord chamberlain.

The countess snorted.

'No, I would not, Cedric,' she snapped. 'If that vulgar little man comes within an inch of my person, I shall leave the opera house immediately.'

'Just as you wish, Isobel,' said the lord chamberlain.

'And you,' said the countess glowering at me over the bridge of her nose, 'deliver me tomorrow a formal invitation with full details of when, where and what you require of my presence.'

'I appreciate your help,' I told the lord chamberlain as we returned to the fireplace.

'Not at all,' said the lord chamberlain. 'You can be responsible for informing the Italian ambassador that he's not wanted.'

CHAPTER 21

'How clever of you to persuade the king,' repeated Madame Prtenchska.

I was in her office with the senior ballet mistresses discussing plans for the production of *The Sleeping Beauty* now that the roles had been changed and Sophie was no longer dancing the part of Princess Aurora.

'And how perceptive of the king to recognise the argument,' repeated Madame Slymnova

'How gracious of him, some monarchs would not have taken kindly to the implications,' repeated Madame Tuillée.

They were so relieved that the problem which had dominated their thoughts for months, threatening the existence of the ballet school and the future of everyone teaching and studying in it, that they kept wandering back to the circumstances of my audience with the king. The following day, true to his word, he had instructed Sophie to surrender the leading role to another dancer and freed from her *prima ballerina* responsibilities the princess was apparently now happily rehearsing the dance sequences for the Lilac Fairy.

It occurred to me that Madame Prtenchska and the senior ballet mistresses were recapitulating their review of the Sophie affair in order to play for time while collecting their thoughts on my suggestion that the royal theatre be involved in the production of *The Sleeping Beauty*. I had proposed that the theatre's director and producer be engaged in providing specialist support for the ballet. The ladies recognised the need for a producer and team of professional stage hands but were struggling with the idea of hiring Pierre.

'He's young, French, charismatic. His job would be to coordinate the visual effects of the production, not interfere with the choreography, in any way,' I said.

'Has he worked with dancers before?' asked the ladies.

'I don't think so. However that could be an advantage. Let me arrange a meeting, so you can question him. Meanwhile please remember I haven't worked with dancers either.'

'But you're special!' gushed the ladies which naturally was very flattering but served to emphasise that the focus of attention was now switching from the ballet school to the opera house, and that responsibility for the success or otherwise of *The Sleeping Beauty* now rested heavily on my shoulders.

The Italian embassy lay in an avenue of handsome buildings in the shade of the castle walls. I stated my business to a man in a frock coat and was led up the central staircase to a waiting room with brochures which encouraged readers to invest in Italian enterprises. Fishing nets and motor vehicles were especially lucrative, according to the glossy publications which I had plenty of time to study because the ambassador kept me waiting for an hour before the man in the frock coat collected me and delivered me to the ambassador's luxurious office.

'Maestro Landour! Forgive me, affairs of state. Come in, sit down. What an honour! I was saying to Maestro Bagnasco only yesterday that our new conductor is a great man to have reinvigorated the Ardaniian symphony orchestra like this. Such depth, such tone. What can I do for you? Nothing is too much trouble, you need only to ask,' said the ambassador embracing me in the Italian fashion, submerging me in a mist of strong cologne remarkably similar to Bagnasco's.

The centrepiece of the office was a reproduction of Michelangelo's statue *Angel di Arca di San Domenico* mounted on a marble plinth. Hanging on the wall behind the ambassador's desk were portraits in gilt frames of Victor Emmanuel III and prime minister Benito Mussolini. The rest of the office was correspondingly opulent, with thick velvet curtains at the windows.

'Yes, it is indeed a reproduction,' laughed the ambassador indicating the statue. 'Donated by the St Frett chamber of commerce, in gratitude for the embassy's humble part in facilitating the export of Ardaniia's fabled olives from here to Rome and Florence.'

I explained to the ambassador that the purpose of my visit was to thank him for ensuring that operatic productions by touring companies from Italy received appropriate ceremonial recognition. Standing in for the royal family his presence in the royal circle over the years had conveyed to visiting artists that the versatility and brilliance of their performances were appreciated at the uppermost levels of society.

'It disturbs me that you have borne the burden alone, however,' I said.

'Think nothing of it, my dear sir,' said the ambassador.

'My intention, having assumed responsibility for the opera house, is to encourage participation by the royal family, at least once during every visit by a touring company,' I said.

'That would be most welcome,' said the ambassador.

'The king is not, I'm sure you know, personally attuned to opera.'

'Alas not.'

'However I am pleased to say that Countess Grigorn, his majesty's second cousin, is familiar with Donizetti's music and has graciously consented to attend Saturday night's performance of *Don Pasquale*,' I said.

'Bravo!' cried the ambassador.

'She is looking forward to the event immensely.'

'It will be my privilege to receive her and escort her to the royal box,' said the ambassador.

'Unfortunately Countess Grigorn thinks you are a vulgar little man and doesn't wish to be received.'

In the interests of diplomacy I decided not to repay the ambassador for keeping me waiting an hour by speaking the truth. Instead I said, 'Unfortunately Countess Grigorn suffers a rare condition. As a result of a tragically unsuccessful love affair, she recoils from contact with men. I hope you understand. I have arranged for you to be seated in the front row of the stalls, where the view of the stage will anyway be better. The countess will occupy the royal box alone, accompanied by her retinue.'

'Unrequited love!' cried the ambassador. 'Of course, I understand!'

On the way out I stopped to admire the reproduction of Michelangelo statue.

'Isn't she magnificent?' said the ambassador proudly, accompanying me to the door.

The St Frett music society was rehearsing *The Mikado* by Gilbert & Sullivan when I slipped into a pew at the back of the warehouse. Lipsky was conducting a small orchestra of approximately twenty players while his wife directed the production from a chair in the wings. The singers were of mixed ages and ability but all cheerfully enthusiastic. Zoe had been given the minor part of Peep-Bo and looked very pretty in the song 'Three little maids from school are we' though her voice was lost in the ensemble, naturally enough. The middle-aged tenor playing Nanki-Poo sang his part very competently but his girth and grey hair ruled him out as a prospective candidate for Rodolfo in *La Bohème*.

Despite my attempts to watch unrecognised from the gloom of the rear pews I was eventually spotted. The Lipskys insisted on dragging me to the stage to meet the orchestra and cast which to my embarrassment applauded my appearance. I told them how pleased I was to have established contact with their society, how the standard of their artistry had impressed me and how I foresaw a valuable partnership between the society and opera house. In liaison with the Lipskys, I said, the current vacancies in the symphony orchestra for which auditions would shortly be held were being reviewed and, in due consultation with the other choral groups, including the university, our respective resources would be combined in selecting the cast for *La Bohème* scheduled for production next year.

Zoe came running across the stage after my impromptu speech, hands clasped tightly together as in prayer.

'Thank you, thank you, thank you,' she said, 'for arranging lessons with Mrs Lipsky!'

'I can't guarantee you a role in *La Bohème*, but work hard in your acting and singing lessons, and let's see what happens,' I said stepping back hurriedly when it appeared that Zoe was about to fling her arms around my neck.

An encounter of a different kind with a young woman of different background and disposition occurred before dinner when I found my route into the palace anteroom blocked by Lady Sarah Delchette.

'Well?' she demanded, hands on hips.

'Good evening,' I said.

'Have you done it yet?'

'That rather depends.'

'On what?

'The nature of your enquiry.'

'You know exactly what I mean. Have you spoken to the bandmaster yet?'

'I regret not.'

'If you continue like this, the maids-of-honour will be forced to take action.'

'What would that involve, precisely?'

'You'll find out.'

'In which case, as a precaution, I shall speak to the bandmaster without further delay.'

'When?'

Pondering my response I reminded myself that since arriving in Ardaniia I had seen little of the countryside. The orchestra was otherwise engaged with rehearsals for *Don Pasquale*. I might as well take the morning off and visit army headquarters in the hills where the band was based.

'Tomorrow,' I promised. 'I shall drive to the barracks.'

'I'll come with you,' she said.

CHAPTER 22

The staff of the motor stables had mostly been transferred from equestrian duties and were inclined to refer to the vehicles as mounts. 'Go easy with the reins today, sir' or 'She's good for a canter, sir' were typical of the instructions issued by the staff when releasing a vehicle to its driver. Approaching the Citroen this morning I was informed that 'she had been fed, watered and brushed down' indicating that the petrol tank was full, the radiator had been topped up with water and the chassis washed and polished. Indeed, the coachwork gleamed as strikingly in the sunlight as the flanks of a well-bred mare.

Waiting in the shade of the castle walls, eyed covetously by the motor stable grooms, was Lady Sarah Delchette. She wore a straw bonnet with blue ribbons, a blue polka dot dress flared at the hem, puffed-up sleeves and light blue shoes the combination of which managed to look simultaneously simple, fashionable and expensive. There was no denying that my passenger was exceedingly pretty, deserving in full the subdued whistles of admiration from the grooms as the Citroen proceeded at a stately pace from the stables to the castle gates.

The road to the fortress where the bulk of the Ardaniian army was garrisoned passed through miles of open country before climbing to the hills. Loose stone walls marked the division between the farms, their houses just visible amidst orange groves and olive trees. The grass verges either side of the road were remarkably trim. I commented on this to Sarah who shrugged her shoulders. Not until we encountered a herd of goats in the middle of the road did the reason for the trimness become clear. The grass verges served not only to enhance the beauty of the landscape but provide goat herders with free grazing.

'What a pity you don't have a title,' said Sarah as we bowled along in the warm sunshine.

'Why's that?'

'Because you can't marry me.'

'The purpose of our trip today is to meet the bandmaster, not discuss your marital options,' I pointed out.

'Perhaps the king will knight you. Then you'd be Chevalier Robin Landour.'

'Frankly, right now, the king is more likely to remove my head.'

The larger estates were set further back from the road, their presence heralded by ostentatious gates, many with coats-of-arms. From the gates gravelled lanes wound through rich fields and vineyards to mansions with turrets rising from the trees. Occasionally an ornamental lake shimmered in the sunlight. Birds floated over clumps of woodland where shooting parties would be gathered in winter, equipped with guns from London and Berlin, and capes from Paris.

'Is your family very rich?' said Sarah.

'No.'

'How many servants do you have?'

'Just a few.'

'What kind of land do you own?'

'Arable mainly, with some cattle.'

'How many farms?'

'Eight or nine.'

'Then you can't be poor!'

'My eldest brother, who inherited the estate, is quite well off. My income from the estate is modest.'

'Then I shall speak to your brother,' said Sarah. 'Though that still leaves the problem of your title.'

The hills in the distance were crowned in pine trees. Beyond them lay the mountains with purple peaks. Somewhere up there in the strands of mist hovering over the valleys was the pass from the border through which marauding hordes in centuries past had attempted to enrich themselves by plundering the nation's wealth. None had succeeded, due in part to the fortress strategically located to intercept the invading forces and to the renowned bravery and discipline of the Ardaniian army.

Although the threat of invasion by land had diminished it suited the army to garrison the bulk of its forces thirty miles from the city, in high country where the soldiers could be kept busy with drills and exercises and the officers amused with polo in summer and skiing in winter when snow covered the slopes. The posting for rank and file soldiers was six months in the fortress followed by four weeks of regimental guard duty in St Frett with occasional nights off for carousal in the local inns. Junior officers were allowed one weekend pass every month. Senior officers could return to the city without restriction and, as we were about to learn, bandsmen playing at ceremonial and ballroom events in the palace travelled regularly to St Frett by coach.

Wheezing and puffing the Citroen reached the top of the final hill and came to rest at the main gate of the fortress. The corporal at the guard room checked the royal crest on the side of the vehicle, snapped to attention, saluted and opened the barrier. 'You'll find the bandmaster's quarters over there, sir,' he said pointing through the gate.

Inside the fortress we took the perimeter road marked 'Motorised Vehicles Only' which skirted the enormous parade ground and headed for the sound of Sousa's *Gladiator March* which grew in intensity as we approached and passed through an archway into a smaller parade ground resplendent with the sight of the royal army band in motion, brass instruments blaring, drums beating. We parked near the archway and proceeded on foot towards a group of non-commissioned officers reviewing the parade. The temperature was cooler up here in the hills. A light breeze accompanied us from the Citroen causing Sarah to clutch the brim of her bonnet. Did I detect a few wrong notes as the bandsmen, turning to complete another length of the parade ground, noticed the breeze tugging the hem of Sarah's dress?

From the shape of his broad shoulders, which I had seen several times before silhouetted in the half-light of the minstrels gallery, I identified the senior of the non-commissioned officers as the bandmaster. He detached himself from the group as we approached and saluted. His face darkened slightly when during the introductions I informed him of my position.

'None of the bandsmen here is permitted to apply for the orchestra, sir. I've seen the audition notices in the newspaper, but the bandsmen are not permitted. Rules and regulations, sir,' he said.

'I haven't come to poach your musicians, sergeant-major, though I am sorely tempted, having experienced the excellence of your ensemble first hand,' I said nodding at the band which continued to march up and down the parade ground delivering Sousa's music competently and with great assurance. 'My mission is simply to enquire into the programming for the dances in the palace ballroom.'

The bandmaster stared hard at me, then at Sarah.

'I have already informed the young ladies of the palace that programming for the ballroom is not my responsibility, sir.'

'I see,' I said.

'The dances are set by Countess Grigorn, sir.'

An hour later, after a tour of the fortress's musical facilities in the company of the bandmaster during which we inspected the practice rooms and bandsmen's living quarters, and consumed strong army-issue tea served in mugs, which Sarah drank from politely without wrinkling her nose, we departed from the fortress on the road back to the city.

'You knew what the bandmaster was going to say,' I said.

'Yes,' said Sarah gaily.

'We have wasted a morning.'

'Not everyone would say time was wasted, when spent with me,' said Sarah examining her fingernails.

'I am not going to tackle Countess Grigorn, and that's final,' I said.

'Coward.'

'Even if I did, she would refuse.'

'Then you must use your influence with the king.'

'If I had any influence with him, I would request a restraining order, against you and the other maids-of-honour.'

From the fortress the road curled down through fields of grass and wheat which thrived in the temperate climate of the hills. Rounding a corner Sarah pointed at a grand residence set in parkland with lawns and terraced gardens.

'If you don't marry me, I might marry him,' she said.

'Who's that?'

'The youngest son of Visconte Ferdinand.'

'A much more suitable match,' I pointed out.

'But what should I do all day, left up here while he went hunting?'

'Manage the household,' I said, 'arrange dinner parties and raise children.'

'Then, after that, what should I do?'

Arriving in St Frett I turned the Citroen in the direction of the castle.

'Not that way,' said Sarah. 'I've booked a table for lunch in the Grand Hotel, in your name.'

Spluttering and protesting that the Grand Hotel was too extravagant I swung the Citroen towards the harbour. I spluttered even more for allowing my affairs to be dictated by Sarah on discovering that the dining room was full of courtiers from the palace who silently followed our progress through the room to our table on the balcony. 'Just good friends, short business lunch,' I murmured to each group of raised eyebrows as I followed Sarah across the floor.

'Heaven knows what they're thinking!' I muttered into the menu.

'It's none of their business,' said Sarah.

'It was most unwise to come here,' I said crossly.

'Don't worry, they won't assume we're engaged, not until you ask me,' said Sarah nonchalantly.

The hotel looked down over a golden-sand beach shared with a small fishing village whose houses decorated the pine tree slopes of the bay with terracotta roof tiles. Fishing boats lolled in the blue sea, their anchors and chains clearly visible.

'Will you take me swimming one day?' said Sarah peering over the balcony.

'Certainly not, you've caused me enough trouble already.'

'We need to establish a common interest.'

'Sarah, we have nothing in common. You don't even like music.'

'Yes I do, it's just that I don't understand it. I like Tchaikovsky though, especially the romantic piece you played with the orchestra the other night, about the lovers, *Romeo and Juliet*,' she said fluttering her eyelashes ostentatiously as the waiter delivered potted shrimps to our table.

'Romeo and Juliet committed suicide,' I pointed out.

'Which I shall probably do too,' said Sarah, 'seeing that you're not interested in me. I've watched the way you look at Yvette de Carbon-Ferriere.'

With mixed feelings I proceeded to the opera house alone after delivering Sarah to the palace. She had had her fun of me, that was true, but the encounter had nonetheless been stimulating and entertaining. Moreover she had raised an important point about the relationship between the sexes. To what extent should there be a common interest? When selecting a bride should a professional musician choose a girl with horn-rimmed glasses capable of analysing the thematic structure of Bruckner's eighth symphony or a pretty maid-of-honour of impish disposition? At the time of writing, the answer eluded me.

CHAPTER 23

The opera house was more than half full for Saturday night's performance of *Don Pasquale* representing an unparalleled turnout according to Soprianti. Attendance at operas was normally confined to the musical elite and the few hundred loyal citizens who could be counted on to support any classical music event.

'The house,' exclaimed Soprianti, 'it is really coming to life again!'

Dutifully I sat in the front row of the stalls with the Italian ambassador looking up over the heads of my orchestra at the stage converted into a theatrical arena. Donizetti's famous opera is a comedy in the *bel canto* style. The proportion of the audience attracted to the hall by the programmes of romantic music I had been introducing struggled with the comparative absence of melodic rapture in the score. However the soloists of the Neapolitan Touring Opera Company were accomplished actors as well as fine singers so the elements of the audience disappointed to find that Donizetti's music was less comprehensible than Tchaikovsky's were nonetheless amused by the plot and applauded loudly when the curtain dropped on conclusion of the third and final act.

My instructions to Soprianti regarding the reception of Countess Grigorn were correctly followed. She was not to be touched, nobody was to extend a hand in her direction, members of the reception committee were simply to bow, attempts at conversation were to be avoided, murmured intimations of gratitude at the countess's presence could be proffered but without expectation of response, walking backwards an usher was to precede the countess and her entourage up the staircase, separately an usher was to ensure that the conductor had observed the countess's appearance in the royal box, whereupon the conductor was to signal the trumpet section to play the fanfare due to minor royalty.

Ten minutes before the end of the opera, as measured on previous nights, an usher would alert the grooms, the carriages from the palace would draw up in front of the opera house, the reception committee would re-assemble in the foyer during the curtain calls and genuflect as the countess descended the staircase. In the unlikely event that the countess expressed a desire to meet the cast she was to be escorted by Soprianti to the stage where I would take over. During the passage from the foyer to the stage Soprianti was to resist the temptation of pleasantries on the lines of 'I trust your grace enjoyed the performance' and keep his mouth shut.

My plans for handling the countess if she ventured onto the stage consisted entirely of transferring her as soon as possible to the conductor Bagnasco who, suitably warned of the perils of attempting to place his arm around the countess's shoulders, would introduce her to the cast. Fortunately the countess had no intention of extending her visit. Within minutes of the final curtain she descended the staircase and departed the opera house for her coach.

Substituting for the countess the Italian ambassador and I walked down the line of the assembled cast, shaking hands and congratulating the singers on their performances. The soprano part, Norina, was sung by an attractive young woman whose voice had impressed me at rehearsals and who could have made a reasonable Mimi were it not for her girth, swollen perhaps by excessive indulgence in the Italian national dish of spaghetti. The young tenor playing Ernesto was equally good looking with an excellent voice, and appropriately slim, rather too self-important for my taste, strutting around admiring his profile in the stage mirrors. The two young stars of the Neapolitan Touring Opera Company had been informed by Soprianti of our forthcoming *La Bohème* production and, when the hand-shaking was over and champagne glasses were being raised, they collared me, pressing for invitations to sing the roles of Mimi and Rodolfo.

'How very flattering,' I said, 'that you should be interested in one of our local productions.'

'Flattering, not at all! We love your opera house!' cried the soprano.

'We love your orchestra!' cried the tenor.

'We love your country!' they cried in unison.

And doubtless they also loved the fees paid to international guest singers, I reflected, informing them of my objective to award roles to resident singers whenever possible but promising to keep them advised of vacancies and associated auditions. From me they moved to LeBreq, his face wreathed in smiles at the well-deserved accolades from the Italian cast at the orchestra's performance, and from LeBreq back to Soprianti who spread his arms and shrugged his shoulders to verify, presumably, that decisions concerning the selection of singers were not his to make.

The carriage park was still full when I returned to the palace later that night. Clambering out of the Citroen I debated whether to venture into the ballroom and try my luck with Yvette de Carbon-Ferrier or proceed straight to bed. Seeking inspiration from the moon which hovered romantically over the bay I decided to risk being intercepted by Lady Sarah Delchette, and proceeded though the castle grounds in the direction of the ballroom.

Maurice Trouville, keeper of the king's pictures, was in the main anteroom bar in his usual seat from which he could peer scornfully into the ballroom murmuring unfavourable comments on the dress and manners of the Ardaniian nobility for which he had little time. The courts of eighteenth century France represented the high point of cultural sophistication in his eyes. Standards of aristocratic conduct had collapsed since then throughout Europe. The courts of Austria and Prussia in the previous century had been little more than beer cellars, in his opinion As for British royalty. . .

He tolerated me by virtue of my role as court musician and because I had selected a work by Ravel for my inaugural concert. He was slimly built with fine features, foppish in his dress, his loose silk cuffs almost completely covering his hands. Deriding the customs of his employers he lived in fear that one of the court's famous paintings might suddenly disappear and that, nominally responsible for their upkeep, he would be thrown into the castle dungeons, a fate that had befallen his predecessor who during his short term of office depleted the royal collection with some under-the-counter sales to a Romanian art dealer.

Trouville's pleas that the pictures mounted on the walls of public rooms in the palace should be fastened into position were rebuffed by the lord chamberlain who refused to insult residents and guests of the palace by implying they were not to be trusted, and pointed out that public rooms were supervised by guards who would scarcely stand by and watch interlopers brazenly remove paintings without authority. Wringing his hands Trouville argued that modern art thieves were more than a match for guards leaning sleepily against their halberdiers but the lord chamberlain was steadfast in his opposition to additional security measures.

Torn between the manifold benefits of his position - the prestigious appointment, handsome salary, academic fulfilment from cataloguing vast numbers of unpublished sketches and drawings from the Venetian and Florentine periods, professional pleasure from handling masterpieces of European art including the collection of French impressionist paintings acquired at the request of the king's mistress before her dismissal - and the prospect of ending up in a dungeon feasting on rats, the fearfulness of the prospect only slightly lessened by the royal physician's observation that the damp conditions in the dungeons would probably promote the growth of garlic with which to season the rodents, Trouville mixed sparsely with his fellow courtiers and settled his nerves by copious consumption of early vintages from the royal wine cellar.

'Success in the opera house tonight, *mon ami?*' he called out when I arrived.

'The Italians acquitted themselves well,' I said settling into the chair next to him.

'They have their strong points,' said the keeper of the king's pictures. 'Art and music. Not much else.'

Concealed from general view within the depths of the armchair I sat listening to Trouville's opinion on the Italian race, hoping to see Yvette waltz past which, in due course, she did.

'Off again, so soon, *mon ami?*' said Trouville as I arose from the armchair timing my arrival in the ballroom to coincide with a full circuit of the waltz. Spotting me standing on the verge of the hall, where I had appeared as if by accident, Yvette lifted her hand from the shoulder of the cavalry officer she was dancing with, and wiggled her fingers.

The household cavalry was the regiment of choice for the eldest sons of the Ardaniian nobility. Without a title and the significant wealth necessary to purchase a commission and afford the lavish lifestyle centring on the regimental polo fields there was no hope of entry. The officers were distinguished by their affected languor and elegance of their white uniforms trimmed with gold. They did not mix well with the officers of other regiments. In fact it would be true to say they did not mix well with anyone, except themselves, their horses and polo ponies, and the royal family, in that order. To approach an officer of the household cavalry was to be subjected to an indolently slow inspection of one's person from head to toe while the aristocratic personage determined whether or not to acknowledge one's presence.

In the ballroom they formed a small group close to the royal canopy as befitted their station. Committed to my course of action, when the music stopped I strode boldly towards the cluster of white and gold uniforms embellished now with the colour of Yvette's ball gown.

'Good evening, my lords. Mademoiselle de Carbon-Ferrier, my honour, I think?' I said.

Yvette glanced at her dance card. I do not know if there was an entry on the card for the slow waltz that commenced as I stood waiting amidst icy glares from the assembled cavalry officers but, if there was, she ignored it and took my arm.

Heart pumping rapidly, I led her away.

I have no clear recollection of the conversation as we danced. I remember informing her of the dinner invitation from the king and being warned of the ceremonial Gallic-Romano tradition whereby the bones of fowl were tossed over the left shoulder in the royal dining room. I remember her giggling into my ear that I should be careful when selecting bones from my plate for disposal, in order to avoid splattering myself with sauce.

And I remember the discussion about Sarah.

'You took her to lunch at the Grand Hotel?' said Yvette.

'She took me,' I corrected.

'You are embarrassed by her attention?'

'She is delightful company, but persistent.'

'You would prefer to be left alone?'

'Frankly, yes.'

'Well then, she must be warned off.'

'Yes, but how?'

'*C'est très simple*. She must catch you in a compromising position with another woman.'

'Compromising?'

'If you are old enough to conduct an orchestra, you are old enough to know what compromising means. Leave it to me. I shall make the arrangements,' said Yvette, hazel eyes lustrous in the light of the ballroom chandeliers.

CHAPTER 24

This morning I convened the first meeting of the opera house ballet production committee. Present were ballet school director Madame Prtenchska, senior ballet mistress Madame Tuillée, royal theatre director Pierre Bonnel, royal theatre stage manager Albert Frenner, *répétiteur* Marcus and myself. We sat round a table in the centre of the stage which, pending shipment of the *Don Pasquale* props, had not yet been reinstated to a concert platform, so that committee members could familiarise themselves with a typical opera house stage performance layout with curtains, backdrops and scenery still in place. Mr Frenner knew the layout intimately from previous productions but the ladies from the ballet school and Pierre Bonnel were unfamiliar with the arrangements of the stage.

In addition to the table and chairs I arranged for an upright piano to be available so that Marcus could play extracts from *The Sleeping Beauty* for members of the committee as required.

As chairman I opened the meeting by inviting the attendees to summarize their perceived roles. Madame Prtenchska said she represented the ballet school's administrative, advisory and support function. Madame Tuillée said she was in charge of production and all aspects of choreography and dancing. Pierre Bonnel said his role was to support the production to the best of his ability. Mr Frenner stated he was responsible for manipulation of props and preparation of scenic designs in accordance with team requirements.

Madame Tuillée eyed Pierre warily. During the preliminaries I had introduced the young Frenchman as director of the royal theatre. Madame Tuillée clearly objected to the implication that he might play a similar role for *The Sleeping Beauty*. In her time the elegant and composed elderly ballerina had taken on the might of the French artistic establishment. She was not going to be outranked by a *jeune dilettante*.

Pierre and I had spoken of this beforehand and he now proved his worth by addressing Madame Tuillée with great charm. Looking directly at her he confessed to limited experience of ballet productions, to great excitement at the prospect of working with such an eminent dancer, how he was totally unqualified to be involved in the choreographic aspect of the production, yet his experience of theatrical performances might perhaps be of some assistance to her, particularly from the viewpoint of the audience. In that respect he saw his role as an off-stage observer, drawing Madame Tuillée's attention to any features of the choreography that might either enhance or clash with the aesthetic aspects of the presentation.

The combination of his deference and charismatic enthusiasm won her over and I was able to obtain unanimous agreement from the committee that Pierre should be given the title of artistic director.

From there we attempted to define the production in terms of fixed boundaries, choreographic and musical. The ballet school had decided to reduce *The Sleeping Beauty* to three acts (prologue and acts 1 and 2, eliminating act 3), exclude a number of scenes and simplify the dance sequences in others. The principal justification for making the cuts was that the students were still at intermediate level, albeit some of them were capable of dancing the full version. The attention span of the audience was another factor. The full version of the ballet took one hundred and sixty minutes. By reducing the performance to approximately ninety minutes there was less danger of restlessness in, for example, the royal box. Dramatically, excision of act 3 could be justified on the basis that the climax of the ballet occurs in act 2 when Princess Aurora is awoken from induced sleep by a kiss from Prince Désiré, and that act 3 consisted of rather overlong wedding celebrations of less interest to the audience than the excitement of the famous awakening scene.

Musically I made it clear that alterations to the score other than those arising from excision of specific acts/scenes were not acceptable. Simplification of dance sequences must not affect the musical notation. Critics were sympathetic to cuts but not to tampering with the inner workings of a score. I did not wish to be accused of presuming to improve upon Tchaikovsky's music. Madame Tuillée nodded at this, while Marcus shifted a little in his chair, aware that my comments were directed in part at his well-meant attempts to assist the dancers through difficult passages by subtly adjusting the tempo when on piano duty as *répétiteur*.

Pierre was delighted by the draft designs for the scenery prepared by the ballet school.

'*Merveilleux*!' he cried.

'Our art classes have been busy,' said Madame Prtenchska proudly.

'The colours!' cried Pierre.

'We have already started on the costumes, so I hope you like the concept,' said Madame Prtenchska.

'Excellent! What do you think, Albert?' said Pierre.

The stage director examined the sketches carefully before suggesting that his set designer prepare a series of final drawings for approval. Where appropriate the designer would include variations on the original drafts. I knew what he was getting at. For me, the drafts were a little too feminine - beautifully executed but rather too wistful.

Technically the most challenging aspects of the production as proposed by the ballet school were the scenes involving the arrival and departure of the wicked witch Carabosse in act 1, and the journey through the forest by Prince Désiré and the Lilac Fairy in act 2. In the original Marinsky version the wicked witch emerges from the darkness of a thunderstorm, an arrangement requiring no more than appropriate sound effects and adjustment of the stage lighting, whereas the ballet school's designs showed Carabosse rising from an underground lair amidst clouds of smoke and flashes of lightning. For the forest journey, Marinsky's boat floats straight across the back of the stage propelled by ropes hidden behind the scenery of tree trunks and grass verges which conceal the river. The ballet school's design was much more challenging, showing the boat with Prince Désiré and the Lilac Fairy onboard floating along the river through the forest above a layer of mist.

Mr Frenner stared at the designs, drumming his fingers on the table.

'What do you think?' said Madame Prtenchska anxiously.

Mr Frenner, a burly man, rose to his feet and treaded his way slowly across the stage testing the planks for strength, as Madame Prtenchska and Madame Tuillée had done earlier when checking the flexibility of the wooden floor for the dancers.

'We're going to need a trap door, so the joists will have to be checked. But they feel all right,' he said returning to the table. 'It's the mist that bothers me. We've never tried that here, though I recall reading that theatres have been experimenting with dry ice in America.'

The penultimate item on the agenda was finance. All three parties involved in the production (opera house, ballet school, royal theatre) were funded by the palace through the treasury under control of the lord chamberlain's office. The opera house was the most heavily subsidised and ran at a loss. The other two, as far as I could ascertain, achieved a small profit, the ballet school from its fees to parents, the theatre from seat sales. Both were banking their profits as reserves against future improvements. As chairman of the committee my duty was to ensure an equitable share of costs and distribution of proceeds from *The Sleeping Beauty* whereas, as director of the opera house, I wanted to protect our cash flow which, right now, was unhealthy. Stalling for time in order to establish an accurate figure for expenditure I asked Mr Frenner to prepare an estimate of production support costs, including materials (props and equipment) and manpower services (himself, Pierre and stage hands) for review at the next meeting.

Lastly we addressed the sensitive subject of publicity, in the form of two questions:

- Could we be certain of filling the opera house for three nights and, if not, what steps should be taken to promote the production nationally?

- If ticket sales were slow, to what extent should we use Princess

Sophie's name in order to publicize the production internationally?

Based on the success of the Tchaikovsky concerts so far I felt confident we would be turning people away from the booking office. However the ballet school was still one or two years from graduating students into the professional dance world, and neither the orchestra nor its conductor had experience of supporting a ballet production. Unanimously we agreed we were not yet ready for an invasion of sensation-seeking journalists from the foreign press.

CHAPTER 25

Orchestral auditions are events of nail-biting stress for the majority of candidates choosing to submit themselves and their talents for judgement by persons who have already achieved the positions and success the candidates seek. Weeks and months of practice, sleepless nights for the candidates tossing and turning in their beds, unnerving dreams of quavers, minims and crotchets peeling from music sheets onto their pillows culminating in the agonising wait on the day of the audition for their names to be called, followed, as the climax to their ordeal, by the walk to the centre of the stage hoping their fingers or lips would remember what to do because their brains were blanketed in terror.

For the persons sitting in judgement, orchestral auditions represented not only an opportunity to fill vacancies but to reassess the musicianship of the ensemble to which they belonged. Brilliant performances at an audition were both a source of professional pleasure and a disconcerting reminder that standards in the outside world continued to rise while the capabilities of the musicians within employment slowly but inevitably declined.

There is a famous story of a conductor who had become so tired of dealing with his self-important violinists that he invited a foreign virtuoso unknown to the orchestra to take part in the audition in the guise of a student. The orchestra's violinists attending the event were quietened by the so-called student's outstanding performance.Even more so when the conductor announced later that the student had turned down his offer of employment on the basis that the orchestra's violin section 'left a lot to be desired in terms of quality'.

The normal practice for an orchestral audition is that the conductor and senior players make up the selection panel supported, at the conductor's discretion, by external experts. Each candidate is invited to play two pieces of music. The first piece is traditionally an extract from a concerto for the instrument, intended to illustrate the candidate's virtuosity. The second piece is supplied by the appropriate section of the orchestra to verify that the candidate possesses sufficient technical coherence to perform competently with other players. Members of the selection panel record their judgements in the manner required by the conductor, normally on paper.

For today's audition I had invited Professor Schmidt, director of the university music school, and Mr Lipsky, director of the St Frett music society, to join myself and the principals of the orchestra on the selection panel. Marks were to be recorded on paper using a simple 1-6 numerical system (hopeless, weak, reasonable, good, very good, outstanding) for each of the candidate's test pieces. In addition to the current and impending vacancies for specific instruments there were gaps in the number of extras/understudies needed for other sections of the orchestra.

Stretching across the stage from one set of wings to the other was a continuous black cotton sheet just over six feet high, tall enough to conceal the identity of the candidates but not so dense as to muffle the quality of music. Flirting brazenly with the truth I informed the selection panel that the reason for the curtain was to relax the candidates by providing them with privacy while they played, and to mitigate against prejudices that might arise within the panel concerning, for example, the performers' ages.

I had adopted this subterfuge with the enthusiastic support of Signora Furcello, the librarian. She was delighted at the idea of women being appointed to the orchestra and at the prospect of female musicians inhabiting the building where until now, in professional terms, she had worked alone. Between us we agreed she would receive the female candidates in the library and keep them apart from members of the orchestra until the auditions started, when she would escort the candidates to my chambers and guide them individually to the stage as their names were called. Male candidates would enter from the opposite side of the stage under direction of Peter Enkhle, the orchestra support manager. Suitably briefed about the subterfuge his role was to summon the candidates, male and female, in the prescribed order and invite them to start and stop playing in response to instructions from the selection panel in the auditorium.

The auditions lasted all afternoon, with excellent results. Schmidt, who had provided most of the candidates, was impatient to know the names of the successful players and stamped off when I refused to publish the results until tomorrow, pending due consultation with LeBreq, the leader of the orchestra. Lipsky - whose contingent had included female candidates in the violin, cello, flute, oboe and harp categories - stayed on until LeBreq and I had finished our review, then joined me in my chambers for a drink.

The sun was setting over the city as Valentino poured the glasses of whisky and soda.

'LeBreq agrees with the verdicts?' said Lipsky.

'Completely. Don't you?' I said.

'It's not my decision.'

'But you agree?'

'I'm delighted with the results, and salute your boldness,' said Lipsky.

Valentino normally retired to the pantry after serving drinks but tonight he hung around the sideboard, wiping glasses, holding them up to the light, shuffling the position of the decanters, glancing over his shoulder in my direction, occasionally coughing into the back of his hand.

'What's the matter, Valentino?' I said irritably.

'Pardon the intrusion, sir, but I was wondering if you have had an opportunity to discuss my prospects with Mr Lipsky yet?' he said.

Lipsky looked at me.

'Valentino has ambitions for the stage,' I told him.

'Would it be useful if I performed a demonstration, by means of a few verses, sir?' said Valentino clearing his throat and taking a deep breath.

'That won't be necessary,' I said hurriedly.

'Ambitions as a singer?' said Lipsky.

'He wants a part in *La Bohème*,' I said.

'I would make a very good Rodolfo, if I say so myself, sir,' said Valentino.

He had chosen his moment well. Mellow with whisky after an exhausting afternoon the director of the St Frett music society and conductor of the Ardaniian symphony orchestra respectively agreed that Valentino should attend the music society's weekly rehearsals for the *La Bohème* chorus and that the opera house would pay for any singing lessons deemed necessary following the society's assessment of his voice.

CHAPTER 26

The resignations came thick and fast.

First the harpist, unable to accept that he would be backed by females when the score called for multiple harp parts. For years he had monopolised the musical scene in Ardaniia. Thanks to St Frett music society I could now fill the parts required by Ravel and other composers of the modern school without him. He was not angry, the harpist told me wearily, just disappointed that his contribution to the orchestra's development over the years had been repaid in such a cavalier fashion. I tried my best to persuade him to stay but he shook my hand and departed to collect his severance payment and oversee the loading of his harp onto a horse-drawn carriage.

Next the principal flautist who, unlike the harpist, was furious. How dare I presume to appoint a woman to his section without the courtesy of prior discussion - my attitude was typical of the young generation - he would not shrink from exposing my conduct to the appropriate authorities! If I had wanted to retain his services I would have responded by showing him the score cards for the lady flautist's audition yesterday on which he had written 'exceptional talent - employ immediately'. But I didn't. Instead I broke the news of his off-pitch problem and my reluctant decision to dispense with his services regardless of his view on women musicians. He deflated immediately. Shoulders slumped, he stared pathetically at the carpet. Return to Vienna, use your well-earned severance pay to consult an ear specialist, I suggested escorting him to the door.

In quick succession followed two violinists, a viola player, horn player and cellist, all adamant they could not associate themselves with an orchestra which employed women, all disgusted with the situation which they felt reflected badly on the management, viz. myself, and all extremely concerned that the female emancipation movement represented a greater threat to international stability than the Russian revolution. None of them were too disgusted or concerned to refuse the severance payments which, having thanked them for their work, I confirmed were available to them on departure.

After the resignations came Schmidt charging red-faced into my chambers pushing Valentino aside at the door.

'What the devil's going on?' he demanded.

'Good morning, professor,' I said.

'What's this about women in the orchestra?'

'Isn't it exciting?'

'Exciting! Is that how you describe what you've done?'

'Progressive?'

'It must be stopped, immediately!'

'Why?'

'You are setting an unacceptable precedent!'

'There are women in your choral society.'

'That's different!'

'And some in your domestic residence, presumably.'

'What's that got to do with it!' snapped Schmidt.

'In fact, if you look around, you will find women everywhere.'

'Not in orchestras!' spluttered Schmidt. 'That's different!'

'In what way?'

'You know exactly what I mean!'

Baiting Professor Schmidt was an agreeable pastime which I endeavoured to curtail because the odds were balanced unfairly in my favour by virtue of my senior position. He was correct that the major European and American orchestras were closed to women. However emancipation was afoot in England and I was not the first conductor to consider it absurd that orchestras should deliberately turn their backs on musical talent.

'To top it all, your females are taking places from my graduates,' said Schmidt waving the list of successful candidates.

'Not any more, as it turns out.'

I told him of the resignations. Quietened by the information Schmidt waited while I summoned LeBreq. Together we sat at the conference table and the professor watched as LeBreq and I worked through the list, promoting existing players into the gaps caused by the resignations and filling their places with candidates who had passed the audition and been placed temporarily in the extras/understudies schedule. By the time we finished, all but three of Schmidt's graduates had been allocated probationary positions in the orchestra which the professor was forced to agree, on LeBreq's prompting, represented a more successful outcome for the university than in the previous few years. Schmidt departed the opera house wearing the expression of someone baffled by a conjuring trick.

The situation following the resignations was now as below ('F' = female, 'G' = graduate on probation, 'H' = head of section, 'M' = male from St Frett music society, or private entry).

Immediate promotion to the orchestra:

Flautist (F), First Violin (F), Second Violin (F), Viola (F), Horn (G), Cellist (G), Double Bass (G), Harp (FH)

Impending promotion to the orchestra (to replace retirements):

First Violin (M), First Violin (G), Second Violin (G)

Additions to schedule of extras/understudies:

Violin (F, M, 2G), Trombone (G), Oboe (G), Harp (F), Timpani (G), Percussion (G).

. . . .

Not unexpectedly the first rehearsal of the new-look orchestra was a ragged affair. Anticipating the disruption I had selected comparatively simple works by Mendelssohn and Schumann for the first half of the next concert, and César Franck's symphonic variations for piano and orchestra for the second half, with Marcus as soloist. I told the newcomers to sight-read the easy sections of the scores and cease playing when the going became difficult rather than risk stopping the orchestra. There was plenty of time before Saturday for everyone to master the pieces, I said, expressing the hope that newcomers would accelerate the familiarisation process by studying the scores in detail before tomorrow's rehearsal.

From the podium the change in the appearance of the orchestra was gratifying. The array of solemn grey beards was now enlivened by bright young faces and sporadic splashes of colour from the brooches and silk scarves of the lady musicians, otherwise modestly dressed in black. Before working on Franck's symphonic variations I asked the violinists scheduled for retirement to give way to their young successors. To my satisfaction, during the last movement the variations, the orchestra delivered a thrilling surge of power.

CHAPTER 27

A reminder from the lord chamberlain was awaiting my return to the palace this evening confirming arrangements for dinner with the royal family. White tie, said the note, cocktails 19.00-19.30 hours in the king's private quarters.

My immediate concern on walking past the guards into the private sector of the palace was the nature of the technique required for throwing poultry bones over my shoulder without showering myself or my neighbours with gravy, and without the bones ricocheting off the wall into someone's lap. So after sinking a strong cocktail and accompanying the royal party through to the dining room I was relieved to see a haunch of venison in prime position on the sideboard, dressed in oranges and glazed with liqueur brandy.

The compensating features of the evening were Prince Ernest, the king's younger son on leave from Sandhurst, an agreeable young man who brought news of England, and Lady Fenella deLoire who sat on the king's left at table feeding his majesty with her fingers and laughing prettily at his asides in the manner befitting a royal mistress. The non-compensating features were Grand Duke Rupert, his overbearing wife, and Countess Grigorn, all of whom pointedly excluded me from their conversations.

The queen, sitting at the opposite end of the table from the king, treated me with great affection. I did not attempt to disassociate myself from the British agricultural delegation which had recently visited the country, with which she continued to connect me. Landscape gardening was a subject of great interest to her and throughout the meal I was spared the need to do much more than nod while she described her passion for hydrangeas and orchids, periodically reaching out with her hand to touch mine.

Fortunately the table was wide and long, with generous spaces between the comfortable gilt chairs, so her attempts to reach me with her feet, of which I was aware by virtue of the rustling sounds of her petticoats, were unsuccessful. Moreover the plumpness of her girth ensured she was firmly anchored in her seat restricting her ability to extend her feet further, sparing me the embarrassment of pretending to be surprised if she suddenly slipped from her chair and disappeared out of sight onto the floor.

It puzzled me that she continued to exhibit in her speech signs of advanced intoxication while confining herself to water, which she drank copiously from a tall crystal glass, ignoring her wine goblets, until it occurred to me that measures of gin were being added to her crystal water jug by the liveried stewards at our end of the table out of sight of the king.

When the ladies had retired from the dining room after dinner and cigars were being lit, Grand Duke Rupert condescended to turn in my direction.

'I gather you're looking for singers for *La Bohème*?'

'What's that?' said the king.

'An opera,' said the grand duke.

'As you are aware, I don't like them,' said the king.

'You'd like this one,' said the grand duke. 'Well?'

'Yes, we are looking for experienced singers,' I said.

'I know one. My niece, Countess Charlotte von Littchnoff. She would be perfect for Mimi,' said the grand duke.

'Is she a professional singer?' I said.

'Vaguely. She recites after dinner, sometimes,' said the grand duke.

'Then I would be delighted to arrange an audition,' I said.

'No need for that, just give her the part, and fill the opera house. Half of Europe will turn up if Charlotte performs,' said the grand duke.

'That sounds very interesting, but there would have to be an audition,' I said firmly.

'Please yourself,' said the grand duke turning his back on me.

There was a rosewood piano in the drawing room where the ladies were drinking coffee and eating assorted chocolates. When we entered the room Lady deLoire pointed at the piano and clapped her hands.

'Can anyone play?' she cried.

The king looked at me.

'Would you mind?' he said.

'Does the darling man play the piano as well? How simply wonderful. A fusion of the arts,' said the queen, 'music and soil management.'

'Mr Landour is conductor of our symphony orchestra, mother,' said Prince Ernest patiently.

'I know that perfectly well, darling, but isn't it wonderful he can play the piano too?'

Grand Duke Rupert and his wife talked loudly with Countess Grigorn as I stumbled through some Chopin waltzes, the worse for half a dozen glasses of wine. Lady deLoire stood beside me while I played.

'That was lovely. How about something a little lighter? A piece of jazz music, the Charleston perhaps?'

She smiled down at me, her pretty face a picture of innocence.

'Would you like to hear the Charleston, sir?' she said turning to the king.

'If you want,' said the king from his chair.

Trapped by the maids-of-honour with no means of escape, I had no option but to improvise a version of the dance while Lady deLoire coquettishly tapped her feet in time to the music.

'Isn't it divine, sir!' she cried to the king. 'Wouldn't it be so much fun to dance it at the ball?'

'What do you think, Isobel?' the king said to Countess Grigorn.

The countess lift her nose haughtily in the air.

'Never mind,' laughed the king. Then lowering his voice he said to Lady deLoire, 'You can dance it for me properly, my dear, later.'

I left the party at the same time as Grand Duke Rupert and his wife. On the palace steps the duke threw his cloak over his shoulder and glowered at me, his hooked nose and dark features illuminated intermittently by the clouds scudding past the moon.

'I shall attend the audition,' he said, 'to make sure that Charlotte gets the part.'

CHAPTER 28

Overnight the newcomers to the orchestra had worked on their scores, and the rehearsal was more successful. Prompted by the exchanges I made yesterday for the Franck variations two of the violinists scheduled for retirement have volunteered to leave now, expressing their relief to LeBreq that they no longer have to practice new pieces of music, an increasingly onerous ordeal for them, and reiterating to me their gratitude for the severance payments by which their futures are now comfortably assured. Indeed one of the faithful old retainers has informed me that he plans to take his wife by steamer to Biarritz, the first time in his adult life he has been able to afford a visit to the city of his birth.

The ladies are settling in well. I am especially delighted with the young flautist. She is the wife of a Spanish fish merchant who recently opened an dockside business here exporting sardines and tuna. She studied music in Madrid. Instead of settling for a string instrument which would have allowed her regular performances with chamber groups she chose the flute which, in her words 'captures the rapture of birdsong'. On merit she deserves to be principal flautist. But that would have been a step too far at this stage, even for me, so I have promoted the elderly second flute to the vacant position of principal, and she has taken his place. If the new principal is wise he will allow his deputy a fair share of the interesting solo passages. If not, he will find himself in my chambers discussing his future prospects over tea and cakes.

The star violinist is French, a mother of two children with a marine engineer husband. Trained in Paris she was hoping for a career as a soloist when she encountered a charismatic young man in white overalls with oil on his face who swept her off her feet and deposited her in the sunshine of Ardaniia. Walking with her husband to his workshop shortly after her arrival she noticed the sign outside a local warehouse. Within a week she was playing for the St Frett music society and within a year became the leader of the Lipskys' small orchestra. In releasing her the Lipskys have demonstrated their generosity and unselfishness, and the first violin section of the Ardaniian symphony orchestra has benefitted immensely.

Amongst the other ladies are a Polish cellist and Italian viola player. The only Ardaniian nationals are the harpists, a pair of delightful middle-aged musicians so thrilled at their appointments to the orchestra that they offered to play without remuneration, a tempting suggestion in view of the current state of the opera house accounts, diminished by the quantity of severance payments, but which of course I adamantly refused. The arrangement between them is that they will take turns at concerts when a single harp is required, using the existing instrument in the opera house. When two or more harps are required, both harpists will play, one of them with their own instrument transported to and from the appropriate residence at opera house expense.

Temporary facilities for the ladies have been arranged in the dressing rooms for stage performers while the unused storage area behind the booking office is being converted into permanent quarters. When completed the new facilities will provide a communal area for refreshments, storage space for instruments, changing rooms and WCs.

Concerned at the cost of the plans prepared by Soprianti's favourite builder, which coincide with plans for roof repairs in preparation for winter storms, I inspected the storage area site this morning and questioned the builder about the choice of fittings, which seemed unduly expensive.

'I want the ladies to be comfortable, not pampered,' I said scrutinising the bill of materials.

'Begging your pardon, sir, but the proposed fittings are in keeping with the standards elsewhere in the opera house,' said the builder, pencil tucked behind his ear.

'Why do they need mahogany shelves, surely plain wood would suffice?' I said.

'Mahogany is the regular fixture for this building,' said the builder. 'Now then, we wouldn't want our standards to drop, would we, sir?'

'Wouldn't we indeed,' I said grimly.

Frustrated at my inability to influence the situation, and determined to review the entire process of contract award for opera house refurbishment, I lost my temper with Soprianti on the way back to my chambers encountering a thick layer of dust in an alcove, all the worse for being illuminated by an overhead light.

'So much for the long-awaited improvement in housekeeping quality,' I snapped pointing at the alcove.

Soprianti spread his arms.

'These builders,' he said. 'No sooner they arrive, they make dust everywhere.'

Morose for the rest of the day my temper was not improved by driving the Citroen into the wall of the Lipsky's warehouse. My intention had been to visit the St Frett music society in order to thank Mrs Lipsky personally for her role in providing the orchestra with an infusion of excellent musicians. I had already thanked her husband during the interlude after the auditions and asked him to convey my gratitude to his wife, but felt that the couple's kindness and generosity warranted a further gesture on my part.

Turning left at the main junction from the central square I was proceeding south down the harbour road at twilight, the sun behind the hills and orange fingers in the sky, when I heard a snapping noise under the bonnet of the car and a rattling sound from the footbrake pedal. Depressing the pedal I found that the link mechanism had disconnected itself from the brakes. The car meanwhile was picking up speed. I switched off the engine, applied the handbrake with as much force as possible, swung the car into the side road leading to the warehouse and managed to reduce the speed sufficiently so that when the vehicle crashed into the wall the only damage was a broken radiator, a profusion of steam, the acrid smell of burning brake pads, some dislodged bricks and a gash on my forehead.

'The brakes failed,' I apologised to the Lipskys who came rushing out to determine why their place of business and residence had been subjected to sudden vibration.

'Next time you want to thank me for something, send a telegram,' suggested Mrs Lipsky dabbing my forehead with a damp towel and applying a plaster to the cut.

By the time I had arranged for the car to be collected and repairs made to the Lipsky's wall, I was late for dinner in the castle. Verifying the validity of the principle that trouble, unlike lightning, strikes its victims repeatedly in quick succession, Sarah was waiting for me in the anteroom.

'I suppose you're pleased with yourself,' she said arms folded.

'About what?' I said.

'How could you!'

'Could I what?' I said taking a cocktail and draining it in one gulp.

'Let us down like that.'

'Sarah, it's been a long day, could you get to the point?'

'Poor Fenella, she didn't know what to do.'

'About what?'

'Why didn't you help her?'

'Are you referring to last night's incident at the piano?'

'Fenella was waiting for your support, having very cleverly given you an opening.'

'Having very cleverly set me up, you mean.'

'You were supposed to tell the king that the Charleston was a marvellous dance, entirely suitable for the ball. Instead, you sat there gulping like a goldfish, apparently.'

'How do you think I got this?' I said pointing to the plaster on my forehead.

Sarah shrugged her shoulders.

'While I was attempting to argue the case for the Charleston, Countess

Grigorn struck me with a brandy bottle.'

Sarah stared at me, her pretty eyes wide open, then burst out laughing. 'You liar!'

'Which is exactly what would have happened if I had pursued the matter. If you want the Charleston, Fenella will have to use her influence on the king, but kindly keep me out of it,' I said.

I pictured Lady Fenella deLoire in her nightdress cuddling up to the king whispering in his ear 'will you do something for me please, kingsy wingsy, darling?' and he replying 'anything for you, my precious' and she saying 'just a little something' and he replying 'whatever your heart desires, my pet' and she saying 'tell the old bat you've decided we can dance the Charleston at the ball' whereupon the king would sit bolt upright up in bed and shout 'the master of music is behind this unseemly interruption to our pleasure, off with his head!'

'Completely out of it,' I repeated.

'All right, I'll tell her,' said Sarah. 'So what happened to your head?'

'I ran into a brick wall.'

Finally, ignoring the principle that persons should not be kicked when down, the lord chamberlain summoned me to the fireplace and informed me that the queen wanted to learn how to play the piano. Until further notice I was to report to the royal drawing room at 1600 hours on Tuesdays for the purpose of providing her with lessons.

He must have seen the pleading look in my eyes.

'Sorry,' he said, 'royal command.'

CHAPTER 29

The cashier is a regular visitor to my chambers, tiptoeing in with the accounts ledger under his arm and a worried expression on his face. If the opera house was a commercial organisation our bank would have withdrawn support by now and forced us into liquidation. Backed by the palace we are in effect a quasi-official department subject to annual audit by the king's treasury, responsible to the lord chamberlain for day-to-day financial management of our budget, and safe from the usual external predatory consequences of fiscal incompetence.

Strictly speaking I should not be relying on support from our bank at all, but the current overdraft arrangement spares me from the need to ask the lord chamberlain for supplementary funds when outgoings exceed the combined total from booking office receipts and the monthly disbursement from the palace. Unfortunately the overdraft figure has been climbing steadily thanks to the severance payments and advance costs of *The Sleeping Beauty* and *La Bohème,* the latter in the form of transfers to St Frett music society to cover chorus rehearsal and voice training expenses.

The blame for the situation is entirely mine. When presenting my pensions and contracts proposal to the lord chamberlain I should have amended the cash flow estimate in the three year plan. Now some expensive chickens have come home to roost and our bank is sounding the alarm.

'Mr O'Reilly has been on the telephone again, sir,' said the cashier adjusting the spectacles on his nose and opening the ledger. He is a small tidily-dressed Ardaniian with bald head and neat handwriting, employed thirty years ago as an assistant clerk, slowly and steadily advancing to one of the most influential positions in the building, subordinate only to the Soprianti and myself. Soprianti normally attends our meetings and, technically, I should insist on his presence but he has taken to assuming an irritating air of condescension, feigning distress at the current status of the opera house accounts and hinting that our finances would be in better shape if managed by his office, without interference.

'Good grief,' I said wincing at the latest figures in the book. 'I'd better visit the bank.'

'Very well, sir,' said the cashier.

'Into the lion's den,' I said reaching for the telephone.

Our branch of the Ardaniian national bank stands in the commercial district of the city, five minutes by motor vehicle and fifteen minutes' walk across the park. The Citroen was still in pieces under the castle walls so I strode over the grass in the park between the trees inhaling the late summer breeze from the ocean preparing my presentation to O'Reilly, the bank manager. The three year plan had been originated by my predecessor Leigh-Winter in response to the lord chamberlain's request as to when, if ever, the opera house might become financially self-sufficient. Confident that I could increase the audience attendance figures, I had accepted the plan and associated cash flow estimate as the basis for quantifying the extent of financial support required each month from the palace. Unfortunately the surplus revenue from increased seat sales had not covered the cost of the recent severance payments, although the overall picture had not changed. A modest temporary injection of cash was required, nothing more.

'The top of the morning to you, it's a grand day to be sure,' said O'Reilly a large Irishman who masked his dislike of the English with boisterous chatter. This was our second meeting. At the first, I had marked him down as a bully, a pre-requisite for his profession, in my opinion.

'The weather will be to your liking, and no mistake,' said O'Reilly.

'It's certainly cooling down,' I said.

'Winter will be here in the shake of a lamb's tail, if they had any. Lambs I mean. Now that's something I miss, good old roast lamb,' said O'Reilly rubbing his large hands briskly.

'Is that so,' I said.

'And how are things in the opera house, settling in nicely? It's been a while since we met, I think.'

O'Reilly flicked through the pages of the diary on his desk.

'You're domiciled in the palace, I seem to remember. How very satisfactory, how civilised, how grand!' he said.

'I find it quite comfortable,' I said.

'The acquaintances you must make! Mrs O'Reilly is always reminding me how much she would like to attend a palace ball, and see all those glamorous dresses and tiaras. Tell me, my wife so badly wants to know, is it true that the king's evening dress uniform is completely white?'

'Your wife may be referring to officers of the household cavalry,' I said.

There was a pause while O'Reilly waited for me to invite him and his wife to a palace ball and, when no invitation was forthcoming, rubbed his hands briskly again.

'Well now, what can I do for you this fine morning?'

'On behalf of the opera house I would like to negotiate a small increase in our overdraft facility,' I said passing across his desk a copy of the three year plan modified to reflect the severance payments.

For fifteen minutes as recorded on the ornate clock on the wall of his lavishly furnished office O'Reilly sucked his teeth, tapped the surface of his blotting pad with his fingers, carried the paper containing the three year plan to the window and examined the contents in sunlight, strode up and down the office stroking his chin, tipped his chair back and stared at the ceiling and finally, when it became clear that an invitation to the palace was not forthcoming and Mrs O'Reilly would have to continue waiting to witness the king in evening dress, announced that unfortunately the bank found itself unable to provide the additional assistance requested.

'Very regrettable of course, but the prime lender, the palace in your case, is always the most appropriate source of supplementary funds,' said O'Reilly bowing me out of his office.

On the way back through the park it occurred to me that the revenue from advanced bookings for *The Sleeping Beauty* might serve to plug the temporary hole in our accounts. Cheered by the thought I awarded an affectionate pat to a passing dog, exchanged cheerful greetings with its owner, then remembered that the posters advertising the ballet had not yet been designed. By the time the artwork had been prepared and approved and the posters printed the opera house would be broke.

As if to emphasize the dire nature of our circumstances I was welcomed on my return by a delegation of singers from the university choral society. Professor Schmidt had finally come off the fence and declared that participation by the choir in *La Bohème* would be permitted only over his dead body, an announcement received with mixed feelings by the younger members of the society who viewed the prospect of the professor's expiration without undue concern yet were bound in loyalty to the choir. Would it be possible, the members of the delegation wanted to know, for the opera house to intercede on their behalf? They did not wish to lose their positions yet were keen to feature in the famous modern opera with the tragic love story and beautiful music which was capturing the hearts of audiences throughout the world.

More expense, I thought. Nonetheless I directed the delegation to the Lipskys, promised the singers that any of them selected for parts in *La Bohème* would have their singing careers protected by me in the event of dismissal from the university choir then, after they had thanked me and bounded enthusiastically from my chambers towards the St Frett music society, dropped my head into my arms.

I was in this position, slumped on my desk wondering how to pay the Lipskys for the additional rehearsal and training time, when Valentino flung open the door of my chambers.

'His grace, the Bishop of Ardaniia.'

Anglican by faith the services at the splendid Roman Catholic cathedral which towered over the city from the slopes of the hill below the castle were not appropriate for my spiritual needs. I had visited the building several times to speak with the organist, a taciturn lecturer at the university music school, and admire the gothic architecture but had never knelt in prayer in the cathedral nor, in the course of many formal occasions elsewhere in the country, had I met the bishop. From conversations overheard at the palace I knew only that he was comparatively young, energetic and admired.

I stood as the bishop entered the room magnificent in his long black cassock, heavy silver cross on a silver chain suspended from his neck, crimson red cap on his head, crimson red sash around his waist. Smiling he extended his hand, palm down. Aware that Catholics were supposed to kiss the holy ring thus presented and ignorant of the appropriate protocol for Anglicans, yet anxious not to be set alight for heresy, I was on the point of lowering my head when, sensing my hesitation, the bishop extended his other arm, reached for my right hand and clasped it warmly.

The range of his musical knowledge was impressive. During our conversation he commented perceptively on the development of church music throughout the ages from plainsong to the great chorales of the classical period, then stunned me by announcing that his ambition was to commission a performance of Verdi's *Requiem* in the cathedral.

'Could you arrange that?' he said calmly, consuming a cream cake served by Valentino who kept crossing himself, so overcome was my steward at status of the visitor.

While waiting for my response the bishop said it was normal practice for the cathedral to invite the university choir and chamber orchestra to perform at Christmas. Favourites with the congregation were Bach's *St Matthew Passion*, Handel's *Messiah* and Mozart's *Requiem*. However this year the bishop sought something different. He wanted the congregation to be challenged by a new experience and stirred by music that at least in part reflected the nation's momentous transition to democratic government. Unfortunately the head of the university music department, Professor Schmidt, had not found himself able to share the bishop's enthusiasm for change and was disinclined to advance his choir's repertoire beyond the classical period. From the opera house, on the other hand, had come glowing reports of exciting new musical programmes.

Duly flattered my immediate reaction was that any arrangements arising from our discussions would materialise after the current cash crisis had been resolved, one way or another, and therefore that the financial implications could be ignored. My next was that we were not yet capable of performing Verdi's *Requiem*. The work required four soloists - soprano, mezzo-soprano, tenor, baritone - which by coincidence matched the requirement for *La Bohème*. I was not yet convinced we would find singers of sufficient accomplishment here in Ardaniia. Auditions for *La Bohème* were still months away. Verdi's *Requiem* was simply not feasible by Christmas. How about Saint-Saëns or Fauré, I suggested?

'How about Rachmaninov?' said the bishop stunning me for the second time with the breadth of his musical knowledge. Rachmaninov was next on my list of outstanding contemporary composers for performance in the opera house. Marcus had already started work the composer's glamorous second piano concerto.

'*Vesna*?' I suggested, 'for baritone, choir and orchestra.'

'Perfect,' said the bishop immediately.

'Celebrating forgiveness rather than death.'

'I much prefer forgiveness,' said the bishop.

'It's shorter than the requiem,' I said.

'Then let us surround *Vesna* with carols,' said the bishop.

We looked at each other with the satisfaction that comes with agreement on a matter of significant moment to both parties.

'How much would you like in the way of deposit?' said the bishop.

'Deposit?' I said.

'The university always insists on advance payment. To cover costs, mobilisation, and similar expenses. Shall we say a thousand crowns?' said the bishop signalling the pair of clerics seated behind him quietly finishing Valentino's stock of cream cakes.

'Do you believe in miracles?' I asked my steward afterwards.

'Yes, sir,' said Valentino eyes glazed from being blessed as the bishop departed from the room.

'Me too,' I said fondling the cheque which, when cleared, would eliminate the opera house overdraft.

CHAPTER 30

After breakfast I went straight to the Lipsky's warehouse to discuss the commission from the cathedral, news of which I had passed by telephone to the couple yesterday. In the excitement of the meeting with the bishop I had overlooked the possibility that the Lipskys might not welcome an extension to their already substantial workload. I was inclined to overlook their ages, approaching seventy five in the case of Mr Lipsky, and was relieved to find them both already at the piano, studying the score of the Rachmaninov cantata.

'Wonderful music!' they cried as I mounted the steps to the stage.

'You're sure I'm not overloading you?' I said.

'Overloading!' they cried, embracing me in turn.

They repeated the story of their flight from Germany, robbery at the border, derelict warehouse, years of sporadic income from piano and violin lessons, slow materialisation of amateur choir and orchestra, slow development of concert hall, first amateur recitals, enthusiastic support from schools but total indifference from the musical elite of the country until, one day, into the warehouse strides a young conductor who in the course of a few months transforms the St Frett music society into a thriving institution for the training of professional opera singers and choristers!

'Having attempted and failed to demolish your warehouse with my motor vehicle,' I said.

'You enjoy it, do it again,' said Mrs Lipsky. 'How is your poor head?'

'This bishop, he knows about us?' said Mr Lipsky.

His point was whether the vocal element of the forthcoming performance in the cathedral should be attributed to the St Frett music society choir or whether the Lipsky's choir should be classified as the Ardaniian symphony orchestra choir, thereby eliminating any awkwardness relating to the Lipsky's religion. I steadfastly opposed the second option, not just for the implicitly ignoble racist aspect of such an artificial arrangement but because I wanted the Lipskys to receive the recognition they deserved There was also the matter of competition from the university choir. The orchestra would be best served by having two large independent choirs in the market place. As far as the cathedral was concerned I was quite certain the bishop would stand no nonsense regarding the Lipsky's Jewish background and, on my part, at the first sign of trouble I would void the commission.

'The performance at the cathedral will be given jointly by the Ardaniian symphony orchestra and St Frett music society choir,' I said firmly.

Coincidentally, signs of unrest at the university choir were manifesting themselves at an opportune time. Yesterday's delegation of mutineers despatched from my chambers to the warehouse had been accepted by the Lipskys for inclusion in rehearsals for *La Bohème,* without guarantee of places in the cast. Now as a result of the commission from the cathedral the mutineers could at least be assured of positions in the choir for the Rachmaninov cantata. The work required a large chorus. More voices were needed. The Lipskys and I spent a mischievous half hour plotting ways of promoting further discontent within the ranks of Professor Schmidt's pampered vocalists.

Arriving at the opera house I found an envelope propped against the silver ink pot on my desk. The writing was feminine and the paper softly perfumed. Valentino watched from the pantry door as I wafted the envelope under my nose. The expression on my steward's face indicated he was struggling to contain himself from bursting into one of the romantic arias from *La Bohème* so I waved him away and, to the sound of coffee cups being clattered in the pantry, sliced open the envelope.

The message was from Yvette. "Important, meet me in the residents' garden at ten o'clock tonight. Wear white carnation. Don't be late."

Judged by their performance at this morning's rehearsal it is clear that the newcomers to the orchestra have mastered their scores. The result is an exponential improvement in the quality of sound. Fewer wrong notes from violinists struggling with the intricacies of their parts, no more high-pitched squeals from off-pitch flutes, a richer depth from the cellos and everywhere a sense of greater alertness and coordination within the sections. I am already beginning to enjoy greater freedom in interpreting the intent of each of the composers we rehearse, an agreeable development especially when accompanying a brilliant pianist like Marcus whose reading of the symphonic variations would surely please César Frank himself.

Returning to my chambers I chaired the second meeting of the opera house ballet production committee. Present, as before, were ballet school director Madame Prtenchska, senior ballet mistress Madame Tuillée, royal theatre director Pierre Bonnel, royal theatre stage manager Albert

Frenner, *répétiteur* Marcus and myself.

Mr Frenner reported that the scenery designs were still being re-worked. Completion of the designs for act 2 could not be accomplished until the method of transporting Prince Désiré and the Lilac Fairy through the forest had been decided. To that end, equipment for manufacturing dry ice and converting the ice to mist was on its way by steamer from the United States for trial. If the equipment worked properly the royal theatre would absorb the cost of the unit into its own budget, foreseeing extensive use for future theatrical productions, not least for Shakespearean plays.

I added to the agenda the requirement for posters and advertising material. Mr Frenner suggested that photographs of the principal dancers be superimposed onto the relevant artwork. Madame Prtenchska, Madame Tuillée and I, concerned that Princess Sophie had yet to prove her fitness for the role of Lilac Fairy beyond reasonable doubt, disagreed with the use of photographs on the grounds that last-minute changes to the cast might occur as a result of injury. Mr Frenner sensibly pointed out that it was normal practice to include photographs of principal members of the cast in the programmes available for sale to the public. Programmes represented a valuable source of revenue, did the opera house intend to perform *The Sleeping Beauty* without them? In accordance with the behavioural pattern of every committee since the dawn of time when faced with awkward decisions, Madame Prtenchska, Madame Tuillée and I agreed that the matter should be held over for deliberation at the next meeting.

The relationship between Madame Tuillée and Pierre Bonnel established at the first meeting of the committee is blossoming into boisterous friendship. Not to be outdone by the royal theatre I had instructed Valentino to procure several bottles of fine wine to accompany luncheon in my chambers. Somewhere between the conclusion of the *filets de boeuf* and the arrival of the cheeses the committee was treated to an impromptu duet between the elegant elderly ballerina in chiffon and pearls and the young director in black beret with a raffish cravat around his neck. Arms linked they rendered for our edification the seven verses of a Gallic ballad of questionable moral status.

Ten o'clock that night saw me bedecked with a white carnation approaching the residents' garden unsteadily. The claret at lunch had been supplemented by burgundy at dinner. I was not so drunk however as to be unexcited at the prospect of the forthcoming encounter. Blood pumped through my veins as I weaved along the moonlit path towards an assignment assuredly not intended to further my understanding of Ardaniian laws on pensions and contracts.

'Pssssst.'

A hand reached out and drew me into a bower of bougainvillea perfumed with Yvette's scent and the night fragrance of the garden.

'You're late,' said Yvette in the semi-darkness.

'The clock has only just struck,' I protested.

'Never mind. Stand still and keep quiet.'

'We're meeting here on behalf of Sarah, I presume?' I enquired.

'Of course. Why else would we be in the garden, alone, in the moonlight?'

'You never know. I thought, perhaps . . .'

'Shhh,' said Yvette.

She looked out from the bower.

'They're coming,' she said.

'Who exactly . . . ?'

'When they draw close, embrace me and say something romantic, loudly, is that clear? Have you been drinking?'

'Only a little.'

'Don't fall over.'

Yvette peered out of the bower again.

'They're nearly here. Are you ready?'

'About this romantic pronouncement, what should it consist of, do you think?'

'I've no idea. You're supposed to know about these things, you're a man. Whatever it is, do it loudly.'

The sound of approaching footsteps and murmured conversation was now clearly audible.

'Get ready,' whispered Yvette.

'I'm really not good at pronouncements,' I said.

A shadow fell across the moonlit opening of the bower as the owners of the voices drew parallel with us.

'Go on!' said Yvette stabbing my leg with her toe.

Clasping her in my arms I shouted 'My darling, your hot kisses have inflamed my senses, I am consumed with desire!'

The silence which followed the declaration was broken almost immediately by Yvette who slipped from my grasp and clutched at the branches of the bougainvillea convulsed with laughter. Outside the bower I saw Sarah standing with her hands on her hips. Scowling at me she spun round on her heels and hurried back through the garden pursued by her companion, a dragoon officer presumably rented by Yvette for the occasion.

'Consumed with desire!' sobbed Yvette. 'Where did that come from?'

'Noel Coward, as far as I recall,' I said stiffly.

Yvette's shoulders were still heaving. Her recovery was clearly going to take time so I bowed, thanked her for cooperating in the matter of Sarah and proceeded to my apartment discarding the carnation grumpily into a flower bed on the way. So much for the prospect of a passionate interlude, I thought. Yvette had skilfully kept her delicious red lips out of range during the embrace.

CHAPTER 31

December. Time is running out. Snow has started to fall in the mountains and the shops are promoting Christmas gifts. In the course of a few short weeks the orchestra will be performing Handel's *Dixit Dominus* with the university choir in the opera house, Rachmaninov's *Vesna* with the St Frett music society choir in the cathedral and Tchaikovsky's *The Sleeping Beauty* with the royal ballet school in the opera house, in addition to the usual Saturday evening concerts.

Time is running out because none of the participants are ready. The university choir is still in rehearsal stage with Professor Schmidt and I am bracing myself for the task of undoing his work. The St Frett music society choir remains under strength and the Lipskys are busy training new recruits, a challenging endeavour in view of the decision to perform the cantata in Russian. The dancers from the royal ballet school are confused by ongoing changes to the choreography, forced by modifications to the scenery arising from constraints in the operation of backstage equipment, and the scenery is still not finished. The orchestra is wilting under the pressure of the considerable workload, several important players are absent with colds and the principal trombone is displaying signs of a nervous breakdown.

If nothing else I have managed to complete my self-imposed tour of duty as *répétiteur* at the ballet school without undue disgrace. By taking Marcus's place in the main rehearsal studio for a fortnight I have accomplished a useful working knowledge of Tchaikovsky's score and, more important, a clear understanding of the passages between and during individual scenes when the orchestra must wait for the dancers.

The role of the opera pianist is different from ballet *répétiteur*. When rehearsing a singer, the pianist dictates the tempo of the music in accordance with the composer's markings and proceeds through the score in whatever sequence he or the conductor deems appropriate, nodding as necessary to indicate points of entry, stopping only to issue suggestions for improvement. He does not have to lift his head from the score except perhaps to determine why the singer has stopped performing. Reasons for this during stage rehearsals include the possibility of the singer being felled by the branch of a newly-positioned tree or tripping over a rope.

Whereas, in the dance studio, the *répétiteur* applies the tempo dictated by the ballet mistress, without any opportunity of proceeding uninterrupted through the score. I am now qualified to state without fear of contradiction that the average ballet class involves more starts and stops than underground trains on the Piccadilly line manage in a day. Angles of limbs are adjusted, hands are manipulated, toes are pointed in new directions, heads are rotated, hip positions are corrected with meticulous detail while the pianist waits, fingering the pages of the score nervously wondering to which bar of music he will be directed to return or, more vaguely, to which section of the dance: 'Go back to the Lilac Fairy's entry, please - one, two, three . . .' commands the ballet mistress clapping her hands.

Nor can the pianist at a ballet rehearsal rely solely on his ears for feedback. He must watch the dancers' movements closely and be alert for loss of synchronisation between music and feet, ready at a moment's notice to nurse a ballerina or the *corps de ballet* back to the established momentum. Anyone doubting the complexity of the *répétiteur's* task should try sight-reading bars 231-306 of the *Pas de Six* in *The Sleeping Beauty*, one eye switching between the conductor's score and piano reduction propped on the music stand in front of him, the other on Violente's feet as she explodes across the wooden floor.

To our relief the dry ice machine has arrived and been found capable of ejecting clouds of thick white vapour which roll across the stage at ground level simulating with extraordinary vividness the effect of mist drifting through a forest.

The artwork for the scenery has been modified to reflect amendments to the design of the boat, duly simplified with the addition of tricycle wheels, pedals and small handlebar in the undercarriage allowing the contraption to be propelled and steered though the trees by a stage hand face down in the compartment below Prince Désiré and the Lilac Fairy. The artist employed by the theatre to modify the scenery designs has sharpened the overall colour scheme and thereby improved the aesthetic effect significantly. Madame Prtenchska and Madame Tuillée were doubtful at first that the new layouts represented an advance from the designs originally prepared by the ballet school but changed their minds after a visit to the theatre workshop where the sets are being constructed. The wardrobe mistress and her team are working late each night updating the dancers' costumes with the sharper colours.

Sophie has settled into the role of the Lilac Fairy and the new principal ballerina, Jennifer, a sweet girl with auburn hair, looks equally beautiful in the part of Princess Aurora. The problem that afflicted Sophie throughout the summer appears to have resolved itself. In the absence of further falls or trips the committee duly went ahead with the production of the promotional material using photographs for the posters and programmes. At the time of writing all four performances of *The Sleeping Beauty* including the children's matinee on Saturday afternoon have been sold out.

So despite the challenges and frenetic pace of current events, I am pleased to record that the financial position of the opera house continues to improve.

Meanwhile the queen has abandoned her plan to become a concert pianist. The most complicated part of my task as her instructor turned out to be keeping her upright on the piano stool, on account of the royal wine intake. Not until halfway through the second lesson did she manage to strike middle C unaided, and by then her enthusiasm had declined.

During the third lesson she exchanged the piano stool for an armchair and requested me to entertain her with a selection of popular tunes. The sequence was repeated for the fourth lesson. She failed to show up for the fifth and, for the sixth, I was received by Countess Grigorn who icily conveyed her displeasure at her majesty's lack of progress with the pianoforte and dismissed my services as tutor.

The queen is not the only member of the royal family to have disrupted my increasingly hectic schedule.

'His Royal Highness Grand Duke Rupert and Countess Charlotte von Littchnoff,' announced Valentino, white faced, at the door yesterday.

Into my chambers strode a woman in her late twenties wearing a full length violet dress. Her hat of the same colour was pierced with flamboyant peacock feathers which struck Valentino on the head as she passed through the door. I would not describe her as handsome but her eyes sparkled with striking vivacity. Behind the peacock feathers came the hooked-nose duke who had ostentatiously ignored me during dinner with the king.

'My niece,' said the duke lowering himself into an armchair. 'You wanted to audition her for the role of Mimi.'

'How simply wonderful, to meet a real conductor,' said the countess extending a gloved hand in my direction. 'And of such eminence, the whole country is talking of your great success with our orchestra.'

While Valentino served coffee and cream cakes, trying to control the motion of his hands which trembled so much that the cups rattled on the saucers on account of the duke's reputation as the fearsome owner of an impenetrable castle high in the mountains with multiple dark dungeons, I invited the countess to acquaint me of her musical experience. Admitting that she lacked formal training, she described a lifelong interest in opera and operettas. As a child she had performed in amateur productions of Franz Lehár's *The Merry Widow* and still frequently gave recitals to friends and guests at her estate in the country. Her husband had been killed in the war. She was thus now appropriately titled to perform Lehár's popular musical, she told me laughing.

I invited her to sing. Safely out of sight in the pantry I could see Valentino draw the palm of his hand across his throat as the sound of the countess's strident voice filled the room.

'What do you mean, mezzo-soprano?' demanded the duke after the countess had completed her recital and I had offered my opinion.

'Her range is slightly different from a soprano,' I explained.

'Maestro Landour thinks my voice would be better suited for Musetta,' said the countess.

'Does Musetta get a dressing room?' said the duke.

'Certainly,' I said.

'Can we see it?' said the duke.

'I haven't got the part yet,' said the countess.

'Why not?' demanded the duke.

'There has to be an audition of candidates first,' said the countess.

'Early next year,' I said.

'Maestro Landour has kindly given me a copy of the score, so that I can practice. Thank you so much for the coffee - the cakes were delicious,' said the countess turning towards the pantry where Valentino had fortunately stopped contorting his face in imitation of the countess's style of vocal delivery.

'You were not impressed, I gather,' I observed to my steward after the duke and countess had departed.

'If she gets the part, I'll eat my hat,' said Valentino.

CHAPTER 32

The star baritone is unquestionably Peter Broch, the youngest son of a local solicitor. Tall and good-looking, he has a commanding voice and forceful delivery in the lower register. Anxious for his future he was amongst the cadre of university singers which mutinied against Professor Schmidt's embargo on *La Bohème* and approached me for advice, ending up at the St Frett music society. He is an outstanding prospect for the role of Marcello in *La Bohème* and will be singing the baritone part in *Vesna* in the cathedral on Sunday.

Professor Schmidt is not yet aware that a section of the university choir has been moonlighting in the Lipsky's warehouse. The professor is due here shortly to watch his choir rehearse Handel's *Dixit Dominus* with the orchestra for the first time and I am steeling myself for the unpleasant task of acquainting him with the singers' revolt. If I delay further, the cat will be out of the bag when Peter Broch appears alongside me in front of the congregation on Sunday and although the professor is unlikely to cause trouble in the cathedral I would prefer to brave the consequences earlier.

The star soprano continues to be Zoe, the scullery maid from the palace kitchens. Her voice is lighter than the other contenders for the role of Mimi in *La Bohème* but she has the best presence, sweet allure touched with waywardness, and her voice is strengthening under tuition from Mrs Lipsky.

No reasonable candidates have yet emerged for the role of the poet Rodolfo or the flirtatious singer Musetta. Rodolfo will be the most difficult to fill. The part demands a tenor with a formidably powerful range. To the amusement of the Lipskys and the rest of the cast rehearsing *La Bohème* my steward Valentino continues to promote his credentials for the tenor role by arriving in the warehouse bellowing arias from the opera transposed downwards so that he can reach the top notes. The teacher appointed by Mrs Lipsky to instruct Valentino resigned after the first lesson. The second teacher is guarded in her opinion other than to remark diplomatically that he makes good sandwiches.

LeBreq and I interviewed the orchestra's principal trombone this morning to determine the reason for his strange behaviour. He has been consistently late, erratic in his playing, distracting the brass players by sighing and fidgeting in his seat during rehearsals. He held out against our questions for a while, denied anything was wrong then broke down and admitted he was seriously in debt thanks to his spendthrift wife. I was faced with two options. The first was to suspend him in the hope that the shock would force him to curtail his wife's extravagance. The second was to authorise a loan from the opera house and remind him gently of the basic steps for controlling domestic expenditure. Rightly or wrongly I chose the latter option.

'What the devil's going on?' said Professor Schmidt bursting into my chambers almost knocking over the principal trombonist as the two men passed each other.

'You've heard, then?' I said.

'Naturally. They tell me everything. We don't keep secrets in the university, unlike other places,' snapped the professor.

'I was going to tell you . . .'

'So I should think. You don't like my tempo, it appears. Everyone is entitled to his opinion, but I conducted my first performance of *Dixit Dominus* before you were born, a performance warmly received in Leipzig, the precursor of many, for which the tempo has never been faulted, to my recollection, until now.'

'I'm sorry, I thought you were referring to something else,' I said.

'What else?' demanded the professor.

'Another matter, which can wait. Meanwhile, I recognise how frustrating it can be when carefully-rehearsed pieces are subjected to change, minor though such changes might be . . .'

'Minor!' snapped the professor.

'. . . and acknowledge that you have far greater understanding of the period than myself. However, in turn, I am sure you acknowledge my right to impose my own interpretation on works selected for performance in the opera house.'

'Interpretation!' snorted the professor. 'It's written down, in the score!'

Dixit Dominus is one of those extraordinary pieces of music that defy classification. Soaring above the gifted compositions of his youth, unparalleled in beauty and originality by anything he wrote later including the *Messiah*, the work is so far ahead of its time that even Wagner struggled to match the thrilling loveliness of the soprano duet. Where on earth, or heaven, did it all spring from? Handel chose psalm 110 as his theme which makes the work even more extraordinary because the psalm in question is a dour, menacing, warlike screed. He incorporated the words of the psalm but almost completely ignored the implications of them in the music which, for the most part, dances through a blissful exposition of love and laughter.

Beethoven surely had *Dixit Dominus* in mind when he described Handel as the 'greatest of us all'. Professor Schmidt on the other hand must have been influenced by the gloom of psalm 110 when he first reduced Handel's joyful masterpiece to a funeral dirge.

I was very careful when rehearsing with the university choir soloists in my chambers yesterday not to criticize the professor. The work had gone through a metamorphosis in England, I told the soloists gathered around the Steinway grand piano, explaining that although Handel was German by birth he had spent most of his adult life in London where the tradition was to play his music with a lighter touch than in continental Europe, a tradition which affected my own interpretations of his work.

The soloists adapted to my revisions without protest and rehearsed very competently. Overall the session was so successful I nursed the hope that the soloists would convey their enthusiasm for my livelier version of the work to Professor Schmidt in advance of this morning's rehearsal with orchestra and full choir. A misplaced hope, evidently.

'They play it faster in England?' said the professor when I had repeated yesterday's explanation.

'Yes, indeed,' I said.

He stared at me doubtfully.

'What else is going on? You mentioned another matter.'

Ordinarily Valentino fussed around visitors to my chambers offering them coffee, tea and cakes, hovering afterwards in the background ready to replenish the array of refreshments. Not this morning. For visits by Professor Schmidt, Valentino had adopted the policy of locking himself in the pantry. Which was a pity. A cream cake might have mollified the professor who stood threateningly in front of me, his expression dark with suspicion.

'They did what?' he barked on being acquainted of the revolt by members of his choir.

'They simply want to extend their range of musical experience,' I said.

'You can hardly describe *La Bohème* as music! Well, they're not coming back to the university, that's final. They can complete the Handel performance here, then they're discharged. You can tell them yourself,' snapped the professor.

'Do think that's wise?' I said.

'Puccini, pernicious rubbish!' snorted the professor.

'Europe's principal opera houses would hardly agree, sold out night after night,' I said.

'More fool they. The university choral society sets standards of musical performance which, under my leadership, shall not be prejudiced. There is no return for members who repay their training by seeking to enrich themselves in vulgarity. Whatever next, shall we be expected to recruit cabaret singers!'

'I really cannot support a position which threatens to suppress artistic freedom,' I said.

'I'm not threatening it, I'm doing it!' snapped the professor.

'In which case, I might have to consider suppressing the opera house's freedom of choice with regard to engagement of choirs.'

The professor glowered at me.

'You can't do that!'

I met his angry gaze firmly.

'I have promised to protect their singing careers,' I said.

'You can't force me to take them back,' snapped the professor.

'No, but I can protect them in other ways,' I said.

'We'll see about that,' said the professor swinging on his heels. 'Play *Dixit Dominus* as fast as you like. I wash my hands of it,' he shouted outside my chambers, slamming the doors as he proceeded down the corridor.

CHAPTER 33

The decision to sing Rachmaninov's *Vesna* in Russian was made by the Lipskys. They were concerned that the first major public performance by the St Frett music society choir might be dismissed as inauthentic. Amongst the Lipsky's acquaintances was a part-time voice teacher of Soviet origin whom they commissioned to instruct the members of the choir in the correct pronunciation. In fact the words are not difficult, the poem by Nekrasov upon which the cantata is based is not long, and the verses are often repeated.

The story is simple and arguably unsuited for a congregation containing children. A wife betrays her vows and confesses her unfaithfulness to her husband as winter sets in. The winter is bleak and harsh and the husband spends the cold days plotting revenge. Deciding that death is the appropriate punishment for his wife he begins to sharpen a knife. The bleakness is accentuated by the orchestra with passages of chilling music and by the menacing tone of the baritone soloist who sings that the "howling voice of winter urges me on - destroy the traitoress".

So why did I propose the cantata to the bishop, and why did he accept it with such alacrity?

Because winter gives way to spring (*vesna*). The music from the orchestra and choir swells in beauty with the arrival of warmth, flowers and sunshine, and the husband's heart softens. He discards the sharpened knife and excuses his wife exclaiming "all thoughts of vengeance have fled - while you can love, forgive, as you would be forgiven".

The pews in the cathedral were packed before the service started. So too were the wide approaches to the altar. Every inch of open space was taken up by music stands and chairs. I had brought the full orchestra with me to accompany the singers. String and wind instruments to the front, harp, brass and percussion instruments to the side, St Frett music society choristers to the rear in three rows positioned on the altar steps, cathedral choristers to the right and left in the choir stalls. More than one hundred and fifty instrumentalists and vocalists in total.

God quite naturally takes precedence over the monarch in church so the national anthem was not played. Instead the congregation stood as the royal party made its way to the front pew accompanied by pageboys and equerries and followed by a long procession of clergymen with the bishop in in the rear.

The colour inside the cathedral was dazzling. Sunlight slanted down through the stained glass windows onto the gold-leafed angels surrounding the altar and upwards to illuminate the great frescoes in the dome. White marble sculptures and purple banners lined the walls. The priests were frocked in red and crimson robes, the choirboys fingering their prayer books and sheets of carol music wore blue cassocks and white surplices. Golden mitres adorned the heads of the bishop and old archbishop, the latter half-asleep in his wooden stall padded with red velvet cushions. Light from the rose window flooded the nave reflecting the silver and gold braid of the uniforms in the congregation, glittering on the emerald and diamond brooches of the rich wives and mistresses. We, the musicians, were dressed formally in black and white. Behind us on the altar, tall candles softly illuminated the gilded arch from which the holy cross was suspended.

From the pulpit the bishop welcomed the congregation. He described how the carols would be split between the cathedral choir accompanied by the organ, and the congregation accompanied by the orchestra and combined chorus (cathedral choir and St Frett music society choir). He talked about the Rachmaninov cantata. *Vesna* was different from traditional Christmas oratorios, he said. Some members of the congregation would be puzzled by the music, others would find it sublimely beautiful but everyone in the cathedral, regardless of opinion, would recognise that the cantata represented a new experience. Much the same way that the nation's transition to democracy represented a new beginning. We must not be afraid of change, said the bishop, but strive to benefit from the opportunities it brings.

Adeptly the bishop concentrated on the word unfaithful when describing the plot, which he explained would be narrated in Russian by the baritone soloist. To the children in the congregation he was aware that the word conveyed a vague impression of sin (mummy must have done something naughty). He was equally aware that the adults would understand only too well what mummy had been up to. The cantata opened with the chorus recalling memories of spring before plunging into bleak midwinter, the subject of one of our carols this morning, said the bishop. But this particular midwinter was much worse than the one in the carol. Angry at the woman's unfaithfulness, disturbed by the storms wailing through the icy countryside, the man planned an unholy revenge. All of us have experienced anger and despair, said the bishop. We know how easy it is to allow our feelings to boil over to the extent we become incapable of rational thought.

Next time anger afflicts you, said the bishop, I pray you will be supported by your memory of Rachmaninov's mighty cantata which will be performed this morning by our national orchestra and chorus as the centrepiece of the carol service. In particular I pray you will recall the transformation which overwhelms the tragic figure of the husband when the music soars triumphantly to herald the arrival of spring. Here are the words you will hear him say, from the mouth of the narrator, as the cantata draws to a close. "Forgive, as you would be forgiven - let God be our judge".

The acoustics in the cathedral were excellent and I kept the orchestra under tight control. Only for the arrival of spring in *Vesna* and the last chorus of *Hark the Herald Angels Sing* did I let the brass and percussion sections off the leash. Momentous waves of sound echoed through the nave and transept as the trumpet, horn and trombone players raised their instruments to their lips.

Rocked by the music and the dramatic magnificence of the service the members of the congregation were slow to rise from their knees after the bishop's blessing at the end of the service. They stood erect in silence as the royal party filed past then relaxed their shoulders and drowned the sound of the cathedral organ with the buzz of conversation. I observed that the conversation was good-natured and that people were animated. Even the children, normally inert after exposure to prolonged religious events, were smiling. Rachmaninov had come through unscathed, I reflected. Time would tell the extent of the spiritual impact of the cantata on the congregation but in the short term I felt convinced that the music would have made a deep impression on the influential assembly in the cathedral, sufficient to promote ticket sales for opera house concerts and productions.

The archbishop was helped from his stall by his chaplains. He summoned me with a gesture of his hand. His fingers were bent stiff with arthritis. They clawed the air slowly in my direction.

'That was lovely,' he said as I approached.

I nodded appreciatively on behalf of the orchestra and choir.

'We were rather hoping for Verdi's *Requiem*,' said the archbishop.

'Next year, your grace,' I replied.

'That's a pity. I'm unlikely to last that long.'

'I pray you are wrong, your grace.'

'Never mind, I shall listen to you from wherever God places me.'

'It is rumoured that the palm court orchestra in heaven plays Verdi's *Requiem* every Tuesday,' I said.

The archbishop issued a strangled cough. The chaplains grasped the elderly prelate's arms. The cough gave way to a wheezing noise in turn followed by a succession of grunts which threatened to topple the golden mitre from the archbishop's head.

'He's laughing,' the chaplains explained.

'It doesn't sound like it,' I said alarmed.

'He will recover in a moment,' said the chaplains.

It occurred to me as I returned to the opera house having congratulated the players and singers on their first class performance that not many conductors were given the opportunity of responding to the award of a handsome commission from a cathedral by nearly killing the archbishop.

CHAPTER 34

The schools have closed for Christmas and the streets are full of children peering into toy shop windows. A chill wind blows from the sea and although the snow is confined to the mountains the weather in the city is grey and wintry enough for Santa Claus and his reindeers. At nightfall the lights of the horse-drawn carriage pierce the evening gloom and the passengers are wrapped in overcoats and mufflers.

By contrast the inside of the opera house has glowed with warm excitement throughout the day. There is something very special about a dress rehearsal. A magic spell is cast, sprinkling stardust onto the stage, quickening the pulse of everyone associated with the production which in our case included the pageboys recruited from the palace to open the curtains upon the fantasy world of *The Sleeping Beauty*. Even the hardened employees of the opera house, veterans of a thousand orchestral concerts and operatic productions, were drawn to the auditorium in their off-duty moments as the building prepared to host its first ballet.

The young dancers arrived shortly after breakfast and scampered along the corridors to the dressing rooms. I had arranged for an early start. The orchestra was fully assembled in the pit as I mounted the podium at nine o'clock.

Madame Prtenchska, director of the ballet school, and Madame Slymnova, senior ballet mistress, were sitting directly behind me in the front row of the stalls alongside the opera house librarian Signora Furcello. Three formidable women, hands folded neatly in their laps, faces composed, masking the anticipation they surely felt. In particular I had become very fond of Madame Prtenchska. The quiet, efficient and stately manner in which she governed the ballet school was a lesson for amateur administrators like myself inclined to stumble from one turbulent event to another. Today's dress rehearsal represented for her the penultimate step on an eight year journey culminating in this weekend's royal command performance. Success or otherwise would affect her international reputation and the future of the ballet school. Raising my baton I was conscious of the importance of not letting her down.

We had gradually introduced the dancers to the orchestra. First by despatching a string quartet to the ballet school to support Marcus's piano accompaniment during rehearsals, then adding a trio of wind instruments. The process was not without difficulty. Despite extensive enquiries Signora Furcello failed to find any copies of Tchaikovsky's reduction for chamber orchestra. I was resigned to the prospect of attempting the task myself when a group of the young recruits to the orchestra, fresh from the university music school and accustomed to such challenges, volunteered to write the reductions for the five and eight piece ensembles, in the process earning themselves flagons of beer paid for from the special expenses fund I maintained in my chambers. The results of their work were admirable, not only in terms of familiarising the dancers with the scope of the orchestral score but in rounding off my own preparations for conducting the ballet.

Then, yesterday, with the orchestra pit in place, while the stage hands completed the final testing of the scenery, equipment and lighting, we let the cast rehearse their sequences for the first time in front of the whole orchestra, including horns, trombones and percussion.

The two pageboys stood proudly in the centre of the stage during the overture. At my signal, they reached into the gap between the curtains and set off in opposite directions towards the wings each clutching a handful of the rich velvet material. Behind the scenes the operation was controlled by ropes and pulleys but to the audience it appeared that the pageboys were magically peeling back the heavy curtains unaided. With each step the pageboys revealed more of the fairytale scene in the castle set for the christening of Princess Aurora, and with each step the cries of delight from the children in the audience, from the poorest schools in the city which we had invited to attend the dress rehearsal free, grew louder.

Madame Tuillée the choreographer and Pierre the artistic director supervised the production from the stalls, standing side by side staring intently at the stage and occasionally making notes. Madame Tuillée corrected some of the dance steps during the intervals between the acts and Pierre adjusted several spotlight positions but the only major disaster, which caused the children in the audience to clasp their hands over their mouths, occurred when the boat carrying Prince Désiré and the Lilac Fairy collided with a tree and brought down half the forest. The stage hand driving the boat had been blinded by the artificial mist. Mr Frenner and his team modified the height of the steering platform on the boat, equipped the stage hand with a diving mask and repaired the broken scenery. Within half an hour the stage was back in action and the children in the audience were rewarded with the famous scene in which the prince wakes the princess with a kiss.

I lowered my baton for the last time in the dress rehearsal shortly before lunch. As the pageboys closed the curtains I turned from the podium to see Madame Prtenchska smiling gently, dabbing her eyes with a handkerchief.

Meanwhile there have been repercussions from last Sunday's concert in the cathedral, manifested in what the Lipskys refer to as 'Professor Schmidt's Revenge'.

LETTERS TO THE EDITOR Daily Gazette

Sir, It has come to my attention that the Ardaniian symphony orchestra and St Frett music society choir appearing jointly at a recent musical event in the city were inadvertently referred to as the national orchestra and chorus. I wish to make it clear that the St Frett music society choir is only one of a number of choral organisations in the country. The university choir, which I am privileged to direct, appears regularly with the orchestra and is commonly regarded as the nation's pre-eminent choral institution.

Professor Heinrich Schmidt, University Music School

CONTROVERSIAL PROGRAMME FOR CATHEDRAL CAROL SERVICE
Daily Gazette Music Critic

The eagerly awaited annual carol service in the cathedral took place on Sunday. As always the cathedral choir was in fine fettle under direction of the organist, Dr Helmut Wittgenstein. Together they performed a selection of national Ardaniian carols and as usual it was a joy to hear the mellifluous congruity accomplished by the well trained choristers in conjunction with the organist. The voices of the trebles in the choir were an especially noteworthy feature of the recitals, their voices joyfully emphasizing the spirit of Christmas. Unfortunately the quality of singing from the visiting choir from St Frett music society was not at the same elevated level and, on the several occasions of performance, tended to dampen the atmosphere of joy generated by the cathedral choristers. Equally dampening was the decision by the Ardaniian symphony orchestra to perform a secular cantata by the comparatively unknown Russian composer Rachmaninov in place of one of the traditional Christmas oratorios so much looked forward to by the cathedral congregation. The playing of the cantata by the orchestra was competent enough although discordant in places and weakly supported by the St Frett choir. It is the fervent hope of this column that the relevant authorities will seek next year to restore the splendour of the traditional Christmas carol service to the cathedral.

Naturally the Lipskys were upset. In the honourable tradition of the journalistic profession Mr Lipsky had informed the newspaper of the conflict of interest arising from his choir's appearance in the cathedral and proposed that an alternative writer be appointed to review the performance. The tone of the article in question indicated that the person selected by the Gazette to stand in for Mr Lipsky was not bound by the same conventions. For all their faults music critics are normally precise in identifying the nature of alleged shortcomings in a performance. In the article in question, examples of specific choral or orchestral weaknesses would have strengthened the substitute critic's case. Instead he had indulged in generalities and, questionably, ventured into matters beyond his jurisdiction, namely the format of the carol service. The article smelled of collusion and spite.

Even more galling for Mr Lipsky was the praise he personally had given to the university choir when reviewing the *Dixit Dominus* concert although, as I pointed out, the praise should have been awarded partly to me for adjusting the stilted tempo foisted on the choir by Professor Schmidt. The professor would not have seen it that way. By praising the choir's performance Mr Lipsky had inadvertently snubbed his nose at the professor's credibility and poured fuel upon the fire.

The Lipskys were experienced enough to know that adverse criticism, malignant or otherwise, was a fact of public life. The matter would probably have rested there but for the intervention of the bishop.

Entering the anteroom for cocktails in the evening I was summoned to the fireplace.

'Have you seen this?' said the lord chamberlain waving the newspaper article.

'Yes,' I nodded.

'The Bishop of St Frett has called me to express his disfavour with the article, on several fronts,' said the lord chamberlain.

'It does leave something to be desired,' I agreed.

'Accordingly I summoned the editor to the palace to convey our joint disapproval. The sub-editor who accepted the article has been reprimanded, and the writer in question disbarred from further work at the newspaper.'

'Thank you, I will inform the orchestra and choir.'

'Kindly do so. The bishop found the subject and tone of the article presumptious, and the criticism of the music unfounded. I share his opinion.'

'The St Frett choir will be particularly pleased to hear that.'

'Concerning Professor Schmidt's letter, do you intend to respond?' said the lord chamberlain.

I shook my head.

'In the spirit of Christmas, we shall forgive, as we should be forgiven,' I said quoting from Rachmaninov's cantata.

'A grossly overrated virtue, forgiveness, in my opinion,' said the lord chamberlain. 'But do as you wish.'

At dinner I was relieved to learn that the royal physician had attended the archbishop's residence earlier and found the prelate to be in excellent form, joking with his chaplains about the palm court orchestra in the sky.

CHAPTER 35

The noise from the dressing rooms on the opposite side of the opera house penetrates my chambers. It is nine o'clock in the morning on the Saturday before Christmas. I am at my desk attending to paperwork listening to the squeals of laughter as the students prepare for this afternoon's matinee and tonight's royal command performance of *The Sleeping Beauty*.

There is no need for the students to arrive so early. There are no rehearsals today. The ballet mistresses and stage hands are sleeping late after three exhausting days and nights and the orchestra won't be here for hours. Yet, captured by the glamour and excitement of the production, the students cannot wait to come to the opera house, to practice for the thousandth time the application of make-up onto their faces in front of the dressing room mirrors and to adjust for the thousandth time the hems of their delightful costumes.

Occasionally driven by curiosity they venture across the stage into the silent corridors on my side of the opera house, tip-toeing past my door, hands clasped over their mouths to muffle their laughter, scuttling back to the stage when Valentino opens the door and scolds them for disturbing my work. He returns from the corridor with a wry smile on his face.

One of my tasks this morning is to update my performance notes for the ballet:

Overture

Tchaikovsky's dramatic introduction fades quickly into the Lilac Fairy's haunting theme (bar 28). Before the audience has caught its breath the curtains are peeled back by the pageboys (bar 66). The violins have to work hard during the dramatic introduction. The semi-quavers wake them up.

Prologue – Christening

The curtains open to reveal a party of courtiers milling about the stage in elegant costumes waiting for the christening ceremony for Princess Aurora to begin. Attempts to conceal the fact that the baby in the crib is not real but played by a wooden doll wrapped in a blanket were temporarily unsuccessful on the opening night. The baby slipped out and hit the floor with a sharp thudding noise which fortunately was masked by the music. Scooped up by a passing fairy the baby has since been secured into its blanket with tape. There are six fairies, invited to the ceremony to bestow abstract gifts like beauty and musical talent, and six children whose job is to deliver practical gifts such as caged birds almost all of which have been dropped onto the stage at one time or another and are now firmly attached to the red velvet cushions on which they sit.

The fairies are dressed in bell-shaped tutus of different colours. They are attended by the corps de ballet and male partners. The Lilac Fairy is the last to arrive on stage. She is greeted rapturously but I do not stop the orchestra for applause until the end of the first dance sequence (bar 2.210) when, arms poised erect, she beams down at the audience. The extent of Sophie's popularity is evident. No life of luxury for this princess, idling her time in the palace eating chocolates and cakes, occasionally opening village fetes. Sophie has chosen to grow up the hard way.

Each fairy performs a dance of varying degrees of difficulty. For some of the sequences Madame Tuillée (ballet mistress) has modified Petipa's original choreography to simplify the steps but not for Violente (scene 3f), a dazzling talented young dancer. The music is unchanged throughout. The flute section played the song bird sequence (scene 3e) very competently, with our new lady flautist on the piccolo.

The arrival of the wicked witch Carabosse, pulled onto the stage on a tricycle disguised with layers of ivy as a venomous coach, propelled by her entourage of rats amidst explosions of thunder and lightning, is the highlight of the act. The rats are zipped into grotesquely realistic costumes with only their feet outside for freedom of movement and an opening in the face for vision and ventilation. Carabosse is played by a gangly young man made up with a hooked nose, warts and long black cloak. He acts the part excellently. A ghostly green spotlight follows him everywhere across the stage. The success of his menacing performance is indicated by the boos and catcalls he receives when holding the poisonous spinning wheel spindle aloft after dancing triumphantly with his rats. I pause the music here (bar 4.215) to allow the boos from the audience to be heard.

Carabosse departs amidst further explosions of thunder and lightning, the music softens and the Lilac Fairy brings the act to a conclusion by commuting Carabosse's curse from death to heavy sleep. Sophie has not put a foot wrong so far, dancing the part of the Lilac Fairy elegantly without a hint of unsteadiness.

Act 1 The Spell

Behind the curtain during the twenty minute interval the stage hands shuffle the scenery around to create a terraced area within the palace. Much of the scenery is the same but reversed to create a different aspect of the palace. This clever use of the props is a mark of Mr Frenner's experience at the royal theatre. The curtains open to reveal three village women ill-advisedly using knitting needles, banned in the kingdom in case Princess Aurora, now sixteen years old, pricks herself and initiates the wicked witch's curse. The three women are caught by the palace master of ceremonies moments before the king and queen descend the steps to the terrace.

During the descent at yesterday's performance the queen accidentally slipped and ended up on her knees. The laughter from the audience made my blood freeze. If the dancer playing the queen slips on the steps in front of the real queen the conclusion would inevitably be drawn that that the opera house was taking advantage of her majesty's affinity for alcoholic beverages to indulge in some mischievous buffoonery at the expense of the royal family's reputation. After the incident I joined Madame Tuillée in pointing out to the abashed young couple the importance of descending the steps slowly. I will have to ensure that the associated musical sequence (commencing bar 5.119) at tonight's command performance is carefully controlled.

In a gesture of mercy the king spares the three foolish women from losing their heads and the villagers celebrate by waltzing across the stage in the famous dance of the flowers (bar 6.37). It continues to amaze me that Tchaikovsky's music is being played here for the first time. The opera house staff are captivated by the waltz. I hear the notes being hummed and whistled everywhere I go, in the corridors, even the booking office.

Tchaikovsky has structured the score to allow Princess Aurora to arrive in the grand manner traditionally adopted by prima ballerinas. There is a stately entrance followed by a complex dance sequence designed to illustrate the brilliance of her technique, in turn followed by a pause in musical coverage while she acknowledges the audience's applause. Nowadays the pause is manipulated by international ballerinas who extend the process for as long as possible, stopping the conductor from restarting the music by continuing to flatter her admirers with deep curtsies and arm gestures until she has beaten the world record for applause or until the conductor has had enough and restarts the music anyway.

The charming young ballerina from the ballet school playing the role of Princess Aurora, originally intended for Sophie, has no time for these sophistries. She skips onto the stage as fast as the music will allow, performs the introductory dance sequence skilfully and has to be persuaded by Madame Tuillée to take a long deep curtsy on completion. Madame Tuillée has simplified Petipa's original choreography but nonetheless the modified version looks impressively difficult.

Even more difficult is the adagio where Princess Aurora, balanced on one toe (*en pointe*), takes the hand of each of the four suitors commended to her by the king and queen, who beforehand have presented her with roses. The transfer from suitor to suitor requires great skill. The musical chords accompanying each sequence must be extended until she is ready to lift her hand. The orchestra focuses intently on my baton. The hours at the piano in the ballet school standing in for Marcus as *répétiteur* while learning the score and familiarising myself with the intermittent holds and pauses required by the dancers were well spent.

Slinking back onto the stage to little shouts of alarm from the children in the audience comes the wicked witch Carabosse with a spindle concealed in her long black cloak. Ignoring the frantic warnings from the children Princess Aurora accepts the spindle from the witch, examines it and pricks her finger. At first it seems the poison has not worked. The princess dances in front of her parents to prove she is not afflicted. The rhythm of the dance changes (bar 9.29) and Tchaikovsky by magical variations in pace and tone conveys the helplessness of the princess's feverish attempts, twirling around the stage, to counter the venom. She collapses into the arms of one of the suitors. The wicked witch laughs triumphantly and is booed again by the furious children in the audience while being chased from the stage by officials. Tchaikovsky reintroduces the haunting theme of the Lilac Fairy while the princess is carried to bed to sleep for a hundred years.

The act ends with Sophie as the Lilac Fairy weaving through the lines of courtiers, sending them to sleep too with her magic wand, disappearing gradually from sight as the stage lights are dimmed, in an attractive scene that should please her father in the royal box.

Act 2 The Kiss

I return to the rostrum for the third and last time. I dislike bowing to the audience from the orchestra pit. The process appears designed to solicit applause for the conductor at the expense of the dancers whereas in fact the intention is to inform the crowd that the performance is about to recommence, asking them to stop coughing and crunching confectionery. I keep the bow as short as possible then launch the orchestra into Tchaikovsky's hunting-theme introduction to act two.

After the curtains have been opened by the pageboys we see groups of splendidly dressed members of the nobility on the edge of a forest preparing to wave goodbye to a group of huntsmen and followers, chatting politely and drinking mulled wine in much the same way people gather in front of the great houses in England in advance of a foxhunt. Prince Désiré arrives and the hunt is delayed for a game of hide and seek and some stately dances. In melancholy mood the prince eventually sets off in a different direction from the hunt and encounters the Lilac Fairy (bar 14.32) who shows him a vision of Princess Aurora (bar 14.100).

Confusingly for the children in the audience the princess, who is supposed to be asleep in the palace, arrives in the forest to dance with the prince. It becomes evident to the children, however, that the princess has materialised in spectral form because the Lilac Fairy, in a delightful musical sequence involving the corps de ballet, forbids the prince from touching her. At the end of the dance the princess disappears and the prince begs the Lilac Fairy to take him to her palace.

Now begins what must be one of the most beautiful scenes in all theatre, the voyage of the Lilac Fairy and Prince Désiré through the magic forest. As if the scene was not lovely enough, our hearts are shredded by Tchaikovsky's music as the boat glides along the river between the trees. Even those of us aware that the boat is being pedalled by a small bald-headed man lying in the bottom of the vessel wearing a diving mask desperately trying to avoid the trees are moved by the tableau.

The wicked witch and her entourage put up some final resistance at the gates of the palace before being overwhelmed by the Lilac Fairy's powerful spells. The prince rushes through the gates to the princess's bedroom and to the delight of the audience resuscitates her with a kiss, bringing the drama to its agreeable conclusion.

I have observed that the length and fervour of the kiss appears to increase with every performance. After the curtains close for the last time tonight Madame Tuillée will probably have to separate the pair forcibly.

CHAPTER 36

There was no hint of the forthcoming disaster. The matinee had been entirely successfully, a lighthearted enjoyable affair. The dancers and orchestra had been relaxed, the conductor had stopped scowling at the second violins, and the children in the audience hissed and booed uninhibitedly at the wicked witch. There was an end-of-term mood in the opera house as the curtains closed. Children tumbled out into the street with their parents and the clock ticked towards evening. The thoughts of everybody associated with the production were focused on the party to be held on the stage later that night when the curtains closed on the production for the last time. After that, there was the palace ball, to which the senior term at the ballet school had been invited. And three days after that it would be Christmas. No wonder everybody was smiling.

The calm before the storm.

I was tightening the bow of my white tie. The ten minute bell had just rung, smartly dressed members of the audience were finishing their drinks in the bar and Soprianti's reception committee was assembling in the foyer to greet the royal family.

The door to my chambers burst open.

'Come quickly!' said Pierre.

I followed the artistic director along the corridor, through the stage door, across the stage where the fairies and corps de ballet were limbering up. The corridor outside the dressing room door marked 'Princess Aurora' was crowded. I forced myself through to find Madame Tuillée and Madame Prtenchska kneeling on the floor examining the young prima ballerina's ankle which was red and swollen like a balloon.

'Why didn't you report this earlier?' cried Madame Tuillée.

'I covered it with ice, and thought it was getting better,' said the injured prima ballerina tearfully.

Madame Prtenchska stood up and took me to aside.

'She can't dance tonight,' she said.

I looked round the room

'Where's her understudy?' I asked.

'Georgina. She's ready, but Sophie wants to have her part back.'

I stared at the swollen ankle.

'What do you think?' said Madame Prtenchska.

'I think that I would prefer to be somewhere else,' I said.

'Me too,' said Madame Prtenchska.

'Preferably half way up the Amazon river,' I said.'

Sophie came towards us holding hands with Georgina, the injured prima ballerina's understudy.

'Georgina doesn't mind, and I would so much like to be Princess Aurora again,' said Sophie.

'Is that really true, Georgina?' said Madame Prtenchska.

'I don't mind at all. Sophie deserves the part, she knows it better than any of us,' said Georgina.

Madame Prtenchska looked at me.

'I think you should decide,' she said.

The first law of crisis management is that emergencies should be handled by the undisputed head of the organisation in trouble. Until a few minutes ago Madame Tuillée, the senior ballet mistress and choreographer at the ballet school, had been in charge of all aspects of production and direction of *The Sleeping Beauty*. Not any longer. Madame Prtenchska, the ballet school director, was now in control. The second law of crisis management is that the person heading the organisation in trouble should endeavour to transfer responsibility for the disaster to another person as quickly as possible. Which Madame Prtenchska was now doing.

With every justification. By allowing myself to become the intermediary between the school and the palace I had ended up in the unenviable position of having to choose between two alternative courses of action both of which were likely to lead to spectacular criticism of the opera house in general and myself in particular. The first option was that the king's daughter should resume the role of Princess Aurora for which she had been declared unfit and, in all probability, prove her unfitness by dancing onto the stage and immediately falling flat on her face. The second option was that the king's daughter should be denied the position of dancing the prima ballerina role despite conclusive evidence that she had recovered sufficiently to resume the part.

'Please!' implored Sophie, kneeling on the floor looking up at me, her blue eyes pleading.

In the auditorium, the five minute bell sounded.

Madame Prtenchska's eyes were searching my face, compassionate and apprehensive.

'You'd better get changed,' I smiled at Sophie. 'Good luck!'

LeBreq was waiting in the wings. Warned by Valentino of the emergency he was sensibly preparing to take over as conductor for the national anthem. I redirected him to the orchestra pit, hurried to my chambers, gulped some water, impatiently allowed Valentino to brush the shoulders of my tailcoat, made it to the rostrum in time for the arrival of the royal family, conducted the national anthem, ducked out of the orchestra pit, up the stairs to the wings, onto the stage.

The pageboys parted the curtains. I stepped forward into the glare of the spotlights and faced the audience.

'Your majesties, your royal highnesses, my lords, ladies and gentlemen. An injury sustained during this afternoon's matinee performance has unexpectedly resulted in changes to the printed programme for tonight's performance. The role of Princess Aurora will be taken by her royal highness Princess Sophie, and the role of the Lilac Fairy by Priscilla Beauville.'

I avoided looking directly at the royal box. Aware that the king's eyes would assuredly be boring quizzically into my back I returned to the rostrum, raised my baton, smiled at the orchestra with as much confidence as my now severely-reduced life expectancy allowed, waited for the auditorium lights to dim then gave the signal for the command performance of *The Sleeping Beauty* to begin.

Statistically the likelihood of completing a short run theatrical production without suffering at least one embarrassing incident in each performance is remote. The odds are substantially reduced when an understudy is involved. When two understudies are involved the chances of getting through a performance without a major incident are zero. If the understudies are deputising for the principal players then the only hope is divine intervention.

Let it be a very minor incident, I prayed as Priscilla, Sophie's understudy for the Lilac Fairy, danced onto the stage. And when the incident happens let it involve the Lilac Fairy not Princess Aurora, I added, which was very unfair on the sweet young understudy but when times were desperate prayers had to be structured accordingly. Mercifully for Priscilla the celestial powers responsible for monitoring earthly appeals were either asleep or not paying attention because they ignored my suggestion and allowed the Lilac Fairy to give an assured performance and see off Carabosse, the wicked witch, in imperious style at the end of the prologue.

Princess Aurora does not make her appearance until midway through the second act (act 1). As the time approached I modified my prayers and suggested to the celestial powers that Sophie be allowed to fall gracefully. Please do not make her slide across the stage in a pantomime slipped-on-a-banana-skin skid. At least allow her the dignity of a swift retrieval. Or a minor loss of balance into the arms of one of her suitors, which might be interpreted by people unfamiliar with ballet as intentional. Or, better still, let her slip during her feverish last dance when everyone would think it was a fanciful response to the poison.

The worst possible time for an incident to occur would be during the Rose Adagio when, suspended *en pointe*, there would be no hope of Princess Aurora making a controlled recovery. Madame Tuillée obviously thought the same. From the podium I could see the ballet mistress standing in the wings with her hands raised in supplication to her lips, like a nun at vespers, as Sophie elegantly transferred herself from one suitor to the next.

Neither of the understudies was required for the hunting scenes which open the final act (act 2). When their turn came Priscilla was first onto the stage, followed by Sophie for the dream sequence with Prince Désiré. From the moment they entered the stage from the wings it was clear that both girls were now full of confidence, moving and dancing beautifully, both looking radiant. It seemed that the impossible was about to happen, that we were going to complete the performance without an incident. Indeed I became so convinced the worst was over that during the voyage of the boat through the forest I allowed myself the luxury of glancing round at the audience to assess their reaction to the scene.

Demonstrating that the celestial powers possess a sense of humour the blow, when delivered, was aimed not at the understudies but the small bald-headed driver of the boat. Momentarily losing his way in the mist he steered the vessel hard into a bank, dislodging a tree.

The audience gasped as the tree swayed perilously showering the stage with artificial apples.

Frantically I thumbed through the score to find a suitable repeat point for the orchestra. Out of the corner of my eye I could see Madame Tuillée mouthing instructions from the wings to the pair of stranded dancers.

With commendable composure the young man playing Prince Désiré dismounted from the vessel, extended his hand to the Lilac Fairy, pushed the boat free of the bank with his shoe and gestured elegantly in the direction of the castle, conveying to the audience that the landing had been planned all along. Thanks to his initiative the stage hands were spared from having to crawl through the mist to free the boat, and the orchestra was saved from the need to replay Tchaikovsky's haunting Lilac Fairy theme.

At the end of the performance, completed without further incident, the young man deserved his kiss on the lips of a real princess. Amidst cries of approval from the audience the corps de ballet and principal dancers lined up in the footlights to acknowledge the applause. Sophie as Princess Aurora in the centre cradling a bouquet of flowers, Prince Désiré next to her, Priscilla as Lilac Fairy on the other side, flanked by Carabosse grinning at the boos he received from the children, flanked by Madame Prtenchska and Madame Tuillée glowing with pride.

'The king will have enjoyed the production, no doubt, sir,' said Valentino as I gulped a large whisky on the way to the reception on the stage.

'I am about to find out,' I said grimly.

CHAPTER 37

It is Sunday morning and I am in bed. My head hurts. The cumulative effect of whisky and champagne has minimised the urge to do anything but slump into my pillows groaning. I acknowledge that my condition is self-inflicted. The need to consider abstinence on a long term basis is evident and I have promised myself an unscrupulously unbiased review of the comparative advantages and disadvantages of teetotalism as soon as the pain in my head subsides.

Meanwhile I have attempted and failed to eat the lightly boiled egg prepared by my valet. The shakiness of my hands dislodged the egg from its cup and splattered it onto the breakfast tray. The spoon is on the floor, together with my napkin and a half-eaten slice of toast, rendering further attempts at consumption pointless. Next to the tray is a copy of the *Sunday Gazette*. According to my valet the front page features a photograph of the king talking to a group of ballerinas at the reception. I look forward to examining it when my vision improves.

Anxious to learn the *Gazette's* opinion of last night's production I asked my valet to read me the article by the newly appointed music critic.

MAJESTIC BALLET Sunday Gazette

Last night in the opera house the audience was treated to a royal command performance of Tchaikovsky's ballet The Sleeping Beauty, making its first and long awaited appearance in the kingdom. The occasion marked the eighth anniversary of the founding of the royal ballet school in St Frett, and celebrated the seventeenth birthday of Princess Sophie. Earlier in the week the princess had danced the important part of the Lilac Fairy. Last night, owing to the unfortunate injury of a colleague, she took the principal role of Princess Aurora.

First, a few caveats. The ballet was shortened to three acts (prologue, act one, act two). The choreography was simplified for some of the dance sequences. None of the students at the ballet school have yet achieved professional status. In short, the production, in terms of ballet dancing, was an amateur one.

So to compare last night's production with the Ballets Russes performance witnessed by this correspondent several years ago would be unfair. The world's most famous dancers were at Mr. Diaghilev's disposal, household names with years of experience on the international stage. And yet, last night, your correspondent found himself captivated by the poise and confidence of the young dancers from the ballet school, at their sense of enjoyment which lifted what could have been a mere exhibition of skillful techniques into scenes of genuine dramatic impact.

Your correspondent was also impressed by the scenery and special effects designed in collaboration between the ballet school and royal theatre, and by the artistry and power of the Ardaniian symphony orchestra which delivered Tchaikovsky's delicious music at precisely the right level. The production was choreographed by Madame Tuillée. The ballet school is directed by Madame Prtenchska. They all deserve our thanks.

In defence of the condition which currently confines me to bed I submit that after those stressful hours on the podium fanned by warm air rising from the orchestra pit, I had become dehydrated and extremely thirsty. The glass of whisky from Valentino in my chambers had exacerbated the situation and the bottles of ice cold champagne on the trestle tables at the reception represented to me the equivalent of an oasis to a parched camel.

I attempt to adjust my pillows, and fail. My head tumbles backwards. Whimpering with pain I sit upright again.

The telephone beside the bed rings.

'Well done! How does it feel, to be lord and master of the universe, with the musical world at your feet?'

I recognise Lipsky's voice in the receiver.

'Would you mind calling again,' I croak, 'later.'

'What's the matter?'

'My head hurts.'

'Have you seen a doctor?'

'Dalrymple-Smith will be in a similar condition.'

'Well, if you must drink . . .'

'Who wrote the article for the *Sunday Gazette*?' I croak.

'Not me. Do you like the photograph on the front page?'

'I expect so, when my sight is restored.'

My valet shuffles back from the kitchen with more coffee. Patiently he resets the breakfast tray. Sundays are the busiest mornings for valets in the palace, he tells me, especially for valets with younger gentlemen to look after. Ballroom nights are a notorious source of aggravation, he says. In hushed tones he informs me there are traces of lipstick on my shirt collar. It is always best to be advised of these matters, he confides, in case plans and arrangements need to be adjusted accordingly. He has taken the liberty of checking the pockets of my dress clothes and found nothing of concern, by which presumably he means indiscreet missives or articles of lady's clothing.

Whose lipstick, I wonder?

Princess Sophie had hugged me during the reception for helping her through the ballet unscathed. She told me that whenever she looked at the podium I was smiling at her, prompting her with the beat, which boosted her confidence. How she managed to mistake what must have been the panic-struck expression on my face for a smile I cannot imagine. Anyway, Sophie's make-up was creamy pink in colour, not red.

Madame Prtenchska and Madame Tuillée had embraced me too, several times, spontaneously and emotionally, after the performance. They were far too sophisticated, however, to imprint lipstick on a man's collar.

The queen had also embraced me, but in the royal manner, by the clutching of hands and mouthing of words. I am very careful to keep her majesty at arm's length. It was certainly not her.

Yvette? We had encountered each other at the ball which followed the reception in the opera house. She was unlikely to have attempted anything in the way of a congratulatory embrace, however, because I am fairly certain I assumed a childish air of reproach, still mortified at the role she played in the embarrassing moonlit bower incident.

Which left Sarah. Shamefully drunk by the time the clock approached midnight I recall her marching up to me angrily, grabbing my hand, pulling me into the stream of dancers and telling me as I stumbled around the ballroom in her arms that I was forgiven for my behaviour. After the decree of forgiveness did we proceed to the Xmas tree and stand together under the mistletoe? I simply cannot remember.

The aspirins are working. My head still hurts and I cannot yet open both eyes simultaneously, but the pain is subsiding. Never again, I chide myself, reflecting guiltily that the only person guaranteed to be in greater discomfort than myself this morning was the driver of boat which had transported the Lilac Fairy and Prince Désiré through the forest.

Attracted by groans from behind the safety curtains during the party on the stage I had excused myself from a group of dignitaries to find the unfortunate coxswain sitting on a crate. He was holding his diving mask in one hand and an empty bottle of rum in the other.

'I did it good and proper, didn't I?' he said blinking at me.

'We couldn't have managed without you,' I assured him.

'I'm going to hang myself,' he said.

'Whatever for?' I said.

'For ruining the ballet.'

'Nonsense, you didn't ruin it. The production was a great success.'

'The disgrace, they'll never forgive me.'

'Now, look here.'

'I shall hang myself, from the roof,' he said pointing upwards.

'I've got a better idea,' I said taking his arm and leading him to the nearest trestle table, 'join me in a glass of champagne.'

CHAPTER 38

First item on the list after the festive break, the cast for *La Bohème*. Zoe is the only realistic candidate for Mimi. Despite their excellent voices the principal sopranos in the university choir are overweight and too old for the role, even if they dared to disobey Professor Schmidt's embargo on the opera, which they won't. Unfortunately the same physical constraints apply to the principal sopranos in the St Frett choir, plump and past their prime. One of the music teachers on the Lipsky's staff is young enough for the part but too shy and lacks allure. I am faced with the choice of inviting applications from abroad or taking a chance on one of the less experienced sopranos, the best of which belong to the university choir, fenced in by Professor Schmidt.

The situation is even less satisfactory for Rodolfo, the lovelorn poet. None of the tenors in the city have the necessary range or stage presence. In his case it appears that I shall definitely have to look beyond our shores and face the prospect of working with the preening young tenor from the Neapolitan Touring Opera Company. Before committing to the disappointment and expense of hiring an international star, however, I have arranged for the churches outside the city to be checked in the hope of discovering a suitable tenor in one of the choirs.

At least we have Peter Broch for the key role of the painter, Marcello. St Frett choir is well off for personable baritone and bass singers. We will not have to search abroad to fill the roles of Marcello's fellow bohemians Schaunard, the musician, or Colline, the philosopher, nor their respective understudies.

Musetta, the flirt, represents a challenge of a different kind. She is the source of comedy in the second act and the counterpoint to the heart-breaking scenes in the snow in act three. The part requires charisma as much as vocal ability. Countess Charlotte von Littchnoff has the charisma but not much in the way of a voice. Luckily two other candidates have been identified. The first is the principal mezzo-soprano of the St Frett choir, the russet-haired young wife of a local businessman. The second is the principal mezzo-soprano of the university choir who impressed me with her singing and vivacious presence in the *Dixit Dominus* concert.

There are several reasons for wanting to put an end to the open warfare which I have incompetently allowed to break out between the opera house and university. Achieving the release of the vivacious mezzo-soprano from Professor Schmidt's clutches is one of them.

Influenced more by an acute shortage of singers than by my veiled threat to establish an opera house choir the professor eventually accepted back the mutineers. He scolded them in front of the university authorities, reluctantly gave them permission to continue their association with the St Frett music society on the condition that the university always had first call on their services, then promptly changed rehearsal times for the university choir to clash with rehearsal times at the warehouse. Forewarned by Peter Bloch the Lipskys juggled their programme for *La Bohème* rehearsals, and have been doing so ever since.

The situation is clearly untenable but I cannot see how to resolve it. Professor Schmidt is so dismissive of the quality of modern music and so opposed to what he regards as the pernicious influence of contemporary composers that he will probably resign if pushed further, which would complicate the situation unnecessarily. Moreover I admit to admiring his integrity and the singularity of his purpose. In my opinion he is quite right to assert that classical music reached perfection of form with Mozart and that everything afterwards represents an adaptation of that perfect form. Arguably, perfection of content was arguably even earlier by Bach and frankly I must confess that if restricted to one period of music I would probably choose the baroque too.

But that would defeat my purpose here. My role as master of music is to educate as well as entertain. Except for the fortunate few born with an intuitive understanding of counterpoint and fugue, the route to the classical and early classical world of music is through the beauty and excitement of the romantic period, then back through the middle period via the high priests Brahms, Beethoven and Bruckner.

Unfortunately in the process of preparing the opera house audiences for the ultimate perfection of Bach I have found the route blocked by an immoveable object. Which of us shall yield, the professor or I? And, of immediate concern, if the two of us continue to brandish fists at each other how shall I free the mezzo-soprano in the university choir from her bonds?

· · · ·

'You are required in the kitchens,' said the lord chamberlains when I called in to his office to deliver the monthly concert programme.

'Whatever for?' I mused.

'The request mentioned you only by name, to attend on a matter of urgency.'

'Something to do with Zoe, I expect.'

'Who is that?' said the lord chamberlain.

'The scullery maid auditioning for a part in *La Bohème*.'

'Possibly. On the other hand, perhaps Mrs Drought wants to acquire a recipe for brown Windsor soup,' said the lord chamberlain drily.

It crossed my mind as I strolled along the garden path, my hat tipped over my eyes to keep out the rain, that the palace kitchens might be about to provide me with another sensational voice, that inspired by Zoe's example another scullery maid had burst into song and Mrs Drought filled with pride at the contribution members of her staff were making to the country's musical development had summoned me to impart the joyful news.

My hopes were dashed on entering the main kitchen to find Zoe standing tearfully in a corner, a suitcase in one hand, a damp handkerchief in the other. Through the clouds of smoke billowing from the ovens Mrs Drought emerged wiping her enormous arms with a cloth.

'You're the one,' she said accusingly. 'Putting thoughts into a girl's head like that. Elevating her beyond her station. Well, you've gone and done it this time, and no mistake. Driving us up the wall by day, keeping everyone awake at night with her caterwauling. I'm not a hard-hearted woman, not accustomed to throwing young people out into the street but I've got an establishment to run, so she's going and you,' she scowled at me before heading back into the smoke, 'can blooming well take her.'

The rain was heavier when we left, pouring from the grey January sky, so we ran for the cover of the car.

'I'm so sorry, sir,' said Zoe alternately wiping rain from her hair and tears from her eyes.

The kitchen staff were accommodated in a dormitory block adjoining the castle walls. To avoid disturbing the other maids when released from the kitchens at night she would open one of the windows and practice her scales and exercises by singing into the dark. Unknown to her the building opposite the dormitory block contained bedrooms reserved for minor officials visiting the palace on government business. Rarely used, they had recently housed a delegation of architects and builders engaged to survey the castle foundations. One of the architects had been awakened by Zoe's singing and complained to the palace clerk of works. The clerk of works complained to the senior keeper of provisions who in turn complained to Mrs Drought.

'I should have anticipated this kind of problem,' I said starting the car.

'It's not your fault, sir. Do you mind me asking, where are we going?' said Zoe.

'To find accommodation for you.'

'I'm afraid I can't afford lodgings, sir. There's my aunt in the country - I've enough money in my purse for the coach.'

'We need you here in the city,' I said.

'I don't want to leave either, sir, but who's going to employ me now?' said Zoe sadly.

Ten minutes later Zoe was being hugged by Mrs Lipsky in the warehouse while I sought advice from Mr Lipsky. Was he aware of any vacancies for live-in maids in local taverns? How appropriate would it be for a prospective opera singer to work in a tavern? Did he agree with my view that I should accommodate her in a hotel while she searched for employment, temporary residence in my apartment being out of the question? If he were in my shoes, what would he do?

At the back of my mind, I suppose, was the knowledge that the Lipskys were very fond of Zoe and possessed a second bedroom in their living quarters, built originally in the hope they might conceive a child. So I was delighted but not completely surprised when after a brief consultation they invited Zoe to stay with them. They also offered her the paid position of secretary to the St Frett music society, exclaiming they were so busy teaching that they needed help with paperwork and general administration and that Zoe's arrival was akin to the descent of a guardian angel from heaven.

'Come, let's look at your bedroom, bring your suitcase, my dear. You can sing out of the window, or anywhere else, whenever you want, night and day,' said Mrs Lipsky to Zoe whose tears had by now given way to a wide smile.

CHAPTER 39

Marcus called into my chambers with his father to say goodbye. He has been accepted by the Royal Academy of Music in London where in addition to his piano studies he will be instructed in harmony and composition. I received a pleasant note from the principal Sir John McEwen who promised to keep a close watch on Marcus's progress and ensure he was given a piano tutor of appropriate eminence.

McEwen is a strict disciplinarian so there will be no risk of distraction at work and Marcus's father, who is accompanying the young virtuoso to England and sharing his accommodation, will make sure he stays on the straight and narrow path. Not that Marcus is wayward. The girls at the ballet school did not appear to attract his interest while he accompanied them as *répétiteur*. If they did, he gave no sign of it. My own assessment is that music so consumes the fabric of his mind he has no time for other interests, though the prospect of the sea voyage clearly excited him. His eyes were sparkling as he shook my hand.

Costs for tuition, travel and accommodation are being met from a special fund instituted by the lord chamberlain to support the development of citizens who contribute to the kingdom's international prestige. There is an allowance for two return trips a year. Father and son intend to maintain their humble lodgings on the outskirts of the city as the base for their return visits although by now they can afford something more comfortable. From his earnings as a soloist in the opera house and the gifts bestowed on him by the royal family Marcus is already comparatively well off. His wealth will surely escalate on completion of his studies when he takes his place on the concert platforms of the world. It is a measure of the prudence and modesty inherent in father and son that they should elect to retain the small rooms in that simple timber building, complete with its old piano and memories of a loving wife and mother.

I shall miss him. The growing popularity of our orchestral concerts is in part due to his youthful presence on the platform and the brilliance of his performances. Within a span of six months he mastered and performed:

Tchaikovsky piano concerto no.1 in B ♭ minor
César Franck symphonic variations

Rachmaninov piano concerto no.2 in C minor
Schumann piano concerto in A minor

They will miss him at the ballet school too. Madame Prtenchska was reluctant to let him go. She yielded only when I promised to find a replacement *répétiteur*. Which reminds me that I need to audition the university piano students before the ballet school opens again next week and starts rehearsing *Swan Lake*, yet another reason for making peace with Professor Schmidt.

Marcus's father was wearing a new suit and looked more secure on the sturdy cane that he has exchanged for his old hand-carved walking stick. He is a bluff, honest man. Years of suffering from his injury and the loss of his wife have marked his craggy face. I am delighted for him now. He deserves the comfort and happiness that his son's extraordinary gifts have brought about. He has been learning English. On departure from my chambers he declared that he looked forward to 'making me quaint again soon.' He will have plenty of time on the steamer to build on this promising start.

Valentino caused a rumpus this morning by accidentally pouring hot coffee into Soprianti's lap. At least I think it was an accident, one can never tell. Soprianti possesses some good qualities but attention to detail is not one of them. Paperwork accumulates on his desk, including petty cash vouchers which may explain the agonised cry at the conference table today as the hot coffee penetrated the general manager's outer garments. Valentino expects prompt settlement of petty cash claims and takes a negative view of having to finance the purchase of cakes and other sundry items with money from his own pocket.

The incident took place at the weekly meeting of the programme scheduling committee. Assembled were Soprianti (opera house general manager), LeBreq (leader of the orchestra), Enkhle (orchestra support manager), Signora Furcello (librarian) and myself. At least the feud between the librarian and Soprianti appears to be over. For months they refused to converse. Only recently I discovered that the cause of the dispute was the condition of the staircase leading to the library, which Signora Furcello claimed was inadequately maintained and which brings me to a matter of small credit to myself.

From the start of my appointment I had been concerned about the cleanliness of the building. My complaints to Soprianti were either ignored or acted upon ineffectually. Angry at the lack of response I withheld from the administrative staff the salary increases and financial packages awarded to the music staff. In hindsight this was a mistake because as soon as I relented and extended the financial umbrella to all employees the dust disappeared from the corridors, the ushers stopped slouching behind the columns and the library stairs became miraculously clean.

With half a brain I should have realised that the staff regarded me as yet another overlord appointed to oversee their underpaid jobs, not perhaps quite so condescending as the previous overlord, but indifferent nonetheless to the insultingly small sums of money they received for their services. My mistake was in accepting Soprianti's assurance that remuneration levels for administrative staff in the opera house matched those for similar modes of employment in the city. The lesson is obvious. Never rely on a single source of information, particularly when the source is an over-groomed Italian.

While Soprianti was hopping around the room mopping his trousers with a tea towel reluctantly provided by Valentino the telephone rang.

'Do you want the bad news first, or the good news?' came Mr Lipsky's voice.

'The good news,' I said.

'Professor Schmidt is in hospital.'

'What happened?'

'Heart attack.'

'What's the bad news?'

'He's expected to recover.'

. . . .

The royal infirmary is the hospital of choice for privileged members of Ardaniian society and non-privileged citizens who can afford the fees. There are no wards, only private rooms, each with a balcony opening onto a manicured lawn with concentric paths for the benefit of patients taking the air after their operations and illnesses, transported in decorative wheelchairs by their nurses. The hospital is approached through an avenue of trees. Photographs of the handsome portico at the front of the building appear frequently in the *Gazette* as the backdrop to the departure of some distinguished personage waving a cigar to indicate to his friends and acquaintances that the course of treatment for his condition has been successfully completed.

Inside the hospital the corridors smell reassuringly of antiseptic. Enquiring at the reception desk I was escorted to a room at the end of a wing. The nursing sister who accompanied me along the corridor told me that the patient had suffered a stroke. His movements and speech were impaired. I was not to excite him. Five minutes, no more.

The professor was awake. As I passed through the door his eyes swivelled from the window. Body motionless, his eyes followed my progress to the bed. They remained fixed on my face as I stumbled through a speech of commiseration founded on the sincere guilt that my ambitions for the opera house might perhaps have been responsible for generating undue stress. I endeavoured to strike a cheerful note. Stupidly I told him Beecham's joke about not understanding why England employed so many third rate foreign conductors when the country had so many second rate ones of its own, then used up the rest of the five minutes explaining that there was no correlation between England and Ardaniia, in case the professor thought I was labelling him second rate.

From the hospital I went straight to the university to be welcomed with a limp handshake by Dr Leisl, head of piano tuition.

'So unexpected, such a sad business,' he said.

'Yes indeed,' I said.

'I shall be standing in for him.'

'My resources are at your disposal,' I said.

'How kind of you. I'm worried about the choir. Very much Professor Schmidt's sphere of influence, if you know what I mean.'

'I should be glad to help, though I doubt the professor would approve. Have you considered using a student from the conducting course to lead the choir temporarily?'

'Let me think about that,' said Dr Leisl rubbing his chin.

'Meanwhile, the ballet school has a vacancy for *répétiteur* which might interest your piano students. At a more appropriate time, I will return to discuss the matter.'

'That sounds very exciting.'

'And, before I forget, the opera house is looking for a mezzo-soprano. Would you mind if I approached your choristers direct?'

'By all means. Normally the professor deals with that kind of thing, but, under the circumstances . . .'

Duplicitous? My meagre defence is that the professor would have done exactly the same if our roles had been reversed.

CHAPTER 40

Spring at last. The snow has disappeared from the hills, buds are bursting in the park, flowers are opening in the herbaceous borders in the palace gardens and the temperature is climbing. One can hardly complain of arduous winters in St Frett. The temperature rarely drops below ten degrees. A cold wind whistles off the sea sometimes and occasionally a damp fog descends on the city. The worst is the absence of sun, obscure for weeks, lost in the grey sky. Not any more, the clouds have disappeared and the countryside is basking in warm sunshine.

I have been invited to join the royal yacht for the traditional spring cruise to Malta. The invitation is an honour, naturally, which I like to think represents an acknowledgement of my modest contribution to the country's artistic progress. However I have an uncomfortable feeling that the queen might have something to do with it. Her open displays of affection are an embarrassment to me.

Grand Duke Rupert will be amongst the guests and it is possible that the invitation was prompted by him as a reward for offering Countess von Littchnoff the role of Musetta in *La Bohème*.

The mezzo-soprano audition was the hardest to judge. There were three candidates, one from the St Frett choir, one from the university choir, and the countess. The grand duke attended accompanied by a crowd of boisterous aristocratic acquaintances whose presence was clearly intended to intimidate the judges in favour of the duke's niece. It must have certainly been intimidating for the candidates, performing in such circumstances in front of the full orchestra. LeBreq conducted. Lipsky, myself and two singing teachers, one each from St Frett and the university, were the judges.

We were not looking for singing quality alone, I reminded the other judges as LeBreq mounted the podium. Musetta was a tease and a flirt, she must illuminate the stage with her presence.

The attractive red-haired wife from the warehouse and the charming mezzo-soprano I had lured from the university while Professor Schmidt lay comatose in hospital, were superior in terms of vocal ability. More experienced, they hit their top notes and held them without vibrato. They were entertaining in their interpretations of the role and if they had been the sole candidates I would have congratulated myself on having two ideal singer-actresses at our disposal. In fact here was so little between them I would have struggled to decide which should be the principal, and which the understudy.

Countess von Littchnoff invariably missed her top notes and wobbled alarmingly in places. I could hear sharp intakes of breath from my fellow judges during the performance and pictured Valentino, sitting behind me in the audience waiting to audition for the part of the toy seller, Parpignol, drawing his hand across his throat. Yet her interpretation was electric. The droll way she mimed her way through the arrival scene in the second act was delightful.

The music teachers favoured the red-haired singer. Lipsky wavered in his opinion. I applied my casting vote for the countess, and carried Lipsky with me, arguing that the selection would be conditional on the countess undergoing a course of tutorials to firm up her voice and improve her breath control.

'You mean I've won?' cried the countess jumping up from the seat alongside the grand duke where she had been anxiously awaiting the result of the contest.

'On the condition that you submit to some expert coaching, which I shall arrange,' I said.

'Of course, of course!'

'Your high notes need attention,' I said.

'I know, I know! Uncle Rupert, darling, isn't that marvellous? I shall be on a real stage!'

'Does she get her own dressing room?' growled the grand duke who seemed fixated on that aspect of theatrical life.

'With her own personal dresser,' I assured him.

The other two mezzo-sopranos took the decision well. Under the circumstances I thought it only fair to invite them both to be understudies, with appropriate financial entitlement.

By comparison the audition for Mimi was straightforward. The candidates were Zoe, blossoming in her new home in the warehouse, and a pair of young sopranos from the university choir. Zoe has increased her weight slightly which gives her voice extra strength without affecting that provocative combination of waif-like innocence and sensuality. The girls from the university were suitably pretty but lacked Zoe's vocal flair and were no match for her on the stage. Zoe amused the audience and judges by hugging LeBreq when the results were announced. Scarlet-faced, LeBreq stepped backwards and was saved by the brass rails on the podium from plunging to the floor.

Peter Broch won the audition for Marcello as expected and, in the absence of competition, Valentino was awarded the role of Parpignol.

'Begging your pardon, sir, it's not the part I really wanted,' he said when I congratulated him.

'Don't be impatient,' I said. 'Not many singers make it onto the stage at the first attempt. What's more, it's an important role. You'll be the centre of attention for at least five minutes. And you get paid.'

'I was aiming for higher things, you see, sir.'

'Be patient and keep practising. Meanwhile when are you going to eat it?'

'Come again, sir?'

'The hat. Now that Countess von Littchnoff is playing Musetta.'

'Oh that, sir.'

'I would like to be there,' I said. 'To watch.'

'As a matter of fact, I don't possess a hat, sir.'

'I'll buy one for you,' I said.

'That won't be necessary, thanking you all the same, sir.'

'Would you prefer a top hat or bowler? Indigestible, both of them, I'm afraid. How about a boater?'

'I was speaking metaphorically at the time, sir.'

'A small trilby, then.'

'Begging your pardon, sir, there are refreshments waiting to be served,' said Valentino lifting his eyes to the ceiling as he departed for the pantry.

The role of Rodolfo has been awarded to the Neapolitan Touring Opera Company which by telegram confirmed the availability of the young tenor who sang Ernesto in *Don Pasquale* here last year. The company has also guaranteed the provision of an understudy of equivalent professional stature in the event of indisposition. I am not happy with the situation but have no choice. None of our local tenors possess the necessary range or experience. I don't care for the young Italian but he is handsome with a good voice. He and Zoe will make a spectacular couple on the stage.

Meanwhile applications are pouring into St Frett music society from members of the university choir seeking positions in the chorus for *La Bohème* and, following the success of *The Sleeping Beauty,* Madame Prtenchska has employed two of the university undergraduate pianists as *répétiteurs* in order to cope with the increased student intake to the ballet school.

What Professor Schmidt makes of this, I cannot imagine. He is recuperating at home, still bedridden, still unable to speak. My visits are uncomfortable events but I force myself to spend half an hour with him on Sundays, chattering inconsequentially under the glare of his eyes.

CHAPTER 41

Moored alongside the naval base jetty in the harbour lay the imposing blue and gold two-funnelled royal yacht *Anastasia*, her paintwork gleaming in the sunshine. The expansive teak decks and immaculate white awnings represented symbols of wealth, comfort and influence. The raffish slant of her masts and sweeping lines of her superstructure promised that her passengers would be transported with a dashing turn of speed. Constructed in Glasgow to plans derived from drawings of the British royal yacht *Victoria and Albert* she was designed for cruising the azure waters of the Mediterranean in style.

According to the brochure from the lord chamberlain's office which accompanied written invitations to the spring cruise, the vessel displaced 3850 tons, was capable of 26 knots, could accommodate fifty guests and was manned by 148 officers and crew.

The royal yacht also doubled as the flagship of the Ardaniian naval fleet, which in total consisted of *Anastasia* and three gunboats. In times of war the yacht could be converted to a corvette-sized warship with the addition of gun turrets and associated armament.

By the terms of the maritime treaty between Great Britain and Ardaniia, the British navy guaranteed the neutrality of Ardaniian waters. Foreign powers unwise enough test the validity of the treaty would find themselves shadowed by battlecruisers of Britain's mighty Mediterranean fleet. Equally the British government could take comfort from the clause in the treaty guaranteeing the support of the Ardaniian government in countering threats to British interests in Gibraltar, Malta and the Middle East, although it was tacitly accepted that the arrival of the small Ardaniian fleet during a naval engagement between Britain and a major maritime power such as France or Italy was unlikely to affect the outcome of the battle.

Nonetheless the treaty was politically important to both nations. The British navy contributed to the spirit of the agreement by appointing a liaison officer to the *Anastasia* to advise on communications protocol and oversee the training programme for Ardaniian sailors posted to British warships.

Not to be outdone by the larger party to the treaty, the commodore of the Ardaniian navy continued the tradition of enforcing standards of seamanship and ceremonial that rivalled those of his British counterparts. The white and blue uniforms of his sailors were neatly pressed, the brass fittings on his ships were meticulously polished, the teak decks on the royal yacht were swabbed vigorously twice a day, and his officers were schooled at English naval colleges under the terms of the bilateral agreement.

A marine band contributed to the tradition of pomp and circumstance within the fleet. Right now the band was lined up on the jetty in the sunshine playing *A Life on the Ocean Wave.* The music added to the gaiety of the guests arriving in their coaches for the royal yacht's spring cruise.

My cabin was on the starboard side of the yacht, two decks down from the main staterooms. I declined the steward's offer to unpack my luggage and spent an agreeable half hour finding space for my clothes and accessories in the mahogany wardrobe and shelved cupboards adorning the walls. The bunk was in an alcove separated from the rest of the cabin by a dark blue velvet curtain on brass runners. The mahogany sides of the bunk could be lowered for entry, and raised as required to prevent the incumbent being ejected from the alcove in heavy seas. Inside the alcove was a brass reading light. The porthole opposite the bunk looked out approximately six feet above sea level. 'Keep Closed when Unattended' warned a notice under the thick brass circular fitting.

Before joining the other guests on the quarterdeck I checked through the list of DOs and DON'Ts in the lord chamberlain's brochure. The consequences of a breach of etiquette would unquestionably be more severe within the confined space of a yacht than in the palace.

HMY ANASTASIA - JOINING NOTES

Lords and gentlemen should not wear peaked yachting caps of the type worn by naval officers, to avoid confusions of command

The practice of discharging liquids or solids overboard is discouraged – if unavoidable, during seasickness for example, check the wind direction first

Lords and gentlemen should precede ladies, not follow them, up ladders

Always use the handrails on ladders, steps and stairs - especially important in bad weather

All passengers must attend lifeboat drills (times to be announced)

Their Majesties will attend all evening functions including cocktails on the quarterdeck 19:00 before dinner 20:00

White tie and decorations will be worn for the Governor's reception in Valletta 19:00 and dinner on last night of voyage

Black tie all other nights

The guest list was posted outside the chief steward's office together with seating plans for the dining room. Neither Yvette nor Sarah were amongst the small group of unattached ladies onboard, and to my relief Countess Grigorn was three chairs away on the same side of the table, safely out of range of conversation and eye contact. Directly opposite me was the American ambassador, a quiet and pleasant man of cultured background whose family owned a chain of bookshops and whose wife, unlike the majority of embassy wives, most conspicuously the Italian ambassador's wife, did not festoon herself with jewellery.

Soon enough I discovered the reason for my inclusion in the guest list. I was settling into a deckchair alongside several other passengers to sleep off the excellent lunch of grilled turbot, hollandaise sauce, salad and chilled burgundy wine. The last of the seagulls had dropped away, the yacht was gliding powerfully through the ocean out of sight of land and a condition of languorous ease had settled upon me when a voice murmured in my ear that I was required by the king.

I followed the steward across the deck, down the stairs in the stern of the vessel to an elegant wood-panelled cabin where the king, grand duke and lord chamberlain were stretched out in leather armchairs smoking cigars and drinking cognac.

'Come in, Landour,' said the king waving his cigar at me. He did not invite me to sit down, negating the possibility that I had been summoned to entertain the three most powerful men in Ardaniia with light conversation, swapping jokes with them, slapping my thighs with mirth and so forth. 'A moment of your time. We seek advice, what future do you see for ballet in the country?'

'Commercially,' said the grand duke.

'In the long term,' said the lord chamberlain.

The king was wearing naval uniform, with the collar undone to reduce pressure on his pink cheeks. The other two were dressed, as I was, in brass-buttoned blazers and white duck trousers, the approved attire for lords and gentlemen on the yacht.

After consideration I responded that the ballet school represented in my opinion one of the best possible investments in the arts and should, in the long term, help secure the financial viability of the opera house.

'There has been interest abroad in future performances of ballet here, is that true?' said the king.

I confirmed that the booking office had recorded high levels of enquiry from home and abroad regarding future ballet productions.

'Which composer of opera would most likely fill the opera house with overseas visitors, Puccini or Mozart?' said the king.

'Puccini,' I said without hesitation.

'Countess Charlotte von Littchnoff will be singing in the forthcoming production of *La Bohème*, is that correct?' said the king.

'The countess is being coached professionally for the role of Musetta,' I confirmed.

'His majesty is aware of the considerable following my niece enjoys amongst our relatives in Europe,' interjected the grand duke.

'Countess von Littchnoff has a unique stage presence,' I said, carefully avoiding the question of what happened if the countess's voice failed to respond to coaching.

'You've been most helpful, Landour We are reviewing certain business opportunities. Your advice will be sought again, without doubt,' said the king dismissing me.

Having earned my passage, I set about enjoying the voyage, playing deck tennis in the afternoon and swimming in the canvas pool. In the evening I mingled on the quarterdeck with my fellow passengers, mainly from the embassies. Protected by the awning overhead from the occasional puff of smoke from the yacht's engines, serenaded by light music from the marine band, moved by the beauty of the moonlight playing on the smooth surface of the sea, fortified by several glasses of Pimms I even managed to survive the company of the British ambassador, arrogant and tone deaf, suspicious of artist types, ill at ease with my position as a courtier with closer proximity to the royal family than himself, anxious that an indiscretion on my part might prejudice relationships with Ardaniia and affect his prospects of a peerage on retirement.

The only really disquieting episode was to find the queen's hand resting momentarily on my shoulder during the cocktail hour, and being informed that she looked forward to 'seeing me later'.

I should have locked my cabin door.

Mellow with wine, somnolent with sea air and sunshine, I had turned in shortly after the king arose from the dinner table. Whether it was the sound of the door opening, or footsteps crossing the carpeted floor, or a nightgown slithering downwards or the curtain being drawn back, I awoke in time to observe the figure of a female, silhouetted against the moonlit porthole, climbing into my bunk.

I flattened myself against the wall. Heart pumping, I groaned silently, the reason for my invitation to the spring cruise now abundantly clear. My presence on the royal yacht had nothing to do with rescuing the opera house from bankruptcy or revitalising the national audiences with new music or triumphantly staging *The Sleeping Beauty* and everything to do with the queen's bounteously affectionate nature.

I flattened myself further hoping that I might drop through the gap between the wall and the mattress and escape across the floor. Too late, her fingers were reaching for my face. The touch caused me to jump, striking my head against the brass reading lamp.

'You do me too great an honour, your majesty,' I gulped trying to retreat down the bed.

'Shhh,' she said, fingers on my lips.

From my lips her fingers moved to my pyjama jacket and started undoing the buttons. Switch on the light and engage her in conversation, that might do the trick, I thought reaching up and coming into contact with those parts of the female anatomy which for a woman of the queen's age one would expect to be sagging a little but which were not.

'What's the matter with you tonight, Charles, do stop playing the fool,' said the voice above me which was much too girlish to belong to the queen.

By now in a state of complete confusion I cried 'My name isn't Charles!' whereupon there was a gasp and a flurry of activity as the owner of the attractive young breasts leapt from my bunk, collected her nightgown and departed from the cabin leaving behind a cloud of unfamiliar perfume in which I lay trembling with shock, staring wide-eyed at the shafts of moonlight streaming through the porthole.

CHAPTER 42

If the grand harbour in Valetta had been developed centuries earlier it would surely have been included in the list of wonders of the ancient world. The sight upon entry from the sea, of the creamy sandstone walls climbing vertically from the deep blue water full of great warships is magnificent. We stood in awe on the quarterdeck of the royal yacht looking up at the fortifications towering overhead in which the Knights of Malta had fended off the Turks, and at the spires and domes of the buildings beyond the ramparts piercing the brilliant sky.

The canons on the ramparts remained silent as *Anastasia* glided towards Customs House quay. This was not a state visit. Instead the ensigns on the vessels of the Mediterranean fleet anchored in the harbour dipped in salute acknowledging the presence of royalty onboard as we passed, dwarfed by the enormous size of the British battleships. A single shell from one of those huge guns would have obliterated the entire Ardaniian navy. The three little gunboats escorting the royal yacht to her moorings looked about as intimidating as ducklings paddling behind their mother.

Never mind, our hearts swelled with pride at the efficient manner the yacht moored alongside the quay, at the smartness of the officers assembled alongside the gangway to greet the governor's ADC and the precision of the marine band marching into position on the quarterdeck. Escort duty accomplished, the three gunboats swung away and hurried from the grand harbour to their moorings in Sliema creek.

I was not on the guest list for the governor's luncheon so I hired a horse-and-cart cab to explore Valetta as soon as the royal party had disembarked. My steward Valentino, deeply upset at being excluded from the list of servants accompanying their masters on the spring cruise, had given me a parcel to post to his mother on arrival. The cab driver recognized the address so instead of stopping at a post office my tour of the historic city commenced on a cobbled street where the residences were tunnelled into the rock, with no natural light other than from the windows beside the door.

Blinking in the semi-darkness I was led by two children to an old woman dressed completely in black sitting in a rocking chair.

'How is he, my son?' said the woman.

'In good health,' I said.

'Is he happy?'

'I hope so. I certainly enjoy his company.'

'He is becoming a famous singer, he tells me in his letters.'

'He's working very hard in that direction.'

'You must be the great new conductor of the orchestra?'

'New, but not great.'

The children had opened the parcel and were gazing hungrily at the collection of chocolate biscuits and candies.

'This is Maestro Landour, the conductor of the orchestra your uncle Valentino works for,' said the woman rising from the chair to boil some water. 'He is honouring us with an unexpected visit.'

'How do you do. My name is Amanda,' said the older of the children shaking my hand.

'My name is Victor,' said the younger child, also extending his arm politely.

'I'm pleased to meet you both,' I said.

'How old are you?' said Amanda.

'Twenty seven,' I said.

'I'm six,' said Amanda,

'She'll be nine next year,' said Victor.

'What comes after six - how many times have I told you?' said Amanda, folding her arms.

Her little brother wrinkled his nose in concentration.

'Four.'

'Boys,' sighed Amanda. 'Can you play the piano?' she said turning to me.

'Not very well,' I said.

'I'll show you, it's easy,' said Amanda taking my hand and leading me further into the cavern. A single light bulb illuminated the darkness sufficiently for me to identify the presence of two large wooden beds, a wardrobe and an old upright piano. Overhead the stone roof glistened with moisture though the interior of the cavern, refreshingly cool after the heat of the street outside, did not feel at all damp.

Duty done for Valentino I continued my tour of Valletta, spread out comfortably legs crossed under the shade of the cab roof, admiring the singular style of architecture in the city, absorbing the noises of church bells and street vendors, occasionally pressing a handkerchief to my nostrils as the cab wheels clattered over the culverts of an open drain. After lunching alone in a restaurant above Sliema creek I took a bus and circumnavigated the island from St Paul's bay to the silent city of Mdina where the vaults of the great houses which constitute the fortified walls are said to contain relics of unimaginable value from the period when the Knights of Malta controlled the island.

'How was lunch?' I enquired of the royal physician as we assembled on the quarterdeck at dusk dressed in white ties and tails.

'Fish,' said the royal physician. 'How about you?'

'Goat,' I said.

'Good?'

'Rather tough, like old chicken.'

'You should be all right, with luck. The barometer's falling,' said the royal physician rubbing his hands at the prospect of something to occupy him between meals during the next leg of the voyage. He had already pinned a note on the sickbay door. QUEUE HERE FOR ANTI-SEASICKNESS PILLS - QUANTITY DISCOUNTS AVAILABLE.

'I wouldn't take them though, if I were you,' said the royal physician.

'Take what?'

'Anti-seasickness pills.'

'Why not?'

'They knock you out,' said the royal physician, 'flat on your back.'

'Isn't that a good thing?'

'Not if it means missing lunch. What do you make of the prime minister?' said the royal physician nodding in the direction of the reception committee lining up at the gangway to greet the governor.

'Pleasant, industrious and committed to an unenviably complicated task. He's rather written me off, though,' I said.

'How come?'

'The government wants to modernise the national anthem. I don't blame them, but the palace is not keen.'

'Quite right,' bristled the royal physician. 'Look out, here's trouble.'

The queen had arrived on the quarterdeck with her entourage of ladies-in-waiting and was proceeding in an admirably straight line towards the king who waited patiently in the stern of the yacht with the grand duke and royal equerries to welcome the governor after the prime minister's reception at the gangway. At the last minute the queen swerved towards us.

'Landour, where were you last night? I wanted to discuss my plans for a cherry orchard in the palace gardens,' she complained, tapping my arm reprovingly with her fan.

I dropped my head and admitted to having retired early, suffering from the after effects of sunshine and sea air, whereupon the queen tutted to the royal physician.

'That's too bad. Dr Dalrymple-Smith, what's your view on sunshine and sea air? Personally I am enervated by them.'

'At my age, your majesty, enervation manifests itself only when lobster thermidor is on the menu.'

The queen laughed. Half-turning to her ladies-in-waiting she said 'Dr Dalrymple-Smith is so divinely amusing.' If she had turned completely she would have observed from Countess Grigorn's pursed lips that her ladies-in-waiting were not all of the same opinion.

My purpose that evening was to trace the identity of the midnight visitor to my cabin. Circulating amongst the groups of attendees at the reception I endeavoured to manoeuvre myself as close as possible to the younger females without attracting attention, sniffing the air in their vicinity surreptitiously in the hope of recognising the perfume. Not unnaturally the male guests from Malta, preening themselves in front of the desirably fresh young females from Ardaniia, were reluctant to yield their positions within the groups and more than once I found myself with an admiral's elbow in my chest being eased away from a subject of my investigation.

The breakthrough came unexpectedly. I had determined that there was a Charles in the cabin next to mine, listed as a major in the dragoon guards. I followed his movements at the reception carefully. Most of the evening he spent talking to army officers from the Valetta garrison in an all-male group but at around eight o'clock, when the reception was about to break up, I saw him wiggle his fingers at a figure in the royal party. Following the direction of his gaze I ran into Lady Fenella deLoire, the king's current playmate.

She immediately took my arm.

'You're not going to denounce us are you?' she said leading me to the side of the yacht.

'Of course not,' I said.

'I'm so embarrassed,' she said.

The king had turned in early and was snoring by midnight. Familiar with his sleep patterns Fenella had decided to visit her paramour, the dragoon guards major, whom she planned to marry when the king tired of her company, which would be soon in view of the frequency of the picnics the king was taking with the Hungarian ambassador's wife, and stumbled into the wrong cabin. She returned to the king's bed and lay awake all night worrying. It would be disastrous for her and the dragoon major if word of the misadventure leaked out. The convention was that the king got bored with his playmates first, not the other way round.

'Of course I won't say anything,' I said. 'However, I seek a favour.'

'Oh dear,' sighed Fenella.

'Please stop promoting the Charleston.'

'Why?'

'Countess Grigorn will never agree, and I've come to share her opinion. The ballroom is too graceful for skirt-flapping dances. Keep the Charleston for informal occasions, in your rooms, or at private parties.'

Fenella thought for a moment.

'All right,' she said. 'If you promise to stop turning your back on us in the palace.'

'What on earth do you mean?'

'Stop walking past us in the anteroom looking gorgeously handsome, ignoring everybody.'

'I look nothing of the sort,' I protested. 'If my conduct seems offhand, I apologise, it merely reflects my commitment to my fiancée in England.'

'You don't have one, we've checked your mail.'

I coughed uncomfortably into the darkness.

'Sarah adores you, why not woo her? If I was a man I should be on my knees before someone so eligible and lovely.'

'This particular man is on his knees trying to run an orchestra.'

'That's no excuse. And be careful of that French bitch Yvette, she's after one of the household cavalry castles. We don't want you getting hurt.'

'How very thoughtful,' I murmured.

'Thank you for being so sweet and helpful,' said Fenella kissing my cheek before hurrying back to the stern of the yacht.

All of which begs the question of what would have happened if I had remained silent during events in my bunk last night. On balance I am inclined to favour the argument that when, in the dark, a girl commences the process of unbuttoning your pyjamas, you should not distract her.

CHAPTER 43

'How was the voyage, sir?' said Valentino.

'Not much in the way of music. Except when I delivered your parcel and was taught how to play the piano by your niece.'

'Begging your pardon, did you say delivered, sir?'

'Yes, there was plenty of time, so I visited your house with the package and had my fingering sorted out.'

'Well I'm blessed. Much obliged indeed, sir. She's a card, is Amanda, right enough.'

'Your mother seemed very well. She made me some tea - even better than yours, Valentino.'

'I'm very glad to hear it, sir.'

'The children enjoyed the contents of the parcel. They've written you a letter, here you are,' I said delving into the briefcase I used for transporting music scores.

. . . .

We have just completed the second meeting of the *La Bohème* production committee. Present were the directors of the St Frett music society Mr and Mrs Lipsky, royal theatre director Pierre Bonnel, royal theatre stage manager Albert Frenner, librarian Signora Furcello and myself as committee chairman. For the brochure and programme the official titles will be director Pierre Bonnel, stage manager Albert Frenner, chorus master David Lipsky, soloists coach Hannah Lipsky, technical adviser Maria Furcello and conductor Robin Landour.

Pierre justly deserves the position of director. The young man is as capable as he is ebullient. For *The Sleeping Beauty* he had been given the difficult task of advising Madame Tuillée on the theatrical aspects of the ballet. Madame Tuillée, headstrong and imperious, was an acknowledged expert on Petipa's choreography, had worked with Gorsky in Russia and trained several internationally famous dancers for the role of Princess Aurora. However she had never directed a full scale production of the ballet. Pierre acted as her eyes from the perspective of the audience, offering suggestions with such charm and diplomacy that by the end she had come to rely on his advice, consulting him frequently, spectacles low on her nose, sheaves of dance papers in one hand, pencil in the other.

It was, he admitted, a completely new experience for him. His first ballet.

La Bohème will be his first opera. The relationship between a play and an opera is much closer than between a play and a ballet, in which the stage is a kaleidoscope of motion. It is the comparative absence of motion in opera, says Pierre, that poses the challenge. I agree with him. Crowd scenes are especially difficult to manage. In a ballet the crowd (corps de ballet) twirls beautifully in coordinated patterns across the stage. In a typical opera the crowd (chorus) stands awkwardly in the background holding cardboard swords trying to remember which side of the stage to exit from when the contralto plunges his dagger into the tenor.

The crowd scenes in *La Bohème* all take place in the second act. Pierre is confident he can handle the noise and bustle. He is, after all, French and at home in that quintessentially French setting, a square in the Latin Quarter of Paris lined with shops and restaurants.

He has already rehearsed a few of the sequences in the royal theatre. To Valentino's embarrassment I happened to be there when Pierre was experimenting with arrangements for the toy vendor's barrow using young students from the ballet school as the children, and an old pram as the barrow. From the expression on my steward's face it was clear he did not regard the task of wheeling the pram across the stage as the crowning moment of his artistic career, until Pierre amused him by clambering into the makeshift barrow and making the children jump to pluck the toys from his outstretched arms. The young Frenchman has the gift of listening patiently to complaints about insuperable problems then, exploding with energy, making the problems disappear. I wish I had his patience when rehearsing my orchestra.

I am equally confident of Mr Frenner as stage manager. He is the complete opposite of Pierre. Quiet, slow moving and blunt, he administers his domain with curt commands, his large hands fearless of the inanimate objects which constitute his trade; scenery props, trapdoors, pulleys, wire ropes, scaffolds, spotlights, gantries and assorted backstage machinery which for *La Bohème* will include equipment for generating snowstorms.

Pierre's designs for the sets, prepared in collaboration with the commercial artist who helped finalise the sets for *The Sleeping Beauty*, have long since been approved by the committee and passed to Mr Frenner for construction.

The most complex set to construct, and for the stage hands to erect and dismantle, is the rooftop garret which features in the first and last act of the opera. Mr Frenner's solution is to build the set in two halves, each half mounted on wheels. The restaurant for the second act and the tavern for the snow-filled third act are built into the rear of the garret. During the interval between the first and second acts the stage hands will uncouple the garret, rotate the half containing the restaurant into position and roll the half containing the tavern to the back of the stage, out of sight. Simple really, says Mr Frenner shrugging his burly shoulders.

Provision of realistic snow coverage has proved to be more difficult. Puccini requires 'snow everywhere'. The instruction can be interpreted to mean that snow should be falling in addition to lying on the ground. For snow to fall, however, stage hands must be located in the rafters provisioned with bags of white confetti and strict instructions not to slip from the heights and follow the confetti onto the stage thereby ruining the performance for the audience and incurring considerable expense and inconvenience to the management. Moreover the pieces of confetti attach themselves to the hair and clothing of the cast below. Stubbornly refusing to melt like snow the pieces have to be brushed off by the performers who have more important things on their minds.

So when Pierre said that snowflakes drifting picturesquely from the sky would enhance the dramatic intensity of the third act Mr Frenner scratched his head.

His answer was yet another invention by our resourceful Americans cousins. On passage from Baltimore to Marseilles by steamer, scheduled to be offloaded for St Frett any day now, is a machine with an electric motor driven fan which sprays droplets of a special fluid into the air. The droplets expand and float gently to the ground, creating a realistic-looking snowstorm. The percentage water content of the fluid is very small so the snow evaporates within seconds of touching the person or the stage, leaving no residue behind. Mr Frenner will have plenty of time to get the machine running. If the equipment doesn't match expectations, the stage hands will be back in the rafters.

Mrs Lipsky's role in the production is to prepare the stars of the show and their understudies for the performance. Normally completely unflappable, she can be forgiven for the anxiety she now expresses at the unavailability of the principal male star, Rodolfo, and the quality of the voice of the candidate I encouraged the audition committee to accept for the part of Musetta.

There is nothing we can do about Rodolfo at the moment. We must rely on the professionalism of the Neapolitan Touring Opera Company to honour the terms of the contract whereby the company provides us with the services of Eduardo Fugarri (the young tenor who sang Ernesto in *Don Pasquale* last year) and his understudy for the week of the performance. The contract guarantees that both singers will arrive fully prepared for the role. I am not happy with the situation but we have no choice. The problem here of course is the absence of a first class tenor with whom the other principals can rehearse the duets, trios and quartets involving Rodolfo. Mrs Lipsky is being forced to use a young tenor from the chorus whose vocal range is scarcely greater than Valentino's.

Nor is there much I can do about Countess Charlotte von Littchnosky who has disappeared on holiday to Austria. I have promised Mrs Lipsky that I will attend a coaching session as soon as the countess returns, and make a final decision about the mezzo-soprano's future in the production then and there.

Meanwhile Zoe has continued to flourish, both in the role of Mimi on the stage and as adopted daughter and secretary in the warehouse. Thanks to Mrs Lipsky's cooking and the passage of time the eighteen year old waif has blossomed into a nineteen year old angel with a voice to match. Mr Lipsky joyfully informs me life in the warehouse is now so full of music that the birds in the small garden do not bother to sing anymore, they just sit in the branches and listen.

Mr Lipsky's job is to train the chorus, monitor the singers with minor roles and allocate tutors as required. Valentino comes under his authority and Mr Lipsky is not satisfied with his progress. My steward has apparently been complaining of a sore throat. This is news to me although I do recall hearing him coughing in the pantry last week. I rather fear that Valentino's hopes of a glittering career as an opera singer may be coming to an end. Fortunately we will have no difficulty filling the part of the toy vendor if he continues on the downward slope.

Signora Furcello's role in the committee is to coordinate Italian aspects of the production. Challenged by her to define what was meant by 'technical advisor' I found myself mumbling about diction and presentation, neither of which she is really qualified to pronounce upon. The opera is being sung in Italian but the diction is the responsibility of the singing teachers and coaches, while the presentation is entirely French. The truth is that I felt sorry for her sitting alone upstairs and wanted her to be involved in the opera, particularly as she had once met Puccini while working in the music library at La Scala in Milan. She says very little at our meetings but from the expression of profound interest on her face during our discussions I think I have made the right decision.

Arriving in the palace anteroom for cocktails this evening I was beckoned yet again to the fireplace.

'Concerning our discussions on the yacht, I am commanded to inform you that the king proposes to attend the last night of *La Bohème*. He will be accompanied by distinguished members of several royal courts in Europe. You are to ensure that appropriate seating is available in the opera house,' said the lord chamberlain.

'Of course,' I said.

'I shall issue a list of invitations and acceptances as soon as possible.'

'That will be very useful,' I said.

'You might as well know that his majesty has decided to participate in the financing of a luxury hotel here in the kingdom. The building will not be ready in time for *La Bohème,* but the success of the opera will help protect the king's investment, if you see what I mean,' said the lord chamberlain.

'Yes, indeed,' I said, seeing what he meant very clearly.

'And it would probably be a good idea to confirm Countess Charlotte von Littchnoff's participation in the opera as soon as possible, for reasons I'm sure you understand.'

'Ah,' I said, understanding the situation only too well.

'If she's no good, get her onto the stage somehow,' said the lord chamberlain. 'In the chorus, if necessary.'

CHAPTER 44

I slept fitfully, like Hamlet, hoist by my own petard.

Impervious to the risk I had strutted onto a foreign podium and set about converting an underpaid and disorientated ensemble specialising in baroque music of limited interest to the general public into a profitable orchestra playing classical-romantic music to an increasingly large audience. In doing so I had trampled over the sensitivities of the musical establishment and hospitalized a dedicated man responsible for educating the corresponding branch of the nation's scholars. Preening my feathers I had devised a programme of musical performances calculated to attract international interest and, blatantly overruling the expert opinion of my peers, had selected a singer not on merit but on the likelihood that the audience would be sprinkled with royalty thereby generating publicity for the opera house and orchestra, simultaneously promoting my career.

Influenced by the consequences of my self-aggrandisement the patrician leaders of the nation had concluded there was profit to be made from the flood of wealthy overseas visitors which would assuredly accumulate at the opera house doors clamouring for tickets for Puccini operas and Tchaikovsky ballets. And thus the patrician leaders had concluded that the royal purse should be opened to finance the construction of a grand new hotel in which to accommodate the flow of well-heeled tourists from Europe and afar.

And thus for me, like Hamlet, the chickens had come home to roost.

However much I tossed and turned in bed, punching the pillows, muttering in the darkness that the problem had arisen from successful execution of my brief, that I had converted an underpaid and disorientated ensemble into a fine orchestra and in the process saved the opera house from bankruptcy, I kept returning to the question of whether my motive for conditionally awarding Countess Charlotte von Littchnoff the role of Musetta had been founded on artistic perception or blatant self-advancement.

Whatever the motive, I climbed gaunt from my bed this morning facing the stomach-churning awareness that the royal finances had been wagered on the success of an operatic production in which the principal performers were either untested or absent.

I called the Lipskys as soon as I reached my chambers and informed them of the position. The lord chamberlain's idea of reassigning the countess to the chorus was impractical, I had no choice but to make a formal announcement to the press confirming that Grand Duke Rupert's niece would be playing the role of Musetta.

After a long silence Mrs Lipsky said 'You do realise that, if we cannot improve her delivery, she will be laughed off the stage?'

'Yes,' I said grimly.

For the rest of the morning I blew off steam at Soprianti who refused to acknowledge that the royal box could be dismantled. Stamping around perimeter of the structure I pointed at the joints in the woodwork where screws would have been inserted, concealed now under layers of lacquer or gold paint. Soprianti shook his head stubbornly.

'The royal box, it has never been moved, not in Soprianti's time, not ever,' he insisted.

'How long have you worked in the opera house, remind me?' I said.

'Twenty two years,' said Soprianti.

'Then you were not here for the coronation,' I said crossly.

'Coronation?' said Soprianti.

'Oh, for heaven's sake! The coronation of the present king, attended by the crowned heads of Europe, who were invited to the opera house for a grand concert after the service in the cathedral, according to the guidebooks. There would never have been enough room to fit several dozen coronets in the royal box, it must have been removed or modified.'

Soprianti summoned the building contractor, the one with the pencil behind his ear.

'The problem you've got here,' said the builder sucking his teeth, 'is expense.'

'Doubtless,' I snapped, 'but what we need to know, regardless of expense, is whether the royal box can be dismantled, stored for a week, then replaced, without damage?'

The builder circled the structure, stopping intermittently to examine the joints in the woodwork which I had pointed out to Soprianti earlier. At the last joint he dropped to his knees and scraped away the layers of lacquer and gold paint to reveal several large brass screws.

'The royal box can be dismantled all right, given time,' nodded the builder, 'and expenditure.'

'How much time?' I said

Removing the pencil from his ear the builder scribbled some figures into a piece of paper retrieved from his overalls.

'Four weeks,' said the builder, 'give or take a week.'

'In its place I want a temporary waist-high enclosure of corresponding quality to encompass fifty seats in the centre of the royal circle, from there to there, and for the entire enclosure to be carpeted in the style of the royal box. How much, and how long, to complete both jobs?'

'I shall prepare a quotation for you overnight, sir. The matter needs careful attention. After all, we wouldn't want our standards to slip, would we?' said the builder.

'No, we don't want our standards to slip, nor do we wish to be overcharged so I shall be asking the stage manager of the royal theatre how much he would charge for the work, and how long he would take,' I said.

'Incidentally,' I said to Soprianti as we descended the stairs to the foyer leaving the builder scratching his head, 'have you instructed the booking office not to sell central royal circle tickets for the last night of the opera to the general public?'

'Naturally,' said Soprianti spreading his arms. 'I tell them very firmly.'

'We'd better check,' I scowled.

In the booking office the clerks produced the seating chart for the Saturday night performance of *La Bohème* and, sure enough, in the area surrounding the royal box, two seats had been marked as sold.

'What is going on here!' shouted Soprianti. 'Who sold those tickets? I demand to know who has disobeyed my orders. You will see, Soprianti does not tolerate disobedience. Now then, who is responsible for this inefficiency?' said the general manager thrusting his chin out at the clerks, a pair of elderly ladies known as Alice and Gertrude.

'I don't remember being told,' said Alice.

'Nor I,' said Gertrude.

'Do either of you happen to know who bought the tickets?' I said.

'We always keep names and addresses of royal circle ticket holders, just in case,' said Alice examining the cards in an index box on the counter. 'Here it is, Mr and Mrs O'Reilly, c/o Ardaniian National Bank.'

Instantly I was suffused with a warm glow.

'Our bank manager,' I said.

'Yes, Mr O'Reilly, I remember him well,' said Alice. 'He seemed very pleasant, a tall talkative man with sandy hair. He likes opera, he told me.'

'Who refused to extend our overdraft,' I said.

'I don't know about that,' said Alice

'Well now, kindly mail Mr and Mrs O'Reilly a refund, with a note informing them that their tickets have been requisitioned by the palace,' I instructed Alice. 'And enclose a pair of complimentary tickets for the upper circle, those two will do, that's right, the seats behind the pillar, with the interrupted view.'

CHAPTER 45

The nightmare is becoming reality.

In a few days' time the harbour will be full of yachts and steamers discharging plank-loads of aristocrats, foreign dignitaries and newspaper reporters clutching tickets for a royal command performance of Puccini's opera *La Bohème* in which the roles of Rodolfo the poet and Musetta the flirt are to be played, respectively, by the dashing young Italian tenor Eduardo Fugarri and the effervescent Countess Charlotte von Littchnosky, niece of Grand Duke Rupert of Ardaniia.

Little do the visitors know as they make preparations for the voyage, checking weather reports for the region from their local newspapers, issuing instructions to their servants regarding appropriate clothes to be packed – dress suits, uniforms, ball gowns, blazers and white trousers for tennis in the afternoons - that the chances of the performance taking place are diminishing rapidly seeing that the dashing young tenor seems to have disappeared and the effervescent countess has still not returned from Austria where she is bedridden with fever.

At least the countess responds to communications. Her most recent cable reported that her condition was improving, she had reserved a cabin for the return journey and I was not to worry, she would be back in time for the dress rehearsal on Wednesday. If the steamer was full she would swim behind the ship towing her luggage, the cable concluded in whimsical vein, presumably to cheer me up which under the circumstances it did not.

In one of her earlier cables the countess announced she had engaged a local singing teacher. By the time she got back to the opera house, she wrote, she would be able to soar through Musetta's high notes like a skylark. Then almost immediately afterwards came the announcement of her illness.

Mrs Lipsky has washed her hands of the matter. She never thought it likely that the necessary improvements to the countess's technique could be accomplished within the limited timescale. Now, in view of the countess's influenza, Mrs Lipsky has shaken her head and declared that the understudies must be mobilised.

Technically the high B flat in Musetta's solo (act 2) and the turbulent quartet outside the snowbound tavern (act 3) are beyond mezzo-soprano range. For this reason Musetta's role is normally sung by a soprano. Personally I like the darker tone of a mezzo-soprano's voice in the part and remain convinced that the countess possesses the necessary reach.

So I shall be deeply disappointed if there is insufficient time to test my theory that the combination of the countess's unusually interesting voice and natural acting ability would result in a spectacular Musetta. I am also naturally concerned that an announcement to the effect that the countess was being replaced by an understudy would increase my chances of ending up in one of the country's dungeons.

In a desperate attempt to remedy the situation I have been exploring the option of dropping Musetta's high notes by an octave. For example, in the act 2 solo, instead of jumping to B flat during the phrase 'tutta ricerca' ('everybody is looking at me') (part 21, bar 13) she would drop to the lower B flat and re-join the orchestra on the G sharp at the end of the bar. Simultaneously I would mask her voice with a surge of the strings and wind instruments.

The ruse might fool the audience but not, alas, the professional press.

Unless the singing lessons in Austria had miraculously transformed the countess's vocal range there were only two viable options, replace the countess with an understudy, in which case I faced the wrath of the visiting aristocrats, or tamper with the score and face the sarcasm of the music critics at having deployed an inept amateur for the role of Musetta.

In other words, death by the sword or the pen.

Death by the sword would be swifter. Shifting uncomfortably I pictured my bloodstained corpse lying amidst flowers in a forest glade, abandoned by a score of scornful duellists, tended only by a passing fawn, which stopped to lick my ashen face.

If the situation with Grand Duke Rupert's niece was serious, with the missing tenor it was potentially terminal.

Seeking to verify the travel dates for Eduardo Fugarri and his understudy, and unable to get through to the Neapolitan Touring Opera Company by telephone, I cabled Naples on Monday, and again on Tuesday. In the absence of any reply, yesterday I called the Italian ambassador in St Frett who promised to investigate and report back to me after lunch, which he didn't. When eventually I got through to the ambassador this morning he blamed a local religious festival in Naples for the difficulty in contacting the opera company.

'You know what it's like. Businesses close down, everybody joins the parade,' said the ambassador.

'Not for an entire week, surely? I've been trying since Monday,' I said.

'Perhaps something is wrong with the telephone lines,' suggested the ambassador.

'That's why I called you yesterday,' I pointed out.

'Leave it to me, I have an excellent contact in the city, I will call you back before lunch, without fail.'

'That's what you said yesterday,' I pointed out.

'My contact was out when I telephoned. That is the trouble with festivals. But, without question, he will be in his office today. I will telephone him now. As soon as we have spoken, I will call you.'

That was three hours ago. I have just been informed by his secretary that the ambassador has left the embassy for the weekend and is not expected back until Monday.

So I have taken the drastic step of booking Soprianti on tonight's ferry to Naples. He should arrive early on Saturday morning. His instructions are to proceed straight to the opera house, wait outside until it opens (ten o'clock according to the brochure in my desk), speak to the duty manager, find out what's going on, if necessary lock the duty manager in his office until the matter is sorted out, then telephone or cable me, before noon at the latest.

Soprianti is wildly excited at the assignment, kissing the female staff and promising to come back laden with boxes of Italian chocolates. Only half in jest I have told him not to come back at all unless accompanied by Eduardo Fugarri and his understudy.

My sense of disquiet is heightened by the absence of Valentino who, following the removal of a tumour from his throat a fortnight ago, is recuperating at his lodgings on sick leave. His place has been taken by an elderly steward called Thomas who shuffles around my chambers disturbing my concentration, serving tea which is too weak and coffee which is too cold. He is slightly deaf and therefore unaware of the noise he generates when dusting the furniture and cleaning the ornaments, activities which I have been forced to insist are carried out before or after my arrival. More than once I have been tempted to ask Soprianti for a replacement but Valentino is due back from sick leave soon whereupon, assuming I have not in the meantime been sacked, executed or imprisoned, normality will be restored to my chambers.

. . . .

I visited Valentino the night before his operation. He was lying in a neatly-made bed halfway down a large ward with a notice on the door marked 'Men's Surgical - General'.

'What if I cannot talk afterwards, sir?' he said nervously.

'Has anyone discussed the operation with you?'

'The surgeon stopped at my bed with some doctors and nurses this morning. They wouldn't know anything until they'd taken it out, the surgeon said. He looked cheerful enough though.'

'Well, that's a good sign.'

'But I can't help worrying, sir.'

'Naturally. However I'm sure everything will be fine.'

'If the worst happens, sir, and I lose my voice, will you take me back?'

'Of course I will, but the worst won't happen,' I said.

'Are you being looked after properly, sir, in my absence?'

'Thomas is doing his best. His cakes aren't up to your standard, but otherwise he's coping well.'

'He doesn't know his way round the market, like I do, sir.'

'You can put him right when you get back.'

'I should have spoken to Mr and Mrs Lipsky before coming in here.

Very nice people they are, exceeding pleasant to me, sir. I'd appreciate you apologising on my behalf for letting them down. Mr Adniss, or young Hugh, either of them can take my part in *La Bohème*, and do it very well, with my best wishes.'

'If you haven't recovered in time, Valentino, then of course I will. But let's not worry about that now.'

His voice was beginning to break.

'If the operation is unsuccessful and I don't make it, I'd appreciate you informing my mother. And next time you're in Malta, sir, perhaps you could give young Amanda and Victor a hug on my behalf. A gesture of love, if you know what I mean.'

He was discharged from hospital a week ago with a bandage around his throat. Thankfully the tumour was benign. The doctors have told him not to attempt to speak until the bandage is removed. To set his mind at rest regarding his future I have sent him a letter instructing him to report back to the opera house to resume his duties as steward as soon as the doctors have pronounced him fit.

Meanwhile the part of the toy vendor has been transferred to Steven Adniss, a member of the St Frett choir, who has been busy pushing the old pram across the royal theatre stage under Pierre's direction.

CHAPTER 46

Saturday evening. I stood at the window of my chambers looking out at the carriages arriving for the last concert before *La Bohème*, my hands clasped behind my back.

Mendelssohn *Hebrides Overture (Fingal's Cave)*
Mozart *Symphony No. 39, K. 543*
Rimsky-Korsakov *Symphonic Suite Scheherazade*

The programme featured yet another masterpiece denied to the Ardaniian audiences by my predecessors. Why had it taken me so long to include Rimsky-Korsakov's adaptation of the fables told by a vizier's daughter to a murderous sultan? I shrugged my shoulders. Perhaps I had been waiting for the orchestra to mature sufficiently to do justice to the brilliant colours in Rimsky-Korsakov's score. More than any other composer the influential Russian was responsible for creating the palette which distinguished the school of romantic music from its predecessor.

Whatever my reasons for delaying *Scheherazade* the matter was of little consequence now. Soprianti had arrived in Naples to discover that the Neapolitan Touring Opera Company had locked its doors, liquidated by its creditors. His cables to that effect were lying on my desk

'Will you be expecting as many guests tonight as last Saturday, sir?' said Thomas, the replacement steward, polishing the glasses on the sideboard.

'Probably more,' I replied.

'I will arrange a transfer of champagne from the main bar. Your stocks are running low, sir.'

'Thank you, Thomas. Incidentally, if the prime minister shows up, he doesn't drink alcohol. Offer him orange juice or water.'

'Very good, sir.'

At the five minute bell LeBreq put his head round the door to announce that the orchestra was assembling on the platform. He added that the seats in the stalls reserved for the press were filling up and that reporters from *Die Presse* in Vienna and *Corriere della Sera* in Milan had been identified.

At the two minute bell I sent Thomas to the foyer to verify that the reception committee had formed. In Soprianti's place I had appointed Peter Enkhle, the orchestra support manager, to greet the royal party. Peter was totally reliable. Never once had he let the orchestra or opera house down. There was no justification for checking his presence in the foyer. If he had been delayed he would have sent a message and organised a replacement in the committee. By sending Thomas to the foyer I was demonstrating the pathetically frail condition of my nerves.

At the one minute bell I collected my baton and walked to the stage door.

'Get a grip on yourself, for heaven's sake,' I muttered, trying to suppress my sense of foreboding as I waited for the signal from the foyer.

'Time to go, sir,' said the usher opening the door, clapping loudly to initiate the applause that greeted my appearance in the auditorium and swelled as, attempting to disguise my feelings with a confident smile, I strode onto the stage past the violinists and mounted the podium.

I turned to face the royal circle. Unencumbered by the royal box the gallery looked different, wider and more spacious. The boundary of the VIP enclosure which had temporarily replaced the royal box was only waist high and thus provided the audience at the back of the gallery with a full view of the stage. Moreover the absence of the royal box with its ornate roof meant that the audience in the galleries above could look down upon the heads of the aristocrats now descending the central aisle to the gilded chairs lining the front of the royal circle.

Heading the royal procession in place of the king and queen was Prince Ernest, the king's younger son, accompanied by Grand Duke Rupert and assorted European noblemen and their wives, early arrivals for next week's opera. The prince stood erect at the front of the royal enclosure during the national anthem.

There is nowhere for the string sections to hide in a Mendelssohn overture. A few errors of timing and tone and the ensemble quickly sounds ragged. So, raising my baton to start the concert, I knew that the opening bars of the *Hebrides Overture* would immediately reveal to the experienced commentators in the stalls the stature of the orchestra.

I need not have worried. The musicians on the stage of the opera house tonight were far advanced in technique and commitment from those I had inherited a year ago. Serenely the violins, violas and cellos soared and plummeted sending the Atlantic waves crashing into the Scottish cave. All that was required of me on the podium was to maintain with my beat the rhythm of the sea, which murmurs restlessly throughout the piece, and the orchestra did the rest.

Nor need I have worried about the Mozart symphony, which the orchestra delivered with triumphant ease. Mozart continues to puzzle me. I am convinced that conductors who resort to reverential pathos in their interpretations of his music are wrong. I simply cannot picture the impish composer staring tearfully at a manuscript overcome by the beauty of the notes he had derived so effortlessly from the gods and goddesses of art, nor can I see him particularly overwhelmed by the tragic events of his darker works like *Don Giovanni*. He was so full of life, so carefree, so irreverent. My solution to the 'difficult' parts of his music is to speed straight through them.

Rimsky-Korsakov on the other hand must have been deeply affected by the forces he unleashed in *Scheherazade*, flattening the audience into their seats with blasts from the trombones and trumpets, beguiling them with oriental flutes and mystical melodies, leading them through the labyrinth of the fables spun by the terrified virgin, culminating in the horrific storm which, when it breaks, rocks the foundations of the opera house.

As the reverberations of the great gong died away, and the solo violin, beautifully played by LeBreq, signalled the end of the voyage, I could feel the audience sigh collectively. The vizier's virgin daughter, on her knees wrapped in silk in the sultan's tent, who had spent one thousand and one nights fighting for her life with fable after fable, had been freed at last.

Standing at the window of my chambers looking out at the carriages departing from the opera house, my hands clasped behind my back, it occurred to me that there were similarities between the virgin's plight and my own. For as long as the orchestra kept playing and the stage remained occupied I was safe. Unfortunately, unlike the virgin who had managed to avoid running out of stories, I had run out of tenors.

CHAPTER 47

SUNDAY

I climbed into the Citroen and drove southeast into the olive groves. For an hour I went, descending from the heights of St Frett into the shaded tranquility of the gnarled trees which carpet with their pale green leaves the central plain of Ardaniia. The Citroen bumped along the tracks of rough red soil squashing clumps of lavender and rosemary under its wheels releasing their musky scent. Sometimes I encountered a herd of goats bleating at the inconvenience of being nudged out of the way by a motor vehicle. There were no other signs of life, except the swivelling dark eyes of basking lizards which observed my progress from the crevices of the old stone walls lining the track.

At a junction of the road I saw an oasis of bright green foliage in the distance. I stopped the car, clambered over the wall and strode across the baked earth under the shade of the olive trees. Approaching the clump of foliage I heard the sound of running water. I parted the leaves and peered down at a stream, bubbling from an underground spring, nurturing a patch of soft green grass.

Here in this appropriately beautiful and dramatic setting I dropped to my knees, squatted on the grass and confronted my future.

Resign or brazen it out?

The honourable course of action was to resign. I should apologise to the king for having prejudiced his investment. Then, if not imprisoned, I should return to England, seek a role in my brother's estate and settle down to the life of a country gentlemen, near a church where, on repentance of my sins, a sympathetic vicar might offer me the position of organist and choirmaster. No one else would be likely to employ an unsuccessful conductor who had sabotaged the musical development of an entire nation, and bankrupted the monarch in the process.

Alternatively I could blame forces beyond my control, grovel at the king's feet and, if not exiled or incarcerated, slink back to the opera house in disgrace. I would seek accommodation outside the palace to spare the courtiers the awkwardness of my presence and avoid the possibility of encountering the king in a dark corridor who, brooding at his fiscal misfortune, might change his mind about incarceration. Diligently I would work to continue the series of successful concerts in the opera house and strive to accelerate the moment when profits from the opera house repaid the lost investment of the crown. With application and good luck, spurred by the inevitable success of *Swan Lake* and future ballet performances, it was not impossible to imagine myself back in royal favour within a couple of years.

No, I said shaking my head, no grovelling, no slinking.

I cupped my hands to drink from the cool stream, then doused my face with water to shock myself into accepting the fact that my career in Ardaniia was over.

MONDAY

The British embassy sat imperiously on the upper slopes of the city. The Union Jack flew from a flagpole amidst copious striped lawns which were used variously for public receptions, garden parties and croquet matches. Fountains played at the gates and liveried footmen escorted visitors up and down the front steps to and from the main entrance.

The ambassador kept me waiting an hour, the statutory period in embassies for minor dignitaries. He made no pretence at being pleased to see me. Plump and self-important he greeted me perfunctorily before seating himself behind an enormous desk under a large oil painting of

George V.

'I suppose I should have expected something like this,' he sniffed after I had outlined the sequence of events.

'In retrospect, it was a mistake awarding the contract for Rodolfo and his understudy to the same company,' I said.

'Surely someone, somewhere, is available to sing the role?'

'Not here, nor - according to the main theatrical agents in Rome - in Italy or anywhere in Europe within striking distance of Ardaniia.'

'Where have the singers from the bankrupt company gone?'

'To America, apparently,' I said.

The ambassador pointed through the window towards the site across the bay where work had commenced on the new hotel. From a cargo ship anchored at the foot of the cliffs, slabs of imported white marble were being slung ashore and transported upwards by convoys of mules.

'You do realise that your flamboyant assurances on the future of the opera house represented a basis for that investment?'

'Hardly flamboyant,' I protested.

'And that the king is involved financially?'

I bowed my head.

'His majesty will not be amused when you cancel *La Bohème*, nor the contingent of visiting crowned heads, left kicking their heels in Ardaniia.'

The ambassador tapped the surface of his desk with his fingers.

'So,' he said, 'what do you propose to do about it?'

'Resign.'

'Well, naturally,' sniffed the ambassador.

'There's no other choice,' I said.

'I hope you don't expect us to smuggle you out of the country. We don't do that sort of thing, I'm afraid.'

'I came here as a matter of courtesy, to acquaint you of the situation, not to seek help.'

'They're unlikely to lock you up. Not with our fleet in control of the Mediterranean,' said the ambassador waving at the window. 'They might want to keep you for a while, though, during negotiations for the updated treaty with London, for bargaining purposes. But you wouldn't be in the dungeons long - a couple of years, five at the most.'

I stared at the ambassador, expecting a hint of a smile, but there were no indications of jocularity on his face.

'If I were you, I would purchase a steerage class steamer ticket to

Marseilles under an assumed name. And be careful of Grand Duke Rupert - another investor in the hotel. I wouldn't go out alone at night, if I were you,' said the ambassador.

'You've been most helpful,' I said.

The ambassador ignored the sarcastic tone.

'Not at all, that's what we're here for,' he said summoning a footman to show me from the room.

CHAPTER 48

TUESDAY

The arrangement was that Soprianti would spend the weekend in Naples tracing the parents of Eduardo Fugarri and his understudy to verify that the redundant tenors had sailed for New York. On Monday he would travel by rail to Rome to visit the main theatrical agents in person in the forlorn hope of finding an available Rodolfo. He would call me this morning to report the results of his endeavours.

The telephone was ringing in my chambers as I climbed the stairs from the car park.

'Mr Soprianti for you, sir,' said Thomas handing me the receiver.

With leaden heart I listened to Soprianti's report, his words interrupted intermittently by the static interference that commonly disrupted overseas telephone calls. He had met Eduardo Fugarri's parents on Sunday and taken them to lunch in a small tavern that served delicious *arancini*. Eduardo's mother was still tearful from waving goodbye to her son at the steamer port in Naples. In Rome, Soprianti had toured the theatrical agents, walking for hours, wearing holes in his shoes, without finding a single tenor capable of singing Rodolfo's role.

After instructing Soprianti to return to the opera house I composed a letter of resignation. I was halfway down the corridor with the letter when the telephone rang again.

'That was Mr Lipsky, sir. He needs you at St Frett music society. Extremely urgent, sir,' said Thomas.

I left the letter on my desk and drove as fast as possible to the warehouse. Hurrying through the door into the familiar gloom I could see a pair of figures on the stage. Mr Lipsky was at the piano in the orchestra pit, with Mrs Lipsky alongside. The music was immediately recognisable, the duet between Mimi and Rodolfo in the snow of the third act in *La Bohème* when the lovers agree to reunite until the spring. Rehearsals for the piece until now had ended with the male voice dropping away when Mimi reached 'how sad to be alone in winter', leaving her to leap to the climax alone.

Scarcely believing my ears, both voices, soprano and tenor, were leaping to the climax in unison. Not only unison, but in blissful perfect pitch.

'Stop!' I shouted reaching the stage.

The music died away.

The bandage had gone from Valentino's throat. His linen shirt was open at the neck. He looked fit and confident, markedly different from the figure cowering in a hospital bed expecting death from a surgeon's knife. The contrast between his dark dashing looks and Zoe's angelically beautiful face was arresting. Neither of the singers was holding a score. They knew their parts by heart.

'Come down,' I ordered Valentino.

I turned to the Lipskys.

'Forgive me. I don't quite understand what's going on, whether it's a miracle or some extraordinary illusion, but whatever it is, I need professional advice. We shall return shortly. Valentino, follow me,' I said.

'But, sir . . .' said Valentino.

'Be quiet,' I said striding to the door.

Valentino clung to the dashboard as I raced through side streets, smoke billowing from the exhaust, chickens squawking from the threat of the spinning tyres. Approaching the main road to the harbour the Citroen hit a pothole, bouncing us out of our seats. Undamaged the car continued along the boulevard, roared through the gates of the general infirmary and skidded to a halt outside the main entrance, brakes squealing.

'What's the name of your surgeon?' I said jumping out.

'Ziegler, sir,' said Valentino.

At the reception counter I drew myself up to my full height.

'Please inform Mr Ziegler that the conductor of the Ardaniian symphony orchestra would like to speak to him, on a matter of extreme importance,' I said to the duty nurse.

Within minutes the nurse returned accompanied by an annoyed-looking bespectacled man wearing a white coat. I extended my hand, which he ignored.

'Yes?' said the surgeon curtly.

'Is this your patient?' I said, indicating Valentino.

The surgeon followed my glance.

'Valentino Borg, isn't it?' he said.

'Yes, sir,' said Valentino.

'What is so important that my rounds have been interrupted?' said the surgeon to me.

'He's been singing,' I said.

The surgeon grimaced.

'A common condition. People have been doing it for years,' he said.

'Not after major surgery, surely?' I said.

'I wouldn't call it major, I removed a small tumour from his neck.'

'After which you instructed him not to speak?'

'Yes, the tumour had aggravated his throat.'

'So he can sing, but not speak?'

'I didn't say that.' The surgeon turned to Valentino. 'How are you feeling, how's the neck?'

'I'm fine, sir.'

'Let's have a look.'

The surgeon turned Valentino's head towards the light from the window and adjusted the top of Valentino's shirt to reveal a small scar. He stared at the scar, turned Valentino's head again, told him to open his mouth, peered down his throat, stared at the scar again and restored Valentino's shirt to its original position.

'The tumour had not damaged the vocal chords, merely impeded them. His throat looks healthy, the incision has healed, he can speak and sing as much as he wants,' said the surgeon turning on his heels and striding off down the corridor.

'I could have told you that, sir,' said Valentino as we walked back out into the sunshine.

'Then why didn't you?'

'You told me to be quiet, sir.

'That's right, so I did.'

'The Lipskys believed me, sir.'

'They don't know you as well as I do. Some people will say anything to get onto the stage. I needed to make sure for myself. Hurry up, we've got work to do,' I said climbing into the car.

'Does that mean I can apply for the role of Rodolfo officially, sir?'

'It's not impossible,' I said hurtling the Citroen through the hospital gates amidst a cloud of dust.

CHAPTER 49

With the exception of the crowd scenes, which are still slightly ragged though improving with each performance, I am pleased with the production so far. Here are my working notes, updated this morning in my chambers as I sit awaiting news of Countess Charlotte von Littchnoff, delayed yet again who, with any luck, will arrive too late for tonight's command performance.

Overture

Puccini does not waste time with the introduction. Dissonant intervals warn the audience not to expect a happy ending though the speed of the intervals indicate that the journey to the finale will not lack passion. The overture is so short that Pierre has arranged for the house lights to be dimmed immediately after the one minute bell, to force the laggards into their seats in time. No pageboys for this production. The curtains glide open powered by unseen forces; stage hands, ropes and pulleys.

Act 1 The Garret

The set designers have produced an impressive interpretation of Puccini's instructions for the garret. A large window looks out over snow-covered gables, the bed onto which Mimi collapses in the last act serves as the table decorated with a pair of candlesticks, freeing space on the stage for the frolics of the tenants. The easel is positioned so that the audience can see Marcello's half-finished painting of the Red Sea. The stove, empty, barren of flames, which emphasises the near-freezing temperature inside the garret and the impoverishment of the tenants, is at the back of the stage near the window.

Seated at the easel and hugging himself to keep out the cold is Marcello, played by Peter Broch, the son of a local solicitor, whose commanding baritone voice has been the single constant feature of soloist rehearsals during the last few months while Zoe developed into the role of Mimi and the search was under way for Rodolfo and Musetta. At the window looking out over Paris is the new Rodolfo, played by Valentino whose conversion from steward to operatic tenor still has me shaking my head in disbelief. Handsome in the classic Mediterranean style, dressed in a ragged coat, he passes convincingly as the lovelorn poet.

Marcello and Rodolfo are joined by Schaunard and Colline, respectively musician and philosopher, played by members of the St Frett choir. Schaunard has been paid for singing to the parrot of an eccentric Englishman. He purchases food for lunch during which the poet and philosopher sacrifice their works for warmth and the stove blazes with burned masterpieces. The challenge for the director is to avoid the horseplay between the youthful tenants getting out of control. There is a danger of too much artificial heartiness and boisterousness disturbing the subtle increase in tension which anticipates Mimi's entry. Cleverly Pierre keeps the singers from moving too far or abruptly from the positions they have been allocated on the stage.

Pierre leaves the best comedy in the first act for the landlord Benoit, played by a local butcher from St Frett who conveys to the tenants his assessment of the physical virtues of women in a wickedly droll voice. Even members of the audience unfamiliar with the Italian language respond to his boastful delivery and I am forced to slow the tempo of the orchestra to allow for laughter.

In the public performances so far Mimi's entry has been greeted with sharp intakes of breath from the audience. Not only is Zoe extremely pretty but the men in the audience instantly recognise the combination of innocence and allure which first captured my attention in the palace kitchens and convinced me she was perfect for the part. Mimi's manipulation of her allure is at the core of the tension in *La Bohème*. For this reason I find it so difficult to understand why international opera houses continue to award the part to elderly overweight females who cannot hope to convince the audience that their hands are either tiny or frozen.

The act ends with the first of the many lovely duets in the opera. There has never been music like this, nor will there be again, to illuminate love. My only quarrel with Puccini is that he hastens the speed of the first kiss. I concede the possibility of love at first sight but am less convinced that prospective lovers can advance from first sight to passionate embrace in fifteen minutes. Zoe and Valentino are still wary of each other physically, and tentative in their love scenes. The wariness needs to be sorted out.

Act 2 Latin Quarter

The success of the second act depends on controlling the crowds of shoppers and children, and on the personality of Musetta. For such an ebullient character, who darts and jumps about the stage himself, Pierre is remarkably effective at restraining the movements of the chorus and stopping the soloists from over-acting while conveying the excitement and bustle of a French market place. There are some masterly touches from him. The superior way the waiters in the restaurant handle the penniless bohemians, for example, and the dismissive attitude of the other diners

Mimi and Rodolfo play a subsidiary role in the second act. Quite rightly Pierre keeps the spotlights off them when they are not singing and concentrates on the vibrancy of the street and restaurant scenes, and on Musetta.

It was a hard choice but Lipsky and I eventually settled on Fiona Bayonne, the russet-haired wife of a St Frett businessman, as understudy for the countess. She is the feistier of the two mezzo-sopranos selected at the audition, and more secure in her top notes. It was a sight to see the expression on Fiona's face when the cable arrived announcing that the countess's steamer had broken down and would not arrive until this morning. Fiona did not know whether to commiserate with the countess or celebrate her own brief elevation to stardom, and settled for the traditional feminine option of weeping into a handkerchief.

Personally I hope the countess's steamer runs aground or blows up. In doing so I also hope, naturally, that the passengers and crew are rescued and delivered to a port sufficiently distant from Ardaniia to ensure the countess cannot reach here today. Fiona has settled into the part so well that the thought of having to exchange her at the last minute and deal with the problem of the countess's missing high notes fills me with dread. Much better the countess swims to the lifeboats of the sinking steamer and I issue a note of regret to the palace that she has been unavoidably delayed and thus unable to sing the part of Musetta before the king and royal guests tonight. For her absence in such circumstances, I surely cannot be blamed.

Act 3 Snow-Bound Tavern

The third act of *La Bohème* contains some of the most gripping scenes in romantic opera. By virtue of its music alone, especially the innovative trio and quartet, in my opinion it represents one the greatest of all operatic accomplishments.

Puccini punctuates the unveiling of Mimi's and Rodolfo's feelings for each other with drunken laughter from the tavern, deepening the sense of impending tragedy. The contrast between the humour and laughter of everyday life and the grimness of the lovers' situation is singularly effective. From the start, by including in the narrative notes to the score the instruction that Marcello's painting of the Red Sea should be replicated on the tavern's signboard with the words 'At the Port of Marseilles' underneath, Puccini announces to the audience that he plans to deploy the device of emphasizing the contrast between high spirits and grief mercilessly.

And, if that was not enough, the action takes place within the nostalgic beauty of a snowstorm.

Mimi arrives through the toll gate to the city in search of Rodolfo who has abandoned her, consumed with jealousy at the way she idly accepts flattery from males. He is sleeping in the tavern, which Marcello accompanied by Musetta is repainting.

In the snow-filled yard Marcello attempts to comfort Mimi. Her cough has worsened through the winter. She hides when Rodolfo appears and overhears him announce that she is terminally ill. The awfulness of the words are aggravated by the simplicity and beauty of the music. 'Must I die so soon then?' says Mimi in the famous trio.

The greatest quartets in opera, from Mozart in *Don Giovanni*, Wagner in *Die Meistersinger* to Verdi in *Rigoletto* are spectacular in their setting and musically overwhelming. Puccini, in his quartet which ends the third act of *La Bohème*, adds to these twin feature the element of derisive laughter. While Mimi and Rodolfo agree to reunite until the spring, snow on their faces, voices soaring, Marcello and Musetta simultaneously embark on a quarrel, explosively and harmonically in conjunction with the lover's duet. The combination of all three features in Puccini's quartet make it, in my opinion, the greatest of all.

Act 4 The Garret

The picture of Mimi as Rodolfo's faithful lover takes a knock when we learn from Marcello in the opening scene of the final act that she has been spotted, dressed extravagantly, riding in an elegant carriage. When we last saw Mimi and Rodolfo they were vowing to reunite until the spring. Something must have happened to part them. We are left to conclude that Mimi's illness (consumption, tuberculosis) has made her decide that the remaining months of her life should be spent in comfort and that thanks to her troublesome allure she has had no difficulty finding a benefactor. Similarly Musetta has parted from Marcello into the arms of yet another wealthy suitor.

Back in the freezing garret Rodolfo tries to write poetry while Marcello attempts a third version of the Red Sea painting. In a mournful duet they recall the days of happiness and pleasure spent with their lovers.

Puccini has not finished with the business of mocking grief with high spirits and thereby making the grief more terrible when it comes. After a sparse lunch of bread and herrings the four bohemians, pretending to be drunk with champagne, experiment with different dances including a fandango which, to the entertainment of my orchestra, involves a brief incursion into three-eighths rhythm. The dancers' partners flirt with each other, which leads to a duel, which stops abruptly when Musetta runs into the garret with the news that Mimi has collapsed in the street outside.

Mimi wants to be with Rodolfo, explains Musetta. She is worried that Rodolfo might be waiting.

How poignant this explanation! How intuitive of Puccini to penetrate so deep into a girl's heart. How feminine that in the face of imminent death, drawn to the person she truly adores, Mimi justifies her decision to return to the garret by telling Musetta that Rodolfo, her lover, the impoverished poet, must be waiting for her.

Rodolfo fails to admit the graveness of the situation as Mimi is carried to the bed, positioned so that the audience can see her full length, wrapped in a blanket, shivering, exhausted with coughing, pale but no less beautiful. The lovers sing tenderly to each other while the bohemians sacrifice their humble possessions to pay for medicines that will do no good and a doctor's visit that will come too late. Colline sings goodbye to his overcoat in an aria of measured pace that matches the footsteps of approaching death.

Elsewhere I have recorded my opinion that Mozart was largely unaffected by the beauty of the music he wrote. There is no evidence to support the theory. My intention was not to disparage Mozart but propose that, at his level of brilliance, the perfection of his output did not surprise him. Conversely I have also suggested that Rimsky-Korsakov could not have written *Scheherazade* without being moved by the magnificence of the musical world he created. Whether he wept or not, as Tchaikovsky certainly did throughout his life as a composer, I do not know. Nor can I be sure of Puccini's reaction to his own music though I think I can see him at the piano, tears welling in his eyes, as he wrote the chords which accompanied Rodolfo's agonized realization on returning to Mimi's bedside at the end of the opera that she had slipped away from him.

CHAPTER 50

'Here I am, at last. Never travel with the Adriatic Steamship Line. The food is awful, the officers are rude, the bunks uncomfortable and the boilers unpredictable,' said Countess Charlotte von Littchnoff walking into my chambers arms outstretched.

'How very nice to see you,' I said laying down my fountain pen.

'I hope you mean that,' said the countess.

'Of course,' I lied.

'Am I too late?' said the countess removing her gloves. She was wearing a full length violet-coloured gown with chiffon cuffs, an embroidered shawl and large feather hat complete with an aquamarine songbird, presumably dead, nestling amidst the white ribbons.

'Probably,' I said.

'You must think me very careless but I could not help being infected with influenza, nor should I be held responsible for the condition of the Adriatic Steamship Line's boilers,' she said dropping her gloves into Thomas's awaiting hands.

'The agreement, I recall, was that you would submit to coaching . . .'

'But I did, madly for days in Riegersburg, and Frau Pichler says there's nothing wrong with my voice,' she said removing her hat and passing it to Thomas.

'. . . here, not in Austria,' I said.

The countess examined herself in the long mirror by the door.

'Frau Pichler is very good. She worked with Caruso. He always called for her, when he visited Vienna,' said the countess patting her hair.

'In which case, I suggest Thomas escorts you to one of the practice rooms, where you can warm up your voice. I will ask Signora Furcello, our librarian, to attend you and refresh your memory on the geography of the building. Come back when you're ready,' I said handing her a copy of the *La Bohème* score.

The countess tucked the score under her arm and laughed.

'Just like a school examination,' she said walking to the door.

'Thomas, on your return, please ask Monsieur Bonnel to spare me a few minutes,' I told my steward. 'You'll find him on the stage, somewhere.'

'She has turned up, then?' said Pierre hurrying into the room.

'Unfortunately.'

'So, what is your plan?'

'In the unlikely event that the countess's range has miraculously increased, you and I shall spend the afternoon alternately rehearsing her at the piano with the other soloists, and on the stage with selected members of the cast.'

In our favour, before her departure to Austria, the countess had rehearsed most of her scenes with Pierre and been measured by the dressmaker. The gowns were ready and, as Pierre pointed out, Musetta's part was not especially difficult to act, not for someone as vivacious as the countess.

To exert pressure on the countess's nerves, simulating the presence of an audience, I invited Pierre and Signora Furcello to attend the test.

'Ready?' I said seating myself at the piano.

'Ready,' said the countess.

'Musetta's song, part 21, bar 1. Don't think of the high notes, think instead of the charmless officers on the steamer, and the defective boilers, then launch yourself,' I said.

Elsewhere in the city, in the palace, in the embassies, several dozen visiting princes, dukes and assorted noblemen and their wives would be settling down to lunch, raising their glasses at the news that the countess's steamer had finally docked and therefore that they could look forward to an enjoyable evening watching Rupert's priceless niece, Charlotte, perform in the opera house - so talented, so divinely amusing. Notwithstanding the trouble her absence had caused me I was as anxious as the countess that she should be acclaimed by her peers on the stage tonight, if only from professional conviction that she was capable of meeting the challenges of Musetta's part.

So when her voice slid away on the C sharp semiquaver before the leap to B flat I felt very disappointed

'Try again,' I said in the embarrassed silence.

The countess cleared her throat.

'From bar 9,' I said.

Once again, her voice slipped away before the leap.

Pierre and I exchanged glances as the countess walked from the piano and slumped miserably onto the sofa next to Signora Furcello.

'Bad luck, never mind,' I said with forced cheerfulness. 'The important thing is that you have an excellent voice throughout most of your range. Some professional training, some attention to your breathing, and you'll be on our list for the next production.'

'I'm so sorry,' murmured the countess.

'There, there,' said Signora Furcello reaching across the sofa as the countess's face started to crumple.

'We will issue a statement saying that conditions on the steamer, resulting from the delayed sailing, exacerbated your influenza and that your throat has become inflamed. Regrettably, under direction from your doctors, you have been forced to withdraw from tonight's performance. Something on those lines,' I said.

'I promise you, I can do it,' said the countess tearfully.

'There, there,' said Signora Furcello passing a lace handkerchief across the sofa.

We sat for several minutes staring awkwardly at the floor.

'I've let you down awfully,' said the countess, dabbing her eyes.

'As a matter of interest,' I said, 'did you sing Musetta's aria to Frau Pichler, the teacher in Austria?'

The countess nodded.

'Did you complete the aria without difficulty?'

'Yes.'

'During a coaching lesson?'

'At an after-dinner recital,' said the countess.

In the vaults of my brain came the tinkling sound of a bell.

'Those recitals of yours, have they always been after dinner?'

'Yes.'

The intensity of the tinkling sound increased. Suddenly I slapped my thighs.

'And did you, during the course of dinner, or afterwards, before the recital, drink anything in the way of, how shall I put it, sherry, wine or similar relaxant?'

The countess sat bolt upright.

'Why, yes. I always have a glass of orange liqueur before singing.'

'Thomas,' I cried from the piano stool. 'Bring me a bottle of orange liqueur. If the sideboard is empty, call our wine merchant, immediately!'

. . . .

We called in the other soloists. The stage hands moved a piano onto the set and we rehearsed all afternoon. I considered mobilising the orchestra but decided against it. There was no point in tiring everybody out. I would rather have a fresh orchestra at my fingertips later, ready and alert for emergencies, than violinists yawning in the semi-darkness of the pit.

Half a glass of orange liqueur had been enough to free the countess's voice. After that she swept through the score imperiously. The alcohol lubricated her throat and relaxed the muscles controlling the operation of her lungs, confirming Mrs Lipsky's theory that her breathing was at fault. It helped psychologically too. After hitting B flat in perfect pitch the countess did not touch the drink again, though the glass sat on the piano within reach all afternoon.

To avoid the prospect of her throat and lungs tightening up when she faced the audience we decided that Pierre should give her a second dose before her entry. Thereafter, in the months ahead, if the countess decided to pursue the career of a fulltime opera singer, Mrs Lipsky's job would be to wean the aristocratic mezzo-soprano off orange liqueur.

I returned to my chambers exhausted. One task remained. At six o'clock I summoned Zoe and Valentino from their dressing rooms.

After three days of close contact, rehearsing, singing and acting together, performing on the stage as lovers, it was reasonable to expect that the couple should have adjusted to each other and be on reasonably friendly terms, if not actually laughing at each other's jokes then at least conversing freely. They filed silently into my chambers and positioned themselves apart, ensuring their shoulders did not touch. The problem, according to Pierre, who uncharacteristically had admitted defeat on the matter, was self-perpetuating. Overawed by Zoe's beauty, Valentino compensated for his shyness by showing off in front of her. Zoe, who did not necessarily dislike Valentino but was irritated by his youthful zeal, snapped at him. After a while she apologised, and the sequence started again.

They had already changed into their *La Bohème* costumes - full blue skirt, white blouse and grey shawl for Zoe - patched trousers, white shirt, red polka dot scarf (donated by Pierre) and tattered coat for Valentino. The make-up on their faces accentuated her exquisite features and his dark good looks.

'In one hour's time, the curtains will open,' I told them. 'When they close, you may never see each other again. You may indeed never act again as Mimi and Rodolfo. Let me put it another way. This opera house is unlikely to invite either of you back unless you are more successful tonight than on previous occasions in convincing the audience that you are in love. You can start by convincing me right now, here in this room, that if nothing else you are capable of simulating an affectionate embrace.'

Zoe and Valentino exchanged sideways glances.

'When you're ready,' I said leaning against my desk.

They stared at me, hoping that I would burst out laughing and admit to be fooling around on the last night of the production, that my real purpose for inviting them to my chambers was to congratulate them on performing so brilliantly and for looking so gloriously romantic together on the stage. When from the severity of my expression they realised I was being serious and that my request represented an instruction they could not afford to ignore they began shuffling their feet. Slowly they turned to face each other. Valentino tentatively encircled Zoe's waist. She placed her hands on Valentino's shoulders and, taking a deep breath, leaned forward to peck his cheek.

'That is about as exciting as a cold bath,' I said

They shuffled an inch or two closer, and Zoe pecked a little harder.

'Affectionate embraces usually involve kissing, not nibbling,' I said.

Inch by inch they adjusted the position of their heads until their mouths were lined up and their lips were touching, whereupon they stopped moving.

I waited. 'Are you still awake?'

The heads nodded in unison, mouths glued together.

'Place your arms around each other properly,' I said.

Valentino extended his grip and Zoe moved her hands from his shoulders to encircle him and then suddenly the barrier of reserve broke and they were at each other like a couple of rabbits on a summer night in a meadow, straining together, kissing ardently, staring into each other's eyes, oblivious of me, responding to the explosive release of latent passion.

'That's the idea,' I said, hurriedly bringing the experiment to a conclusion. 'Back to your dressing rooms, please, and repair your make-up.'

CHAPTER 51

From my bed I can see the tops of the flagpoles. The centre pole, the highest of the three, is reserved for the national flag. The pole on the left is for the royal standard which flies when the king is in residence. The one on the right normally remains bare, so the white and gold ensign flapping from its masthead this morning caught my attention.

'What's that for, do you know?' I asked my valet.

'Investiture, sir. Some of his majesty's visitors are being awarded the Royal Cross of Ardaniia this morning.'

'Is that so.'

'Was the egg to your satisfaction, sir?' said my valet removing the breakfast tray.

'Perfect.'

'I'm glad to see you looking so well, sir,' he said which meant he was relieved that, unlike the previous occasion which had involved breakfast in bed, I had not spilled coffee over the bedclothes or thrown up in the bathroom.

On that occasion I had been guilty of consuming excessive quantities of champagne and whisky. This time, responsibility lay with the exhausting sequence of events which had nearly scuppered *La Bohème* and sapped my customary energy. So lethargic was my condition on awakening this morning that I decided to treat myself to the pleasure of a breakfast tray.

I was already half dead when the time came to mount the podium last night. Barely taking in the splendour of the royal enclosure gleaming with tiaras and gold braid I launched the orchestra into the overture praying that the worst was over and that the celestial authorities responsible for the wellbeing of conductors would take pity and allow the production to proceed without incident. The authorities must have agreed that the law of averages had been working against me recently because not only did they refrain from blowing up the snow-making machine or collapsing the scenery but encouraged the cast into such magnificent performances that when I finally laid down the baton and nodded gratefully at the orchestra the opera house erupted with thunderous roars of approval and applause.

Zoe and Valentino were magnificent as Mimi and Rodolfo. They are still young compared with today's international celebrities. It was their youthfulness that made the love story so particularly convincing and Mimi's tragic death so harrowing. There is a delightful scene in act 1 where Mimi drops the key of her apartment to the floor. Rodolfo finds it but pretends to continue the search alongside her, both singers on their knees. The tenderness of the look they exchanged last night when their hands touched was enchanting. So too was their embrace at the end of the act, allowing me a moment of self-congratulation at the effectiveness of the ordeal I had put them through in my chambers.

The star of the show however was Countess Charlotte von Littchnoff as Musetta. Gloriously attired in crimson and black she led her elderly admirer, played by the droll butcher from St Frett, onto the stage by the ear, dismissing him imperiously to a table when she caught sight of her ex-lover Marcello and initiated the wicked scenes of flirtation which dominate the second act. The secret to comedy is timing. Her interlude with the misfitting shoe represented a masterclass in audience manipulation. The laughter the scene generated from the audience in the stalls behind me was almost drowned by the well-bred growls of amusement from the royal enclosure above.

The orchestra played exceptionally well. It is a measure of my confidence in the players that I have reduced the span of my beat by at least half since the early days of my tenure, which is less tiring for me and allows more precise control of the music. Conducting the orchestra now is like driving the Citroen through an orange grove, sunlight flashing between the leaves to mark the vehicle's passage, a simple touch on the steering wheel there, a simple adjustment to the throttle here, the engine responding and purring gracefully in harmony with nature, butterflies hovering like grace notes over the bonnet.

Lipsky told me afterwards that one of the foreign music critics had been overheard saying that with such an excellent orchestra and soloists the Ardaniian opera house would soon rival the best in Europe. I was too far gone by then to take in the comment but smiled contentedly this morning at the recollection.

In the long history of opera I doubt that so many personages of royal and noble blood have ever stood on the same theatre stage at the same time. The ushers had sealed off the corridors to everyone but members the royal enclosure and press box. Even then there was scarcely room to manoeuvre across the wooden floor. Most of the noble throng had come to congratulate the countess. Still wearing her make-up and glamorous crimson and black gown she circulated amongst them, squeezing through the crowd, laughing, clutching hands and embracing her admirers.

The queen, puzzled as usual to find that her favourite landscape gardener had been conducting the Ardaniian symphony orchestra, was greatly affected by the plot of *La Bohème*. She made straight for Valentino, arms outstretched. 'My poor darling, what a terrible loss - you must be so sad!' Valentino was indeed sad. Moments earlier he had been proudly holding hands with Zoe, waiting with the rest of the cast for the arrival of the guests, when Grand Duke Rupert, swooping like Count Dracula from his castle, escorted her away to a corner of the stage where he could be observed leering at the lovely young soprano.

'Bereavement is so stomach-churning,' said the queen to Valentino who watched helplessly as Rupert, cloak spread, imposed upon the pretty victim his well-practised prelude to seduction.

From the stage door I could see what was going on and sympathised with Valentino. Unfortunately when the owner of multiple royal dungeons takes a fancy to your girlfriend there is not much you can do except grit your teeth. Most other options involve the prospect of chained legs and head loss. Poor Valentino had to wait until the royal party departed for the palace before reclaiming Zoe's hand.

I followed shortly afterwards, so tired that I nearly stumbled over the wheelchair parked in the corridor outside my chambers.

'He's been waiting for you,' said the grey-haired woman standing beside wheelchair whom I recognized as Professor Schmidt's wife. 'He wants to apologise.'

A claw emerged from the wheelchair and grasped my arm. I leant down. The professor's lips were moving but no sound came from his mouth. Except for his eyes, fixed on mine, the rest of his face was frozen.

'You have nothing to apologise for,' I said to the professor. 'Quite the reverse.'

'Sometimes you can hear what he's saying, sometimes not,' said his wife.

The image disturbed me as I lay in bed, sipping coffee, looking out at the flagpoles. For what reason had the professor apologised? Driven to despair by the production of *La Bohème* in the opera house, had he arranged for me to be assassinated by a gang of cut-throats and was apologising in advance or, having sat through the production, had he been surprisingly converted to the lyrical beauty of Puccini's score?

My thoughts on the subject were interrupted by a knock at the front door.

How inconvenient, I thought, sinking back into my pillows.

'An equerry, sir. I have shown him to the drawing room,' said my valet.

Sighing I wrapped myself in my purple and white striped dressing gown, purchased in Jermyn Street, and strode from the bedroom.

'What's up?' I said.

The immaculately attired equerry wearing the uniform of a household cavalry lieutenant, with gold epaulets to signify his special duties as a royal aide, stared at my dressing gown, eyebrows raised.

'Your presence is required in the investiture hall,' he said.

'Whatever for?'

'I would suggest a morning suit,' said the equerry, continuing to eye my dressing gown. 'As soon as possible. Ten minutes at the latest.'

He was not impressed by my morning suit either. Admiring myself in my changing room mirror I thought the combination of elegant grey tailcoat and black striped trousers, tailored for me at considerable expense in Saville Row, looked rather dashing. The trouble with cavalry officers is that they regard themselves as arbiters of fashion. Without exception they have that irritating habit of looking you up and down, however well presented, and then sniffing. as if you have just crawled out of a drain pipe.

The investiture hall was full of hushed groups of people, each group consisting of aides centred around a figure wearing a crown or coronet, the central figure adorned with an ermine cape around his shoulders.

'I'm not quite sure what I'm doing here,' I said on being handed over to a second equerry, this one a captain in the household cavalry, even smarter and grander than the first.

The equerry examined his list.

'Mr Robin Landour. Chevalier, first class. Citation: "For services to the arts." You'll be going in last,' he said.

'Good grief,' I gulped.

'It's only a knighthood, I'm afraid, but . . .' said the equerry eyeing me up and down, implying by his unfinished sentence that someone with my taste in clothes could scarcely expect more.

Head spinning, caught totally unawares, I stood watching the regal figures being prepared for entry to the throne room. As a British citizen, was I allowed to accept the honour? Had our ambassador been informed? Should I ask to speak to him? No, I snorted to myself. Acquainting the ambassador, out of courtesy, of the grave situation facing me concerning *La Bohème* his advice had been to purchase a steerage class steamer ticket to Marseilles. Let him see the value of his advice.

'Any minute now,' said the equerry returning to my side as the sound of trumpets indicated that the last of the royal figures was making his way through the double doors. 'The procedure is quite straightforward. Walk directly to the throne. Hold your hat like this and kneel on the stool. After the citation the king will touch your left shoulder with his sword. Count to three, and stand. If his majesty ventures no comment, bow and reverse six steps. You may then turn and proceed through the open doors to the garden, and join the party on the lawn.'

The equerry glanced in the direction of the throne room.

'Off you go,' he said.

No trumpets announced my entry through the doors. The main business of the morning having been completed the senior officials of the court lined up behind the king were making preparations to disperse. My arrival, I felt, was something of an inconvenient anti-climax, delaying the distinguished assembly from transferring itself to the ministrations of the wine stewards on the lawn

For heaven's sake don't trip up, I said to myself, proceeding as fast as decency allowed to the throne.

At least the pageboy standing beside the king seemed pleased to see me. I recognised him as one of the curtain pullers borrowed from the palace for *The Sleeping Beauty.*

'Chevalier first class, for services to art,' piped up the pageboy reading from a roll of parchment as I knelt on the stool. 'In as much as our loyal servant, Mr Robin Landour, hath brought great music to our state . . . '

It occurred to me when the sword touched my shoulder that I should experience a sense of profound diligence, an awareness of responsibility for performing good deeds and an abundance of humility and forgiveness. The latter was important because on my way to the throne I had spotted the Italian ambassador on the lawn. He had been avoiding me since his inept handling of the Neapolitan Touring Opera Company situation and I needed as much humility and forgiveness as possible to avoid lunging at the scented diplomat's throat.

'A word with you,' said the king, passing the sword to the pageboy who swivelled it playfully before sheathing the blade in the scabbard.

I followed the king across the room to a small table by the window covered in a white linen cloth on which stood an ice bucket containing a bottle of champagne, already opened, presumably for the king's personal use.

The king poured two glasses. Handing me one, he said 'Well done, richly deserved. *Swan Lake* for Christmas?'

'Yes, sir.'

'With Sophie in the main role?'

I nodded.

'She will be ready, sir.'

'What about opera?'

'You enjoyed *La Bohème*, sir?"

'Very much.'

'Then I suggest *Madame Butterfly*, by the same composer.'

'If you say so.'

'Followed by Wagner's *Die Meistersinger von Nürnberg.*'

'Whatever you think. We want you to stay, you know. You must choose one of our maids-of-honour and settle down.'

'Thank you, sir.'

'Or, if you don't want a maid-of-honour, how about our attractive French advocate, the one you dance with sometimes?'

'I am rather outnumbered by the household cavalry there, sir.'

'Let me think. I've got it, you can have the queen.'

'Your wife, sir?'

'It could be arranged, you know,' said the king.

'I'm lost for words, sir.'

'She's not extravagant, and fond of music.'

'I'm honoured at the thought, sir.'

'Well, what about it?'

'I couldn't possibly consider such a generous bequest, sir.'

The king sighed and emptied his glass.

'Pity,' he said.

OTHER BOOKS BY
Jonathan Diack

Old English Press is in the process of publishing the
following books by Jonathan Diack through Amazon and
major booksellers

No Barking Please
The Quince River Parchment
A Gentleman's Guide to Women, Commoners & Cooking
A Gentleman's Guide to Cooking
Dangerous Flotilla
The Escape of MV *Duchess*
Peter the Perpendicular (reissue)

For details of the books visit the publisher's website
www.oldenglishpress.co.uk

79669620R00130